MONSTERS
IN OUR
MIDST

Tor books by Robert Bloch

American Gothic
Fear and Trembling
Firebug
The Kidnapper
The Jekyll Legacy (with Andre Norton)
Lori
Midnight Pleasures
Monsters in Our Midst
The Night of the Ripper
Night-World
Once Around the Bloch
Psycho
Psycho II
Psycho House

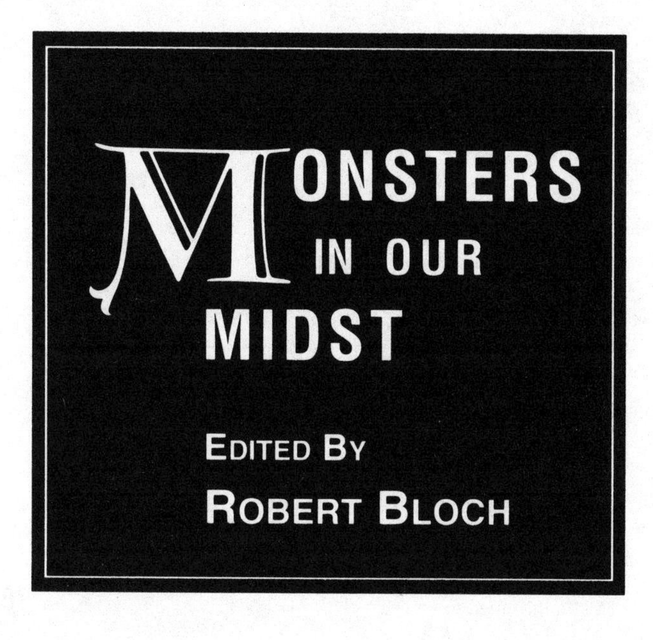

A TOM DOHERTY ASSOCIATES BOOK
NEW YORK

This is a work of fiction. All the characters and events portrayed in this book are fictitious, and any resemblance to real people or events is purely coincidental.

MONSTERS IN OUR MIDST

This book is printed on acid-free paper.

A Tor Book
Published by Tom Doherty Associates, Inc.
175 Fifth Avenue
New York, N.Y. 10010

Edited by James Frenkel

Library of Congress Cataloging-in-Publication Data

Monsters in our midst/edited by Robert Bloch.
p. cm.
"A Tom Doherty Associates book."
ISBN 0-312-85049-2
1. Horror tales, American. I. Bloch, Robert.
PS648.H6M65 1993
813'.0873808—dc20 93-26552
CIP

Printed in the United States of America

Acknowledgments

Introduction by Robert Bloch.
Copyright © 1993 by Robert Bloch.

"Snow Man" by John Coyne.
Copyright © 1993 by John Coyne.

"A Gentle Breeze Blowing" by Robert E. Vardeman.
Copyright © 1993 by Robert E. Vardeman.

"For You to Judge" by Ramsey Campbell.
Copyright © 1993 by Ramsey Campbell.

"The Child Killer" by Steve Rasnic Tem.
Copyright © 1993 by Steve Rasnic Tem.

"The Lick of Time" by Jonathan Carroll.
Copyright © 1993 by Jonathan Carroll.

"The Edge" by Richard Christian Matheson.
Copyright © 1993 by Richard Christian Matheson.

"How Would You Like It?" by Lawrence Block.
Copyright © 1993 by Lawrence Block.

"The Moment the Face Falls" by Chet Williamson.
Copyright © 1993 by Chet Williamson.

"Judgment" by Ed Gorman.
Copyright © 1993 by Ed Gorman.

"Reality Function" by J. N. Williamson.
Copyright © 1993 by J. N. Williamson.

"Sacrifice" by Kathleen Buckley.
Copyright © 1993 by Kathleen Buckley.

"Name That Tune" by Charles L. Grant.
Copyright © 1993 by Charles L. Grant.

"Taking Care of Georgie" by Lisa W. Cantrell.
Copyright © 1993 by Lisa W. Cantrell.

"Fish Are Jumpin', and the Cotton Is High" by S. P. Somtow. Copyright © 1993 by S. P. Somtow.

"It Takes One to Know One" by Robert Bloch.
Copyright © 1993 by Robert Bloch.

"The Lesson" by Billie Sue Mosiman.
Copyright © 1993 by Billie Sue Mosiman.

"Fee Fie Foe Fum" by Ray Bradbury.
Copyright © 1993 by Ray Bradbury.

This book is dedicated, with gratitude and admiration, to its talented contributors. And to Martin H. Greenberg, whose assistance was a major contribution in itself.

Contents

MONSTERS
IN OUR
MIDST

Introduction

Robert Bloch

What exactly is a psychopath?

"A mentally disturbed person; one with a poorly-balanced personality structure."

That's one definition, but it doesn't tell us much. Most of us experience varying degrees of mental disturbance from time to time, even when sitting behind the steering wheel or standing in line at the checkout counter. But the antisocial thought is not the deed, and what constitutes a poorly-balanced personality structure varies from one culture to another.

There are other definitions, plenty of them, though none give us the answer we need. About all they agree on is that a psychopath is capable of committing capital criminal offenses with complete awareness of what he or she is doing, but without any guilt feelings, pangs of conscience, or empathy for victims. In other words, a used-car salesman.

Because of the ability to understand the nature of his/her crimes, the psychopath is not considered legally insane, and psychotherapy's diverse definitions distinguish the psychopathic from the psychotic.

But enough of this. The clinical approach doesn't get us very close to our subject, and that's why we have to find our own psycho-pathways.

The accomplished writers represented in this volume will be our guides, helping us explore *terror incognita.*

When invited to lead the way, no limits were placed on the direction they might choose to go. It came as a surprise to find that many of them didn't seem to stray too far afield. Most of their stories are set in ordinary surroundings and deal with people who, at least on the surface, seem little different from those we might meet on the street—or in a mirror.

It is then that our gifted guides usher us into the realms of the unexpected. Sometimes a sudden twist in the straight and narrow path takes us from the familiar into the labyrinth of nightmare. Sometimes a single step leads us into the looking-glass so that we see what really lurks behind surface appearances.

These writers also lead us to conclusions.

Under the outward conformity most of us assume, there are nonconformist urges and emotional responses, instincts and impulses many of us suppress—but which are all too recognizable when succumbed to by the characters in these stories. When such characters explode, we can't help wondering if our own fuses could be lit—or are already smoldering.

Maybe our old friend Norman Bates best summed it up long ago when he said, "I think perhaps all of us go a little crazy at times."

Speaking of Norman, I've been accused of opening a Pandora's box and loosing a new horror—the mentally disturbed menace—upon the world. Such charges cite novels like *The Scarf, The Kidnapper* and *Psycho,* plus examples from shorter fiction.

Truthfully, I can lay no claim to so monumental a

disturbance. Many illustrious predecessors—Messrs. Poe, Stevenson and de Maupassant among them—created the unbalanced anti-hero. All I might have done is help revive the concept and place the character where you're likely to find him today: down the street, next door, or even in your own home.

In so doing, I tried to indicate that horror can take root in reality as well as the supernatural. And in order to deal with it, one must understand it.

The first step towards understanding involves confrontation, and it's there that we begin.

Medical science has not been spectacularly successful in this area. It took almost four hundred years to progress from belief in demonic possession to the theory of multiple personality. Hardly a quantum leap, and still regarded by some as jumping to conclusions. Definitions keep changing, but terminology—be it label or libel—isn't always a clarifying agent.

Treatment too has changed, and new methods of therapy are employed, but largely to the same old ends of restraint or sedation, which in themselves do not constitute cure. And in-depth examination of individuals is often disappointing in terms of overall results.

A few years ago Harold Schechter's *Deviant* offered its factual account of the Ed Gein murder case as a clever but minor pulp chiller. Interspersed with its obvious shock-treatment of Ed Gein's unchivalrous behavior are statements from psychotherapists who examined and/or evaluated him. None of these quotations answers the question of how a seemingly harmless little man could lead a longtime secret life as a ghoul, necrophile and murderer. It was revealed that Gein, as a small boy, witnessed his parents butchering a hog. Apparently this had been a traumatic experience—but there's quite a gap between a child's terror over what was then a commonplace occurrence in farm life and a grown man's urge to fashion a belt made from the amputated nipples of female corpses.

It is this sort of gap which psychotherapy has been unable to bridge. Thus it remains for fiction to construct a span. In the past, Dostoevsky offered more intelligible insight into motivation for murder than Krafft-Ebing. And today, despite clinical advances and advantages, it is in fiction that we tend to discover the clearest concepts of the criminal mentality.

But in what sort of fiction will one find it?

There's a tendency today to classify fiction as either mainstream or genre. One genre—the "mystery"—can be indiscriminately applicable to puzzle stories, espionage, police procedure, capers, detectives and private eyes ("straight" or "hardboiled"), psychological suspense, and horror.

These highly-disparate designations represent a desperate attempt on the part of writers and readers to establish individual criteria for separate categories. But to the literary establishment, the only basis for evaluating genre fiction is a commercial one. How well does it sell? Is the published product's appeal limited to special tastes, or will it have a mass-market audience?

The sort of mystery in which we seek some understanding of antisocial behavior generally has little mass-marketing potential, and the reasons for this are fairly obvious.

The typical mass-market male customer can be identified by his baseball cap and mustache; in one hand he carries a six-pack of Lite beer, and in his other, a take-out pizza. He is apt to be dissatisfied with his job and disappointed with his sex life. Reading is often a form of escapist activity when there are no sports programs available on TV, and also serves as a concomitant to chronic constipation.

Mystery fiction which doesn't cater to mass-market males or to devout Agatha Christian females is regarded as something of a pariah. Or almost so.

The past decade has seen a gradual revival of the short story form, and it is in this area that the more specialized adjuncts of the genre flourish today. Both horror and psychological suspense enjoy greater consideration in the pages of magazines and anthologies. And there's a slowly increasing awareness of original efforts as opposed to the gross-out imitations of splatter-films and comics.

It is in the insightful work that we will find probings and portrayals of the psychopathic personality, rendered by writers whose voices are clear rather than strident; writers who know that a whisper is sometimes more penetrating than a scream.

I believe in the power of suggestion. It stimulates the imagination, stirs emotion, evokes glimpses of worlds beyond the words. Those capable of using this power are the true creative artists.

Tourists today can fly to Brazil, board a train there and tape the sounds of their travel. Yet that tape, however stereophonically enhanced, can never equal the feel and essence of the journey captured by Villa-Lobos' brief and deceptively-simple tone-poem, "The Little Train of the Capeiras." Modern photography is a marvel, but had the camera been available in Leonardo's day, it could not have given us a *Mona Lisa.*

Knowing what to select and what to omit, what to emphasize, what to subordinate—these discriminations distinguish the artist from the artisan in other fields, and is of preeminent importance in the writing of fiction. Exactitude, used to extreme, reduces creative writing to reporting, and nowhere is this more evident than in the so-called horror genre, where emphasis on the explicit reduces the genuine to mere journalism.

Subtlety is also an important ingredient. Big is not necessarily better, louder is what stand-up comics become when their routines don't register with the audience. Villa-Lobos' little train wouldn't benefit by a musical transformation into an Amtrak express or a jumbo jet; the enigmatic lady popularly known as the *Mona Lisa* doesn't need the aid of a face-lift, nor does her appeal depend upon giving her more cleavage.

Suggestion, subtlety, selectivity—these are major criteria which helped govern the selection of stories for this anthology. But everything is a matter of degree. I hasten to issue fair warning that there's violence aplenty lurking in the pages that follow; violence which lurks waiting to leap out and strike at your most vulnerable sensibilities.

After all, the writers of these stories can only be restrained up to a point. It is very difficult to keep a ghoul on the Pritikin Diet.

About writers of horror fiction, now: They tend to come in all shapes and sizes, ranging from self-styled amateurs like the late H. P. Lovecraft to seasoned professionals fully capable of writing a manual titled *How to Raise Hackles for Fun and Profit.* Both extremes have their place in this volume. In between are a round (but never square) dozen others, representing a variety of ages and backgrounds. What they have in common is their uncommon ability—their talent for terror.*

Another shared characteristic is their gift for characterization. Using that gift, they have achieved one of the

*Sounds like a good title for an anthology. Somebody will steal it—wait and see!

objectives of this anthology, giving us some understanding of psychopaths as people.

One of the most effective methods they employ is to explore motivations. It's easy enough to describe psychopaths as walking time-bombs, but we're not as much interested in the explosions as we are in what makes them tick.

Creating explosions and explosive situations is fairly easy. But it's the ticking that makes for suspense, and devising ways to keep it going requires a special *expertise.* The contributors represented between these covers are thus endowed. They are horologists of horror, constructing the mechanisms of madness with clockwork precision.

Explosions startle with their abruptness and stun through the sheer volume of their sound. Yet no matter how big the bang, its echo will die. And in the end, it's the ticking you're most likely to remember; the constant nerve-wracking ticking which compels you to concentrate on its source, its significance, its reason for being.

As a sometime writer myself, I once devised a novel, the previously-mentioned *Psycho,* which was later filmed. In the book I killed off my heroine early in the story, while she was taking a shower. The film version followed this procedure, but expanded the murder with vivid details. Thanks to the skill of the director and his production crew, audiences were shocked by the sequence; anyone mentioning *Psycho* would automatically refer to the "shower scene."

That was the "explosion."

Because of the noise it made at the box office, the film and its famed episode were widely imitated. Girls screamed in shower stalls and similarly-confining areas, while undergoing femicide at the hands—and weapons—of various mad slashers. Somehow none of these pseudo-*Psycho* offerings seem to stand up well under long-term critical scrutiny, and while some enjoyed brief success in ripping up heroines and ripping-off the original, few are frequently recalled or revived today.

Meanwhile *Psycho* endures, but with a noticeable and intriguing shift in emphasis.

During an era of escalating overkill, today's hapless heroines frequently suffer a death worse than fate, sometimes before we are even introduced to them by name. And the effect of the once-horrendous "shower scene" has been so watered down by imitators that its chief function now is to serve as a study-project for classes in film-editing.

This being the case, what has kept *Psycho* alive, both in print and onscreen?

Here's where that shift in emphasis comes in. Readers and viewers have come to realize that this is not a story about a "shower scene." The story is about a man named Norman Bates.

Norman isn't a psychopath, but a full-fledged psychotic. In order to divert suspicion from him in a visual medium, the film depicted him as younger and thinner than he appeared in the book, and deprived him of the alcohol which sometimes fueled his fugue. In other respects more important than appearance, however, he emerges as the central character, the *diabolus ex machina* whose madness is more memorable than his method. We remember Norman because of the way he "ticks."

And *why*.

It's the *why,* as well as the way, which writers represented in this anthology explore. To do so without turning stories into mere case-histories earns them my admiration and profound gratitude. Any editor would be grateful for contributors like these. If you share my sentiments, then by all means seek out other offerings by the same writers in the bookstores and on the magazine stands. Their work goes far beyond mere gimmickry; they are not gratuitous goremongers but true storytellers.

I think a great many stories included here will keep ticking away for a long while to come. Particularly if one bears in mind that such tales of death and dementia are not fantasies.

Recent scientific studies have indicated that the mortality rate for the human race is close to 100%.

As for the prevalence of mental disorders, it was H. P. Lovecraft who posed the question—"Where does madness leave off and reality begin?"

Perhaps you'll find the answer in the following pages.

Snow Man

John Coyne

When Marc entered the classroom, "Peace Corps Go Home" had already been written on the blackboard. It was neatly done, and that eliminated all but two of the Ethiopian students.

They were watching him, but he only laughed. Stepping up to the board, he erased the words, deliberately sending a spray of dust into the room. The girls near the windows waved their arms to keep the dust away, and Kelemwork stood and opened one of the windows.

Nothing was said.

Marc arranged his books on the teacher's desk, making sure he looked busy and important before them. The second bell rang and he looked up at the class. A few faces turned away. They were unsure of what he'd do and that made him feel better. Still, he had to take a couple of deep breaths to put a stopper on a wave of his own fear.

"You're unhappy about the quiz," he began, speaking slowly. Even thought they were in the third year of secondary school, they still had a hard time understanding English. He spoke slowly, too, because it helped to calm his nerves. "All right! I'm unhappy, too! A teacher must set standards. You understand, don't you?"

He wondered how much they did understand. He crossed the front of the room, pacing slowly. No one was watching him.

"What do you want from me?" he shouted. "All hundreds? What good will that do you? Huh? How far will you get? Into fourth year? So what!" He kept shouting. He couldn't stop himself. His thin voice bounced off the concrete walls.

Still they sat unmoved. A few glanced in his direction, their brown eyes sweeping past his eyes. In the rear of the classroom Tekele raised his hand and stood.

"We want you to be fair, Mr. Marc."

"Am I not fair?"

Tekele hesitated.

"Go ahead, Tekele, speak up." Marc lowered his voice.

"You are difficult."

"Oh, I'm difficult. First I am unfair, now I am difficult."

Tekele did not respond. He looked out the window, and then sat down.

They kept silent. Marc stared at each one, letting the silence intensify. He could feel it swell up and fill his eardrums.

"All right," he told them. "We will have another test."

They stirred immediately, whispering fiercely in Amharic. Marc opened the folder on his desk and taking the mimeographed sheets began to pass them out, setting each one face-down on a desk, telling them not to start until they were told. When he came back to the front of the room he announced, "You have thirty minutes. Begin."

No one moved.

He walked slowly among the rows, down one, then the next, and when he reached the far left rear corner of the room, he said, "If you do not begin, I will fail everyone. You will all get zeros."

They did not move.

He went again to the front of the room, letting them have plenty of time.

"All right!" he said again, pausing. If just one of them would weaken, look at the quiz, he would have them. "That's all!" he announced. "You all get zeros. No credit for the quiz and I am counting it as an official test." He gathered his books into his arms and left the classroom.

As the door closed, the room ignited. Desks slammed. Students shouted. He turned from the noise and went along the second floor corridor and into the faculty room. Helen was there grading papers. She glanced at her watch when Marc entered and smiled, asking, "Did you let your class go?"

He shook his head.

"What, then?" She watched as he went to the counter and made himself a cup of tea.

"They won't take my quiz."

She waited for his explanation.

"I left them in the room."

"Marc!"

"They wrote 'Peace Corps Go Home' on the blackboard."

"My, they're out to get you." She smiled, sipping her tea and watching him over the rim of the cup. She had a small round face, much like a smile button, and short blond hair.

Marc wanted to slap her.

He heard footsteps on the stairs, voices talking in Amharic, and then silence as the class walked by the open door of the faculty room. The students were headed for the basketball court.

"What are you going to do?" Helen asked. She was trying to be nice.

"Nothing."

"Aren't you going to talk to Ato Asfaw?"

"Why should I? He said discipline was our problem."

Helen put down her cup. "Marc, you're making a mistake."

"You're the one who thinks it's so goddamn funny."

"Okay! I'm sorry I made light of your tragedy." She began again to correct her students' papers.

Marc sat with her, waiting for something to happen. The faculty room was hot. The dry, hot early morning of an African winter. Through the open windows, Marc could feel the hot winds off the Ogaden Desert. He was from Michigan and that morning he had heard on the shortwave radio that the American Midwest was having a blizzard. He tried to remember snow. Tried to remember the wet feel of it under his mittens when he was only ten and walking home from where the school bus left him on the highway.

He was still sitting staring out at the desert when the school guard came and said in Amharic that the Headmaster wanted to see him. Walking to the office, Marc glanced again at the arid lowlands and thought of snow blowing against his face. It made him feel immensely better.

"Mr. Marc," Ato Asfaw asked, "why are 3B on the playground?" The small, slight headmaster was standing behind his desk.

"I left them in class. They refused to take my test." Marc sat down and made himself comfortable. He knew his casualness upset the Headmaster; it was an affront to the Ethiopian culture. In the two years that he had been in Ethiopia, he had learned what offended Ethiopians and he enjoyed annoying them.

"But you gave them a quiz last week." The Headmaster sat down behind his enormous desk, nearly disappearing from sight. With his high, pronounced forehead and the finely sculptured face of an Amharia, he looked like the emperor Haile Selassie.

"Yes, I gave them a quiz. They did poorly, so I decided to give them another one."

Asfaw nodded, hesitated a moment, then said, "3B has other complaints. They say you are not fair. They say you call them monkeys, tell them they are stupid."

"They're lying."

"They say you left the classroom, is this true?"

"They refused to take my quiz."

"Perhaps you may give them another chance."

"Why?"

"Because they are children, Mr. Marc. And you are their teacher." He spoke quickly, showing his impatience.

His desk was covered with papers typed in Amharic script. Stacks of thin sheets fastened together with small straight pins. How could he help a country that couldn't even afford paperclips, Marc wondered.

"I don't see them as children," he told the Headmaster. "Some of those 'boys' are older than I am. They know what they're doing. They wrote 'Peace Corps Go Home' on the blackboard." Marc stopped talking. He knew it sounded like a stupid complaint. Helen was right, yet he wouldn't back down in front of the Ethiopian. Americans never back down, he reminded himself.

"You have been difficult with them," the Headmaster went on, still speaking softly, as if discussing Marc's sins. "They are not American students; you are being unjust, treating them as such." He stood again, as if to gain more authority by standing.

"I am not treating them as American students or any other kind of student, except Ethiopians," Marc answered back. He crossed his legs, knowing it was another sign of disrespect.

"Mr. Marc, your classes in Peace Corps training taught you Ethiopian customs. Am I correct?"

Marc nodded, watching Ato Asfaw, waiting for the catch.

"You learned that we have our own ways. Your teaching methods are, what do you call it, 'culture shock'?" He smiled.

Marc shrugged. They had all been told about culture shock, how everything in the new country would disorient them. But he had weathered "culture shock" of his own, he reminded himself, and said to the Headmaster, "This country has a history of school strikes, am I right?"

"Not a history, no. There have been some strikes. But over nothing as trivial as this! This quiz!" His voice rose as he finished the sentence.

"Well, what are you going to do?" Marc asked. He hooked his arm over the back of the chair.

Asfaw picked up a sheet of paper off his desk.

From where he sat, Marc saw the paper was full of handwritten Amharic notes.

"There are many complaints on this paper," the Headmaster said again. "The students are sending a copy to the Ministry of Education in Addis Ababa. Did I mention that?" He looked over at Marc, enjoying the moment. He had the brown saucer eyes of all Ethiopians. In the women, Marc found the eyes made them timid-looking and lovely. The same eyes made the men look weak.

"These complaints are lies. You know that!" Marc

stood. "I want an apology before consenting to teach that class again." He turned and walked out of the Headmaster's office without being dismissed. It made him feel great, like the protagonist of his own life story.

The students in 3B were still on strike at the end of the week. Marc kept out of sight. He stayed in the faculty room when not teaching his other classes, spending his time reading old copies of *Time* magazine. None of the teachers, including the other Peace Corps Volunteers, ever mentioned the strike. The Volunteers stationed at the school were the Olivers, a married couple from Florida, who lived out near the school, and Helen Valentino, who had an apartment next to his place.

The town was called Diredawa and it was built at the edge of the Ogaden. There was an old section which was all Ethiopian, mostly Somalis and Afars, and the newer quarter where the French had lived when they built the railway from Djibouti across the desert and up the escarpment to Addis Ababa in the Ethiopian highlands.

Marc never saw his students in town. He had no idea where they lived. Unlike the other Volunteers, he had never been asked to any of their homes for Injera and Wat. He thought about that when he was killing time in the faculty lounge waiting out his striking class period.

He did see the students from his class, saw them as they passed along the open hallways, going and coming from one another class. They watched him with their brown eyes and said nothing, did not even take a sudden breath, as was the Ethiopian custom when making a silent note of recognition.

He thought of them as brown rabbits. Like the brown rabbits he hunted every fall back home on the farm. He liked to get close to the small animals, to see quivering brown bodies burrowing into the snow, and then he'd cock his .22 and fire quickly, catching the fleeing white-tail in mid-hop, splattering blood on the fresh whiteness.

Marc raised his hand and aimed his forefinger at his students lounging in the shade of trees beyond the make-shift basketball courts. He silently popped each one of them off with his make-believe pistol.

"Singh has had classes with 3B for the last week," Helen told him. "I just found out."

It was the second week of the strike when she came over to his apartment with the news. He was dressed in an Arab skirt and sitting on his bed chewing the Ethiopian drug chat. The chat gave him a low-grade high and a slight headache, but it was the only drug he could get at the edge of the desert.

"That bastard," Marc said.

"Singh is telling the students that they can't trust the Peace Corps Volunteers. He's telling them we're not real teachers."

"That bastard," Marc said again.

"What are you going to do about it?" she demanded.

Marc shrugged. The chat had made him sleepy.

"We're all in trouble because of you," Helen told him. She was pacing the bedroom, moving in and out of the sunlight filtering through the metal shutters. The only way to keep the apartment cool was to lower the shutters during the long hot days.

"It's my class," he told her, grinning.

They had been lovers in training at UCLA, and during the first few months in Diredawa.

"Yes, but we're all Peace Corps!"

"Screw the Peace Corps."

"Marc, be serious!" She was in tears, and she was holding herself, trying to keep from crying.

"I am serious. I don't give a damn."

"I'm calling Morgan in Addis. I'm getting him down here," she shouted back.

He wanted to pull away the mosquito netting and ask her climb into bed with him, but he didn't have the nerve.

"I don't want him here. I'll handle this," he told Helen.

"You just said you're not going to do anything. Look at you! Sitting here all day chewing chat!" She waved dismissively.

"Want some?" he asked, grinning through the thick netting.

Helen left him in his apartment. The chat had made him too listless to keep arguing, to go running after her, to pull her back to his bed and make love to her. Besides, he knew she would call Morgan. She was always trying to run his life.

Marc went to the airport to meet the Peace Corps Director. It might have been more dramatic to let Brent Morgan find him, to track him down in one of the bars, to come in perspiring from the heat with his suit crumpled, his tie loosened. But then Helen would have had first chance at him, and Marc didn't want that.

The new airport terminal was under construction and there was nowhere to wait for the planes, so Marc parked the Peace Corps jeep in the shade of palm trees and watched the western horizon for the first glimpse of the afternoon flight from Addis.

He himself had first arrived in Diredawa on the day train. It was their second week in Ethiopia and all the Volunteers were leaving Addis Ababa for their assignments. They were the only ones traveling by train.

The long rains were over and they could see the clouds rolling away from the city, leaving a very pure blue on the horizon. It was still chilly, but not the piercing cold they had felt when they first arrived in country. No one had told them Ethiopia, or Africa, could be so cold. But they were going now, everyone said, to a beautiful climate, to warm country, to what Africa was really like.

It had been their first trip out of the city. They did not know anyone, and everything was new and strange. They sat together on metal benches and watched the plains stretch away towards the mountains as they dropped rapidly into the Great Rift Valley.

The land, after the long rains, was green and bright with yellow meskal flowers. On the hillsides were mushroom-shaped tukul huts, thick brown spots on the green hillside, in among the yellow flowers. There were few trees and they were tall, straight eucalyptus which grew in tight bunches near the tukul compounds.

In the cold of early morning, Ethiopians were going off to church. They moved in single file across the low hills towards the Coptic church set in a distant grove of eucalyptus. A few Ethiopians rode small, short-legged horses and mules, all brightly harnessed, and everyone on the soft hills wore the same white shammas dress and white jodhpurs.

Marc had never been so happy in his life.

Now, sitting in the shade, he saw the Ethiopian Airlines plane come into sight; and, spotting it, he realized his eyes were blurry and that he was crying.

Marc wondered why he was crying, but also he knew that lately he was always finding tears on his face and having no idea why he was crying.

The Peace Corps Director was the first off the plane. His coat and tie were already off and his collar was open. From the hatch of the small craft, he waved, then bounded down the ramp, swinging his thick brown briefcase from one hand to the other. He came over to where Marc sat in the front seat of the open jeep.

Marc reached forward and turned over the engine.

"Tenastelign," Brent said, jumping into the front seat.

"Iski. Indemin aderu," Marc answered in Amharic and spun the vehicle out of the dirt lot.

Brent grabbed the overhead frame as the small jeep swayed.

"Where do you want to go?" Marc shouted, glancing at the Peace Corps Director.

"School . . . ?"

Marc nodded, and spun the jeep abruptly toward the secondary school.

Brent kept trying to make conversation, shouting to Marc over the roar of the engine, asking about the others, telling Marc news from Addis. Marc kept quiet.

He was being an asshole, he knew, but he couldn't help himself. He wanted Brent to have a hard time. It was crazy, but he couldn't stop.

When they reached the school, a few students were standing in the shade of the building, leaning up against the whitewashed wall and holding hands, as Ethiopian men did. Brent straightened his tie and put on his coat as they went to the Headmaster's office.

Asfaw stood when they entered the office, and he came around his desk to shake hands with them both, gesturing for them to sit. Brent began to talk at once in his quick, nervous way, telling the school director why he had come to Diredawa, explaining that the Ministry of Education, as well as the Peace Corps, was concerned about the situation with Marc's class.

Asfaw listened hard, frowned, nodded, agreeing with everything, as Marc had known he would. He nodded to Brent's vague generalizations about the Headmaster supporting the faculty, and the Ministry supporting both.

Marc wondered if Brent really believed all this bull-shit.

"Of course, Mr. Marc has been very strict with his pupils," Asfaw finally said, not following up on what Brent had said.

"Well, perhaps," Brent answered, gesturing with both hands, as if he were trying to fashion some meaning of the situation from the hot desert breeze. "But that really isn't the question. I mean, in the larger sense." He pulled himself forward on the chair, straining to make himself clear. Then he stopped, saw Asfaw was not comprehending, saw a film of confusion cross the Headmaster's brown eyes, and asked, as if in defeat, "What do you think is the solution?"

"Mr. Marc is not very patient with our people. They are not used to his ways."

"There are certain universal ways of good behavior," Marc interrupted, raising his voice. "They deliberately did not take my test. That's an insult! And you! They know you're too afraid to do anything."

"All right! All right!" Brent spoke quickly, halting Marc.

Asfaw nodded, then began. "If you do not mind, Mr. Brent Morgan, I would like to say something." He looked for agreement and Brent nodded, gesturing with both hands.

"We have a strike in our school. Now this is something not unknown in our country. We have had many strikes. I have been in strikes when I was a student. I say this because I do not want Mr. Marc to feel he is being subjected to prejudice by his students. So, we must not say why do the students strike, but how can we bring them back to school.

"For Mr. Brent, you have said education is the most important for Ethiopia. We must not be so hidden by these petty problems, and look instead towards the larger issues. Do you not agree? Is this not what you have said?" He glanced at both of them, his face as alert as a startled rabbit's.

"Why, yes," Brent answered hesitantly. "We can certainly agree, but let's not dismiss some basic educational principles."

"And what is this?"

"That a teacher commands a position of authority within the community, that the students respect this authority," the Peace Corps Director answered quickly.

"A teacher, I was told when I studied at Ohio University, achieved respect by proving to his students that he deserved it."

"Yes, this is very true, but it is difficult to achieve when the students know the teacher is alone in his authority," Morgan answered.

"Or when they would rather have a passing grade than an education," Marc butted in.

Asfaw smiled at Marc and said softly, like a caring parent, "To be truly honest, Mr. Marc, you, too, were probably concerned mostly with point averages, I believe the term is, when you were in school."

"Let us try," Brent began slowly, "to look at this issue again." He maintained a smile, adding, "We have been missing the main point. The strike must cease. The students must return to school. Now what avenues are open to us?"

"But I have made my decision!" Asfaw seemed surprised. He looked from face to face, his brown eyes widening.

"Certainly, but do you really think Marc should return to class without an apology from the students?"

"Oh, an apology is such a deceiving thing. Yes, perhaps in America, it is important, but you must remember this is Ethiopia. We have our own ways, don't we, Mr. Marc?" The Headmaster smiled, and then shrugged, as if it were all beyond his power.

"And in Ethiopia the mark of a clever man is his ability to outwit another person," Brent answered. "You must realize if Marc returns to his classroom without an apology, or some form of disciplinary action taken, he will be ineffective as a teacher."

The small man leaned forward, putting his elbows on the desk. "I will first lecture the class. I will tell them such demonstrations will not be tolerated. And Mr. Marc, if he wishes, can have them write an essay, which I will also see is done."

"And what happens the next time I give a test?"

"I should think, Mr. Marc, as a clever person, you will review your teaching methods. I think you are aware none of the other teachers, including the Peace Corps, are having difficulty with their classes."

"I have to remain in authority in my class."

"I think Marc is correct. We must be united on this point. Take a firmer position," Brent added, making a fist with one hand.

"How might you handle it?" Asfaw asked Marc.

"Give them some manual work."

"They cannot do coolie work! They are students!"

"That's the point! They don't deserve to be students. A little taste of hard labor will prove my point. They won't mouth off again."

"It could be symbolic, I should think," Brent suggested. "You could arrange a clean-up of the compound, perhaps. It would be very instructive, actually."

"Nothing less than three days. The first day it will be all a joke, but the next two they'll work up a little sweat!" Marc smiled in anticipation.

"You are asking very much." Asfaw shook his head. "It is against their culture to work with their hands."

"I'm asking only enough to let me return to that classroom with the respect given a teacher."

Brent kept glancing at Marc, who in turn, kept avoiding Morgan's eyes. He liked pushing the Headmaster up against the wall.

"If you have them do at least three days of work around the school," Marc finally said, surrendering to the pressure of the moment, "I'll forget about the apology and go back to teaching."

Brent glanced quickly at Asfaw.

The Headmaster hesitated.

He was thinking of what all that meant, Marc knew. He wasn't going to be outwitted by this ferenji.

"It is not completely satisfactory," the Headmaster responded slowly, "but the students are not learning. I must put away my personal feelings for the betterment of education in Ethiopia. I will call the boys together and explain the requirements." He smiled.

Brent slapped the knees of his lightweight suit and stood. He was beaming with relief even before he reached across the Headmaster's desk and shook the small man's hand.

Marc drove back into town after he dropped Brent at the airport. He drove past the Ras Hotel where they went to swim, and where they ate lunch and dinner on Sundays, the cook's day off. He turned at the next block and went by the open-air theater, then slowly drove along the street which led to their apartments and the piazza.

The street was heavily shaded from trees and the houses with big compounds, built up to the sidewalks. It was one of the few towns in Ethiopia which resembled a city, with geometric streets, sidewalks, traffic signs. But the bush was present. Somalis walked their camels along the side streets, herded small flocks of sheep and goats between the cars and up to the hills. Behind the taming influences of the foreign houses was Africa. Marc felt as if it were beating against his temples.

The apartment the Peace Corps had rented was not what Marc had imagined he'd be living in. He had visions of mud huts, of seamy little villages along the Nile. But not Diredawa. It was a small town with pavement, sidewalks, warm evenings filled with the smell of bougainvillea bushes, and bars with outside tables. It was a little French town in the African desert.

He parked the jeep in front of the apartment building, then walked over to Helen's apartment and, going onto the porch, knocked on the door. When she didn't answer, he walked in and went into her bedroom, whispering her name. When she still didn't answer, he walked in and sat on the edge of her bed and watched her sleep. She had taken a nap, as always, after her last afternoon classes.

She continued to sleep, breathing smoothly, her arms stretched out at her sides. He could see she was naked under a white cotton sheet, and he watched her in silence for awhile before leaning forward and kissing her softly on the cheek. She stirred and blinked her eyes.

"What time is it?" she asked, waking and pulling the sheet closer.

"After three. Morgan's gone. I took him to the afternoon plane."

"Why didn't you wake me?" She turned on her side.

"I didn't know you wanted to see him."

She shook her head, pressing her lips together.

"You want to have dinner?" he asked, not responding to her anger.

"I can't. I'm going out."

Marc watched her for a moment, and then said, "Do you want me to ask with whom?"

"I have a date with Tedesse. We're going to the movies."

"When did this start?" He kept his eyes on her.

"Nothing has started." She shifted again on the bed, sensing her own nakedness under the sheet.

"What about us?" he asked weakly, wanting her to feel his pain.

"Marc, I have no idea what our relationship is, not from one moment to the next." She was staring at him. "Sometimes, you're great. You can't do enough for me. The next day, you know, you barely say hello. What do you expect?" Her eyes glistened.

"The school's bugging me, that's all. You know that. Can't you understand, for chrissake!"

"There's nothing wrong with the school," she answered. "You've created half the problems yourself." She had pulled herself up and was wide awake.

"And you top it off by dating some Ethiopian!"

"Marc, quit all this self-pity. It's very unattractive."

"I wanted to go to the movies."

"Then go!"

"Sure, and have you there with Tedesse?"

"Do what you want." She turned her face toward the whitewashed bedroom wall. "Now please leave. I want to get some sleep."

"Are you in love with him?"

"I don't want to talk about it."

"I need to know."

"Marc, don't badger me."

He slammed the apartment door, leaving, and a Somali knife on the living room wall fell down with a crash.

The students began to move rock on Monday. Marc

walked out to the field behind the school and watched them work. It was malicious of him, he knew, but he enjoyed it.

He stood on a mound overlooking the work area and did not speak, but he knew they were aware of him. He saw them glancing at him, whispering to themselves.

They continued to work and after a few minutes he turned and started back toward the school. It was almost two o'clock, time for his afternoon classes.

The first stone flew over his head. Marc didn't react to it. He wasn't even sure where it came from. The second one clipped his shoulder, and the next hit him squarely in the back. He wheeled about, ducked one aimed at his head, and started back at the students.

There were no obvious attackers. He saw no upraised arms. They were working as docilely as before. He stopped and cursed them, but no one looked his way, no satisfying smirks flashed on any of their brown faces.

He stayed away from the work site for the next two days, but watched them from the second floor corridor, making sure they saw him, standing there, grinning, while they sweated under the hot sun.

On the Thursday morning the class was to return, he decided to begin teaching immediately, not to dawdle on their punishment, or the rock tossing. He planned to teach just as Mr. Singh, the Indian, did, with no class discussion, nothing but note taking. He would fill the blackboard and let them copy down the facts. No more following the question where it led. No more trying to make his classroom exciting and interesting. He didn't care if they learned anything more than what they could memorize.

He rode his bike out to school early, getting there before the students or teachers, and went upstairs to the faculty room to wait for the first bell.

A few of the teachers said hello as they arrived, but when Helen arrived on her bike shortly after seven, she asked what was wrong with their students.

Marc didn't know what she was talking about. Helen went to the front windows and watched the compound.

The students were too quiet, she told him. Something was wrong.

Marc stepped onto the breezeway and looked up at the three stories of classrooms. The railings were crowded. The students stood quietly, waiting and watching. A few, mostly girls from the lower grades, were playing on the basketball court. The others in the compound were in small groups of three and four. There was a little talking, but only in whispers. Gradually they turned and noticed Marc, and watched him without expression, their soft brown eyes telling him nothing.

He stepped back into the faculty room.

The Sports Master, an Ethiopian, had just come in. He scanned the teachers until he spotted Marc and came directly to him.

He had once played football for the country's national team and had a small, well-built body. Around his neck a whistle dangled from a cord. The man was sweating.

"We're having a strike," he told Marc. "Asfaw has sent for the army."

As he spoke, two Land Rovers swung into the compound and a half-dozen soldiers tumbled out. The students' reaction was immediate. The passive, quiet assembly rose up clamoring. Those students on the three tiers of the breezeway began to beat the iron railing. Girls began the strange high shrills they usually saved for funerals. And then rocks began to fly.

The windows of the Land Rovers were broken first. The officer was caught halfway between the school and the Rovers; he hesitated, not sure whether to keep going or rejoin his men.

And then the barrage escalated. From all sides, from everywhere, came the stones and rocks. One soldier was hit hard, faltered, and grabbed his buddy. From the second floor faculty room, Marc could see the blood on the man's face. And then from everywhere in the school compound came the stones and rocks.

The officer ran back to the Land Rover and grabbed his Uzi. Spinning around, he opened fired on the students, spraying them with a quick burst of bullets. The small bodies of boys and girls bounced backwards, smashed up against the whitewashed walls of the school.

Time magazine was sold at a barber shop near the apartment. The barber saved Marc a copy when it came in on the Friday plane and he picked it up on Saturday, the day after the shooting at school, to read in the Ras Makonnen Bar. There were soldiers in the piazza, loitering in the big square facing the bar.

Occasionally a jeep would careen through the open square, its tires squealing. There were no students in the piazza, but periodically Marc heard gunfire coming from across the gully. He wondered if it had to do with the students. Were they catching more of them, chasing them down in the dark alley of the Moslem section? He smiled, thinking that might be happening while he had a peaceful breakfast.

He ordered orange juice, pastry, and opened *Time,* flipping rapidly through the pages for articles about the Midwest.

There had been another ice storm in Chicago, he read, that had closed down O'Hare Airport, caused a forty-five-car pile up on I-94. Marc read the article twice, lingering over familiar names and the details of the storm.

He kept smiling, thinking of home, wishing he were there for the storm. He imagined what his Michigan town might looked like, buried deep in ice and snow. He could feel the sharp pain of the wind on his cheeks, feel the biting cold. He looked up, stared through the thick, bright, lush bougainvillea bushes.

There were tears in his eyes. Cold tears on his face. He didn't know that he was crying.

He wiped his face with the small, waxy paper napkin, and looked out at the bright square and the loitering soldiers, who had found shade at the base of several false banana trees. They had abandoned their rifles, left them propped against a tree. He wondered why the soldiers weren't cold.

He thought again of the killings at the school, how the officer with the Uzi had killed eight in the first burst of gunfire.

Helen had begun to scream. She was holding her ears, trying not to hear the students' cries, but still she couldn't look away from the slaughter.

He couldn't either. Several of his students, long, lanky kids, jumped and jerked when they were hit. The bullets tossed them around, made them hop and dance, before they were slammed back against the whitewashed walls of the school where they splattered like eggs, breaking bright red yolks.

Helen wouldn't stop screaming, even after silence fell in the school yard, after the lieutenant stopped firing, after the students scattered, those who were still alive.

She was standing at the windows, screaming. Marc couldn't go to her; he couldn't figure out how to walk. Mr. Singh finally seized her, pulled her away from the window as the Headmaster began screaming in Amharic at the soldiers.

Marc walked out the door then and down the stairs. He walked straight by the soldiers as if what had happened meant nothing to him. He walked away from the school, went across the open brush land to the dry gully river, which he knew he could follow into town. From the river bed, he heard the sounds of an ambulance coming out from the French hospital.

He walked to his apartment and locked himself inside, then crawled into bed and slept through the heat of the day. Helen came to get him after dark. She had told him martial law had been proclaimed and that she and the Olivers were leaving, going up to Addis Ababa on the night train. It was no longer safe in town, she told him. But he wouldn't leave, he told her. He wouldn't let the students drive him out of Diredawa.

Marc stood and walked out of the cafe bar and into the piazza. It was empty except for the soldiers. He wondered where everyone had gone, why no one was on the streets. He was lonely, knowing that he was the only Peace Corps Volunteer in Diredawa. He thought that perhaps he was the only white man left in town.

But it wasn't true. There were French doctors at the hospital, missionaries from the Sudan Interior Mission, French workers with the railway. Tourists. Yes, the desert town was full of white people.

Still he hurried, cut across the open square, going home, back to his apartment where behind locked doors he'd be safe until the Peace Corps staff came to get him. They wouldn't leave him alone, he knew. This was a mistake, he thought at the same moment, crossing the empty street. He shouldn't have left his apartment and taken a chance on the streets. There might be students around.

He broke into a run.

A rock hit him on the side of the head and bounced off like a misplayed golf shot. He stumbled forward, but knew he was okay. It had only been a rock. They couldn't kill him with rocks. He was too tough. Too much of an American. These were just people in some godawful backward Third World country, half starving to death every few years.

He pulled his hand away from the side of his face and his fingers looked bright with blood.

"Shit!" he said, thinking of the mess to his clothes. And he hated the smell of blood. He stumbled forward, finding his feet, knowing he had to keep running. They couldn't catch him in the middle of the street.

A half-dozen soldiers were still loitering by the entrance of the movie theater, less than a dozen yards from him. He waved to get their attention and shouted out in Amharic. Another rock hit him in the mouth.

He tumbled over on his back and rolled in the dirt, coughing up pieces of his teeth and globs of blood and spit. Marc raised his hand and tried to shout at the soldiers. Why weren't they helping him?

He crawled forward, still going toward the apartment, thinking only that if he could get to the gate and behind the iron fence, he would be safe.

He coughed up more blood and in his tears and pain knew he had to run, that they might swarm out of the trees, or wherever they were hiding deep in the palm-lined street, and seize him, take him back into the Old City, where it was another tribal law that would deal with him. An eye for an eye.

He got to his feet and ran.

There were more rocks, coming from the right and left, showering him, bashing his head, knocking him over once more. He fell forward, into the gutter, and smashed his head against the concrete.

If he stopped he was dead. His only hope was to reach the iron gates. Gebra, his zebagna, would keep out the crowd of students.

Why weren't the soldiers helping him? They hadn't hesitated to shoot when they were pelted, why couldn't they protect him?

He burst through the metal compound gate, startling Gebra. Marc shouted at him to bolt the compound door. It was the guard's job to protect him now.

He ran up the stairs to the second floor apartment and slammed the back door, locking it behind him. Running from room to room, he pulled the wide cords that dropped the heavy old metal shutters, shutting out the sunlight and sealing the apartment in the shadowy dark.

He fell in a corner, sweating from fear and exhaustion. Then he reached up and touched his forehead, felt for the rock bruise. When he took away his hand, he couldn't see his bloody fingers in the darkened room.

His hands were shaking. And he was freezing. He crept across the floor, going toward the bed, keeping himself below the windows, afraid the students might figure out which ones were his. The shutters were metal, but he couldn't be too careful, he told himself.

His whole body was trembling. It was funny, he thought. How could he be so cold in the middle of Africa? At the edge of the desert?

He thought of when he was in school, waiting on the road for the school bus and standing in the freezing cold. He shivered, and crawled under the mosquito netting, covering himself with the sheets. He would be okay soon, once he was warm. Why didn't he have a blanket, he wondered.

He watched the slanting sunlight filter through the

metal window shades. The sunlight stirred the dust off the desert. It lit the room with shafts that looked like prison bars. He felt his face and wondered why there was no blood. He waited for the rocks to begin again. He thought about waking in the warmth and comfort of his farmhouse in Michigan, where he knew everyone and everything, where he was safe, and no one was different. He shivered, freezing from the cold. He opened his eyes again and saw that it had begun to snow in Africa. The flakes falling through the sunlight filtered into the room.

He would be all right, he knew. He understood cold weather and deep snow. Ethiopians knew nothing of snow. He smiled, thinking: let them try to shovel snow! They'd need him. He knew about snow. It was part of his heritage. He would teach the students how to make a snow man, he thought, grinning, and realized that everything was going to be okay. He was in the Peace Corps, and he had a job to do.

A Gentle Breeze Blowing

Robert E. Vardeman

Charley Ferguson leaned forward on the counter, inspected the glass carefully and wiped off a greasy fingerprint only he saw, then spread out the tabloid. He shook his head as he scanned the lurid pictures and let his eyes march down the columns of smeary print rife with the latest reports on the government's misguided efforts and how they stifled America's free enterprise system.

The Econo-Stop Gasateria's door opened and a draft of air sent Charley fumbling to keep the paper from scattering. With the gust of wind would come dirt he'd have to sweep up, but in a minute. The paper still held his attention.

"Damned bureaucrats," he muttered, his mind on the article he'd been reading. "They don't want innovation. They want to keep us all down."

"I've heard that," the customer said.

"Yeah, me, too," said a second man. Charley looked up then. He hadn't noticed the second man come inside. Truth to tell, he hadn't noticed the first, either, except from the hot wind as the door opened to let in the dust.

"Don't turn rabbit on us," the first man said. The second was already moving to block the exit from behind the counter. Charley's heart jumped into his throat. He'd never been robbed before.

"Don't hurt me," he got out, his mouth filled with cotton. "Don't get blood all over me. The place is insured. There's no problem with me just handing over the money."

"You got it all wrong, Mr., uh—" The first man looked at the second for confirmation.

"Ferguson," the second said. "Charles J. Ferguson of 219 Sandstone Place, LA. I forget the ZIP code."

"Right. Now, Mr. Ferguson, we just want what you owe. Pay us two hundred and eighty-seven dollars and we'll be on our way."

Charley stared. He didn't understand.

"The chemicals, numb-nuts," the second man snapped. "You've been buying stuff from Priority Chemical Supply and you ain't been paying."

"The chemicals," Charley muttered. "I need them. I—"

"Can it, Ferguson. We just want the money."

"Isn't this unusual, sending men out to collect?"

The second man barked harshly, sounding more like a dog than a human. The first man said, "We got other business. Our boss told us to stop by and collect while we were out this way." As he moved, Charley saw the hint of a gun butt poking out of the man's well-tailored suit.

"I was going to send a check. Next payday. My work's important—"

"Yeah, right, you a gas jockey in some podunk burg just outside LA. You're doing rocket scientist stuff and can't be bothered."

"My work is important," Charley said, as if reciting

something he had memorized but didn't quite understand. "I'm developing a petrochemical fuel additive to eliminate pollution. You see, there are octanes and heptanes. They're all alkanes. I'm so close. I . . ."

The second man hit him expertly just behind the left ear, making his head spin. Charley fell forward, the tabloid slipping to the floor. Through his daze all he could think of was the blood getting on his shirt and how dirty his hands were from the floor. He ought to sweep it more often.

"Pay up. The boss didn't tell us to get tough with you, but he won't like it if we come back without your money."

"A check?" Charley came to a sitting position, trying to wipe the grime off his hands.

The man hit him again.

"Don't get smart, you little faggot. Cash. Now, or we beat it out of your worthless hide. It might take a month to find your parts if we strew 'em out over the desert."

Charley Ferguson paid his debt from the cash register. The men turned and left, talking and acting as if nothing remarkable had happened. Charley tried to get his breath back. His heart refused to stop racing and his hands badly needed washing. Then indignation replaced fear.

Dammit, he *needed* the chemicals for his research. In a way it was only fitting that Econo-Stop Gasateria pay for them, he decided. His invention would help them. It'd help all the gasoline companies.

He went to the rest room to clean up. He felt dirty after dealing with men like that.

"Let me get this straight," Mr. Pendergast said, his pale blue eyes narrowed to slits like a killer pig's. "You were robbed and you didn't even have the good sense to call the cops?"

"I called," Charley lied, his face emotionless and his gray eyes locked onto Pendergast's. "I dialed 911 and they kept putting me on hold. So I tried another number, but they kept shifting me around. I gave up since you were going to be here soon."

"You didn't report a robbery of almost three hundred dollars?" Pendergast shook his balding head, then rubbed the bare patches of skin with both hands to capture the sweat before it rolled down his face. "Ferguson, you're one stupid son of a bitch."

"What do you mean, Mr. Pendergast? I tried."

"You been coming up short in the register for almost three months. Now this."

"There've been a lot of drive-offs. Those damned gang kids. They fill up and then roar off without paying. And I explained the other shortage, the one for fifty dollars."

"Yeah, yeah, a fast-change artist. That happened to me once when I was starting out, but this kind of thing is happening a hell of a lot to you, Ferguson. Drive-offs, shortages, fast-change artists, now a goddamn robbery. I got to tell the company something."

"I'm telling the truth," Charley said with a straight face.

"Damned if I don't believe you," the supervisor said, staring hard at Charley and not seeing a chink in the man's façade. "All right, we'll get the cops out here, and you'll cooperate with them one hundred percent. If they tell you to jump, you ask how high on the way up, you got that?"

"Yes, sir," Charley said. He'd be off duty and home within an hour. He could finish the last of his tests. If only he hadn't come to work tonight. "Whatever you say, Mr. Pendergast."

* * *

As Charley Ferguson drove along the seventy-eight miles to his home, he passed by one of the huge Long Beach refineries. Impulse made him steer to the visitors parking lot, but he didn't go to the administration building. Secretaries kept him out. Bureaucrats like the ones described in the tabloids put up a barrier ordinary people couldn't penetrate. The oil companies didn't want to listen to inventors like him because he'd ruin their profits. He had found the ultimate additive, and there'd be no need for the millions of dollars of other shit they put into the gasoline to puff up their corpulent profits.

Charley hopped out of his car, wiped the seat clean with a dry rag, and then dug around in his trunk for a minute until he found the tarp. He followed the twelve-foot-tall fence with the barbed-wire top away from the office building. He'd get in. He wasn't like the others who could be stopped by a phalanx of secretaries and their bureaucrat bosses. He'd find the process engineer in charge and talk with him this time. The man would have the training and good sense to see right away how important the anti-smogger additive was.

The hole under the fence was obscured by a low-growing shrub. Charley pushed the bush out of the way, dropped the tarp so he wouldn't get his clothing dirty and slithered into the refinery, as he had done a half-dozen times before. Then, he had been studying the refinery's procedures. This single plant shipped more than fifty million gallons of gasoline a year all over the United States, and maybe the world. And at least ten percent of the output was used right here in LA where the smog was so bad Charley could taste it day and night, even out in the desert at the Econo-Stop Gasateria.

"Hey, you, put on a hard hat if you're going in there," came the sharp command. Charley turned to the burly man carrying a roll of blueprints under his arm.

"I'm looking for the project engineer," Charley said.

"Here, use this one." The man tossed him a hard hat from a rack near one of the tanks. "I don't know where McQuire is. Haven't seen him all morning. Who are you?"

"A chemist," Charley said without hesitation. "I've got a new additive that'll totally remove all pollutants when the gasoline burns."

"And I'm a monkey's uncle," the engineer said. "What do you call this wonder chemical, fairy gold?"

"It's my anti-smogger," Charley said. The man stopped and stared at him, then reached for the walkie-talkie at his belt.

"They told me about you," he muttered. He thumbed on the call button and spoke rapidly. To Charley, he said, "They told me a nut was always coming around making wild claims. How'd you get inside the fence?"

Charley almost panicked. They had thrown him out twice before. The last time the anti-American bureaucrat had promised to have him arrested. Charley didn't answer. He ducked through a door, then sprinted away. The engineer followed, but he was paunchy and out of shape. Charley led him a fine chase, knowing the layout better than the engineer, then saw a half-dozen security guards arrive in two jeeps. Charley clenched his hands into fists so tight the nails cut into the palms and caused tiny crescents of blood to form.

Why wouldn't they listen to him? He could make this plant into a producer of non-polluting gasoline overnight. All it would take was a drop or two of his anti-smogger. Why wouldn't they listen?

He gave them the slip, wiggled back under the fence and got to his car. It took several minutes using the alcohol-moistened towelettes to get his hands clean. Red lights flashed inside the refinery and a siren began to wail. He had to get home, he had to get to work. He'd show them. Charley Ferguson might not have a college degree but real inventors didn't need worthless pieces of paper given to toadies by pompous bureaucrats. What kind of schooling had made Edison the genius he was? He'd show them all!

Charley Ferguson put the small vial on the counter top and stared at the amber liquid sloshing inside. Ten millimeters, just the way the scientists measured stuff. He stared at the liquid and felt a warmth building inside at the magnitude of his achievement. It had taken years to develop and more failures than he cared to admit, but now he was ready to try it out. They'd always had it in for him, but he'd prove he was right. Charley sneered at the memories welling up. They all worked for the Japanese. All the bureaucrats wanted to keep down American ingenuity, the one thing that had made this country great. They were all traitors and had sold out to foreigners.

But Charley Ferguson would show them it could still be done. He snatched up the small glass bottle and hurried outside. A dry desert wind blew across the parking lot at the side of the Econo-Stop Gasateria. To Charley it felt like the breath of a new day. The best way of testing his gasoline additive was to demonstrate to users how it cut down on pollution.

Using the special key, Charley fumbled at the bottom of the small well and finally unlocked the underground gas tank. He pulled up the plug and leaned back as the heavy gasoline fumes rocked him. He sucked in a lungful of hot air and then bent over. He poured half the vial into the tank of unleaded gasoline. The other half went into the regular tank; Econo-Stop Gasateria didn't bother with the highfalutin premium brands. Mr. Pendergast said people needing gasoline out on the edge of LA just wanted enough to get into the city. They weren't looking for performance as much as they were for cheap fuel to keep them going a few more miles.

Charley would show them. He'd *give* them performance. No more smog. He wiped his hands off on a clean rag and smiled. Satisfied with the night's work, he went back inside. The new shipment of tabloids had arrived, but he held off his curiosity until he had swept the place spotless. Only then did he read through the horrors of a rabid pet weasel devouring a woman's small child and finally come to the new pieces on how American competition was being stifled.

Charley had done his part. He wondered if he should write to the paper and let them know.

"God, Ferguson, you can't believe the hell I've been going through the past couple days," Mr. Pendergast said. "The company's not buying the robbery, not all the way."

"You're firing me?" Charley Ferguson wasn't too disturbed at this. It had been two days since he had put the anti-smogger into the station's main tanks. The testimonials from hundreds of satisfied drivers not having to suck up their own auto's filthy pollution would make him rich.

"We can't get anybody to take your place, so you got a job for a while longer. Besides, you keep this place cleaner than any three guys ever could." Pendergast shook his head and pressed the heels of his hands into his eyes. He wasn't thinking about Charley or the job. "But that's not the half of it. The feds are on my case now."

"The EPA?" Charley feared them almost as he did OSHA. Damned meddling bureaucrats.

"Why them? No, this is the FBI. They got this bug up

their ass that the gassing deaths were caused by something from this station."

"What deaths?"

"Hell, if you'd get your nose out of those scandal rags and watch the TV you'd know. There's been a dozen deaths in the last couple days. Doesn't sound like anything more than coincidence but you know how they are."

Charley Ferguson knew. Bureaucrats.

"There they are now. Who else but an FBI agent would wear a coat and tie in this heat?" Pendergast wiped his face with a handkerchief and went to the meet the two federal agents. Charley watched from inside as they flipped open small wallets. Gold badges gleamed in the light from the exterior neon sign.

"We'll have to take samples," said the one obviously in charge. "It's been cleared with your main office." Charley stepped back so that he stood in shadow. He didn't want them seeing him. How they meddled, how they tried to hold hard-working Americans back.

"Why here?" complained Pendergast. "There must be a hundred other stations supplied by the refinery. That's where the trouble is, you know."

"We think it might be eco-terrorists," the second agent said. "It might not be your fault at all, but we have to check."

"Yeah, sure, sure," Pendergast said, "but why single out this station?"

"Gas receipts. All from this station. It's the only link we can find with eight of the deceased. And five others might have been through here in the past couple days."

"It's all a crock," Pendergast muttered. "A quirk of fate."

"The deaths had a few other elements in common,"

the second agent said, "but the overriding factor was the extreme toxicity of their car exhausts."

Charley Ferguson slipped away, going out the back door to his car. He didn't want to hear their lies. They were out to get him. The FBI was nothing but a bunch of bureaucrats like the EPA and the oil company executives. There wasn't anything wrong with his anti-smogger. They just wanted to keep polluting the nation's skies so they could keep everyone in check. Well, he wasn't going to let them!

Charley listened to the phone ring the next morning. He didn't answer. It would have been Mr. Pendergast wanting to know why he'd bugged out like he had. After he was supposed to be on duty and didn't show up, there weren't any more calls. Charley began to relax on that score, but he seethed at the injustice being heaped on his head. He was humanity's greatest benefactor since Alexander Fleming and the newspapers were calling him an eco-terrorist, a Green Fascist, a lunatic poisoning the nation's gasoline supply. They didn't come out and name him, but he knew they meant him.

Charley finished his dusting and clicked on his portable black and white TV. He never watched anything except *Jeopardy!* and the occasional Nova special on PBS. He just didn't have the time for frivolous viewing when there was so much research to be done, but now he watched the news. As always, it made him furious. Nothing good was ever shown. Only the bad was shown to demoralize American citizens. Even his anti-smogger was being run into the ground.

Charley snorted in disgust as he saw the lead news item.

". . . new eco-terrorist activity has brought about eight more deaths. All deaths occurred while the driver was stopped in traffic. It is theorized that the toxic gases seeped into the cars from tainted gasoline. Less than one minute's exposure to the poisonous exhaust is needed to cause unconsciousness. Death follows within minutes. The FBI claims that they are close to making an arrest but decline to say what eco-terrorist group is responsible. If you have any information, call Crime-crushers at 555-3465."

Charley Ferguson turned off the set with a savage twist of its volume knob.

"Lies, all lies. Eco-terrorists," he sneered. "The FBI's making it all up—or worse." He sat down when the full enormity of it hit him. The people *were* dead. And the government had killed them to keep word of the anti-smogger from spreading. The very people he had relied on for endorsements were all dying. What better way to keep the skies polluted?

Charley ran to the window and cautiously looked outside. He went cold when he saw the black car parked across the street. It hadn't been there an hour before. They had his house staked out and were waiting for him to make a mistake.

"I'm not going to let them screw me over," he muttered. He hastily packed a few belongings in a knapsack and slung it over his shoulder. He'd have to travel light and fast or they'd toss him in jail and pin all the FBI-caused deaths on him. His anti-smogger worked. He was benefiting everyone, and they were spreading those lies about him.

He'd have to do better. Sitting around had been a mistake. He should have been showing the world his genius. He went to the garage and looked at his process equipment. Twenty gallons of anti-smogger had been generated before he ran out of feedstock chemicals. Charley knew better than to call up Priority Chemical with their hoodlum collection department, but no one else would advance him the chemicals. Over the years the bureaucrats had slowly tightened the noose around his neck and cut off his supplies. But it wouldn't matter. He had invented the perfect anti-smog additive, and for all he knew it might even give better mileage than untreated gasoline.

Charley lugged the four five-gallon cans from the garage and hid them in the trunk of his car. He froze when he heard people at his front door. They were coming for him. He jumped into the car and took off the emergency brake, letting the car coast a way down the alley before he hit the ignition. The old car asthmatically coughed to a sickly life and Charley gunned it.

Taking the corner too fast, he screeched off before the FBI agents could get back to their car and follow him. He was breathing hard. It had been close. But what was he going to do now? As he drove, a thought slowly came to him. By the time he was heading out of town and going into the desert for the Econo-Stop Gasateria, a broad smile had crossed his lips. This was going to be about perfect.

Charley Ferguson pulled up behind a billboard a few hundred yards down the road from the Econo-Stop Gasateria and got out of the car. He climbed the rickety billboard and got to the ledge just below the peeling advertisement for the Desert Mystery Spot eighty miles on into the heat and dust. He sat cross-legged in the grime and watched the station for what seemed an eternity, but finally his patience paid off.

The EPA, along with two men who looked like clones of the FBI agents he had seen there earlier, came in and took over the station. Charley imagined he could hear Mr. Pendergast's screams of protest all the way down the road. Eco-terrorists, they had said. Charley knew better. *They* were the problem.

He waited for the off-white panel van to pull out. He jumped to the ground and got into his car. He'd show them. He managed to pull in behind the van as they wheeled back into town. The white and blue government plates were his beacon through the night until the EPA inspectors stopped at another Econo-Stop Gasateria station on the outskirts of the city. Charley hadn't even known this station was in operation. He watched as the inspectors dropped their lines into the station's underground tanks and removed samples. When they left, Charley drove in.

"Fill it up, mister?" the attendant asked, still standing in the station's doorway. He showed more diligence than Charley ever had in trying to foist off the polluting gasoline on a customer.

"I'm looking for the EPA guys," Charley said. "They're supposed to be here any time now."

"You with them? You just missed them. Not more 'n five minutes ago," the attendant said.

"Damnation. Did they check your tanks?" Charley asked, knowing that they had.

The attendant nodded. Charley said, "They're supposed to make a second test. Did they?"

"Don't know. Can you do it? I don't like you guys poking around here. No offense."

Charley kept from laughing. This was too easy. "Sure, no problem. Let me get my kit." He grabbed a small vial of his anti-smogger. Within seconds he had added it to the tanks already checked by the EPA and within minutes had caught up with the white panel van.

Through the night Charley Ferguson followed them, adding his revolutionary anti-smogger to tanks checked and declared free of contaminants. It was a good night's work.

Charley Ferguson didn't dare check into a motel. The FBI was capable of scrutinizing all records anywhere in the U.S. using their computers. He slept beside the road, in a small park where truckers dozed. His battered car was hardly noticeable among the huge eighteen-wheelers. Charley stirred and then yawned as the sun hit his eyes. He shook himself, his belly grumbling from lack of food. He glanced at the dashboard clock, but it hadn't worked in more than six years. He stretched and turned on the radio. He got the six o'clock news.

"The government is advising motorists against all unnecessary driving during this crisis. More than two hundred commuters were killed during a rush-hour gridlock forty-five minutes ago on the Santa Monica Freeway."

Charley sat up and rubbed his eyes. He could scarcely believe the U.S. government—*his* government—would go to such lengths to suppress his invention. They were slaughtering hundreds!

"The original source of the unknown and still undetectable contamination has been located at a service station east of LA on Interstate Highway 10—"

Charley took grim note that the news reader didn't mention Econo-Stop Gasateria by name. They refused to give the people a choice, a chance for cleaner air. But it hardly mattered since Charley had seen the government agents close the station. That was why he had followed the EPA inspection team to eight other stations. The American people had to be given the chance for cleaner air.

"The eco-terrorists have succeeded in contaminating an unknown number of other individual stations. Special Agent Guerrero of the LA office of the FBI advises everyone to drive as little as possible and to not use your vehicles if you have refilled your tank within the past seventy-two hours. This—"

Charley couldn't listen to any more. He turned off the radio. All he had wanted to find out was the time. Instead he had heard the paranoia and fear fostered by the government, twisting perceptions and creating fear when there ought to have been joy.

The sun was setting and the blood-red glow through the smog was pretty, in its way. But Charley wouldn't miss it. He preferred clean air, fresh air and letting the pure wind caress his face and blow through his short, neat blond hair. He snapped out of the reverie and looked around at the huge trucks. It was a pity his anti-smogger didn't work on diesel fuel, but the government didn't put all the additives in it that they did in regular gasoline. When he had made his mark with cleaning up the air from regular gas-powered vehicles, he could turn his attention to the trucks and buses. By then, Charley expected to be rolling in the money.

He keyed his car to a fitful life and roared off. The EPA would be closing down all stations and being careful about dispensing from the ones he had already tried to clean up. He had to be smarter than them, and he knew how. Charley drove carefully, watching the speed limit and being sure not to break any laws. The government was after him; it wouldn't do to be arrested on some trumped-up charge before he made his real contribution to the environment.

At one in the morning he pulled into the visitors parking lot at the refinery. The place was deserted but this didn't bother him. The security force patrolled the far side of the complex until almost two. He had an hour to work before anyone noticed the solitary car in the lot.

He lugged one can of his anti-smogger to the hole

under the fence without getting too dirty. Sliding the awkward can under the cyclone fence was a chore, but Charley didn't hurry. He had to do this right the first time or the EPA and the other anti-American bureaucrats would stifle his invention forever. He had to show them—and he would, he would!

Climbing to the top of the first massive tank of refined gasoline took five minutes. It took only seconds more to pour in a half-gallon of his anti-smogger. By the time he had poured his additive into nine more tanks, he was filthy and needed a bath, but Charley held his impulses in check. There was so much work to do and so little time. He had to succeed the first time or they would grind him under as they had done countless others he had read about.

From his lofty vantage point atop the eight-story tank, Charley studied the refinery. Every batch of unleaded gasoline the refinery had produced during the past two weeks now contained his anti-smogger. Some of the gasoline would be distributed in the Los Angeles area, maybe ten percent. The rest would be shipped across the country and perhaps the world.

Charley didn't like the idea of cleaning up Tokyo's atmospheric pollution for free, but it was a price that had to be accepted. The State Department could bill them for the services later. He walked down the spiraling metal stairway. At the base, he checked his watch and saw that it had taken much longer than he had thought.

He heaved a sigh and left. Time would send his anti-smogger gasoline from this plant. But what of others? He still had fifteen gallons of anti-smogger. Charley's excitement mounted as he wiped down his seat using an aerosol disinfectant, then got into his car and drove off. There were other, smaller refineries along this road, and he had enough anti-smogger for them. It would be a long night for him, and a dangerous one, too, but he could rest later—as a hero.

Asleep on his feet, Charley Ferguson finished his work just before the morning shifts came into the fourth refinery he had treated with his wonderful additive. He sat on the hood of his car and watched the workers pour into the plant. The satisfaction he got from triumph was almost more than he could bear.

But a small detail gnawed at the back of his mind. Charley had the feeling of something left undone. When he touched his shirt pocket and found a tiny vial of his anti-smogger—the last of it—he knew what was missing. He had been so rushed, so harassed by the EPA bureaucrats, he had forgotten to use it in his own tank.

The sunrise was especially bright this morning, Charley thought as he drove off slowly, getting stuck at a busy traffic light leading into the plant. He felt a little dizzy, but that was all right. He was giddy with success. As he sat at the long red light, he fancied the air was already cleaner, purer, better for what he had done. Sucking in a deep breath, he knew he had done the right thing, but why were pioneers never appreciated?

The rising sun grew and grew and grew until it filled his entire field of vision. Charley Ferguson slumped forward, rejoicing at his success.

For You to Judge

Ramsey Campbell

Throughout the reading of the charges Foulsham felt as if the man in the dock was watching him. December sunshine like ice transmuted into illumination slanted through the high windows of the courtroom, spotlighting the murderer. With his round, slightly pouting face and large dark moist eyes, Fishwick resembled a schoolboy caught red-handed, Foulsham thought—except that surely, no schoolboy would have confronted the prospect of retribution with such a look of imperfectly concealed amusement mingled with impatience.

The indictment was completed. "How do you plead?"

"Not guilty," Fishwick said in a high clear voice, with just a hint of mischievous emphasis on the first word. Foulsham had the impression that he was tempted to take a bow, but instead Fishwick folded his arms and glanced from the prosecuting counsel to the defense, cuing their speeches so deftly that Foulsham felt his own lips twitch.

". . . a series of atrocities so cold-blooded that the jury may find it almost impossible to believe that any human being could be capable of them . . ." ". . . evidence that a brilliant mind was tragically damaged by a lifetime of abuse . . ." Fishwick met both submissions with precisely the same attitude, eyebrows slightly raised, a forefinger drumming on his upper arm as though he were commenting in code on the proceedings. His look of lofty patience didn't change as one of the policemen who had arrested him gave evidence, and Foulsham sensed that Fishwick was eager to get to the meat of the case. But the judge adjourned the trial for the day, and Fishwick contented himself with a faint anticipatory smirk.

The jurors were escorted past the horde of reporters and through the business district to their hotel. Rather to Foulsham's surprise, none of his fellow jurors mentioned Fishwick, neither over dinner nor afterwards, when the jury congregated in the cavernous lounge as if they were reluctant to be alone. Few of the jurors showed much enthusiasm for breakfast, so that Foulsham felt slightly guilty for clearing his plate. He was the last to leave the table and the first to reach the door of the hotel, telling himself that he wanted to be done with the day's ordeal. Even the sight of a newsvendor's placard which proclaimed FISHWICK JURY SEE HORROR PICTURES TODAY failed to deter him.

Several of the jurors emitted sounds of distress as the pictures were passed along the front row. A tobacconist shook his head over them, a gesture which seemed on the point of growing uncontrollable. Some of Foulsham's companions on the back row craned forward for a preview, but Foulsham restrained himself; they were here to be dispassionate, after all. As the pictures came towards him, their progress marked by growls of outrage and murmurs of dismay, he began to feel unprepared, in danger of performing clumsily in front of the massed audience. When at last the pictures reached him he gazed at them for some time without looking up.

They weren't as bad as he had secretly feared. Indeed, what struck him most was their economy and skill. With just a few strokes of a black felt-tipped pen, and the occasional embellishment of red, Fishwick had captured everything he wanted to convey about his subjects: the grotesqueness which had overtaken their gait as they attempted to escape once he'd severed a muscle; the way the crippled dance of each victim gradually turned into a crawl—into less than that once Fishwick had dealt with both arms. No doubt he'd been as skillful with the blade as he was with the pen. Foulsham was reexamining the pictures when the optician next to him nudged him. "The rest of us have to look too, you know."

Foulsham waited several seconds before looking up. Everyone in the courtroom was watching the optician now—everyone but Fishwick. This time there was no question that the man in the dock was gazing straight at Foulsham, whose face stiffened into a mask he wanted to believe was expressionless. He was struggling to look away when the last juror gave an appalled cry and began to crumple the pictures. The judge hammered an admonition, the usher rushed to reclaim the evidence, and Fishwick stared at Foulsham as if they were sharing a joke. The flurry of activity let Foulsham look away, and he did his best to copy the judge's expression of rebuke tempered with sympathy for the distressed woman.

That night he couldn't get to sleep for hours. Whenever he closed his eyes he saw the sketches Fishwick had made. The trial wouldn't last forever, he reminded himself; soon his life would return to normal. Every so often, as he lay in the dark which smelled of bath soap and disinfectant and carpet shampoo, the taps in the bathroom released a gout of water with a choking sound.

Each time that happened, the pictures in his head lurched closer, and he felt as if he was being watched. Would he feel like that over Christmas if, as seemed likely, the trial were to continue into the new year? But it lacked almost a week to Christmas when Fishwick was called to the witness box, and Fishwick chose that moment, much to the discomfiture of his lawyer, to plead guilty after all.

The development brought gasps from the public gallery, an exodus from the press benches, mutters of disbelief and anger from the jury; but Foulsham experienced only relief. When the court rose as though to celebrate the turn of events he thought the case was over until he saw that the judge was withdrawing to speak to the lawyers. "The swine," the tobacconist whispered fiercely, glaring at Fishwick. "He made all those people testify for nothing."

Soon the judge and the lawyers returned. It had apparently been decided that the defense should call several psychiatrists to state their views of Fishwick's mental condition. The first of them had scarcely opened his mouth, however, when Fishwick began to express impatience as severe as Foulsham sensed more than one of the jurors were suffering. The man in the dock protruded his tongue like a caricature of a madman and emitted a creditable imitation of a jolly banjo which all but drowned out the psychiatrist's voice. Eventually the judge had Fishwick removed from the court, though not without a struggle, and the psychiatrists were heard.

Fishwick's mother had died giving birth to him, and his father had never forgiven him. The boy's first schoolteacher had seen the father tearing up pictures Fishwick had painted for him. There was some evidence that the father had been prone to uncontrollable fits of violence against the child, though the boy had always insisted that he had broken his own leg by falling downstairs. All of Fishwick's achievements as a young man seemed to have antagonized the father—his exercising his leg for years until he was able to conceal his limp, his enrollment in an art college, the praise which his teachers heaped on him and which he valued less than a word of encouragement from his father. He'd been in his twenties, and still living with his father, when a gallery had offered to exhibit his work. Nobody knew what his father had said which had caused Fishwick to destroy all his paintings in despair and to overcome his disgust at working in his father's shop in order to learn the art of butchery. Before long he had been able to rent a bed-sitter, and thirteen months after moving into it he'd tracked down one of his former schoolfellows who used to call him Quasimodo on account of his limp and his dispirited slouch. Four victims later, Fishwick had made away with his father and the law had caught up with him.

Very little of this had been leaked to the press. Foulsham found himself imagining Fishwick brooding sleeplessly in a cheerless room, his creative nature and his need to prove himself festering within him until he was unable to resist the compulsion to carry out an act which would make him feel meaningful. The other jurors were less impressed. "I might have felt some sympathy for him if he'd gone straight for his father," the hairdresser declared once they were in the jury room.

Fishwick had taken pains to refine his technique first, Foulsham thought, and might have said so if the tobacconist hadn't responded. "I've no sympathy for that cold fish," the man said between puffs at a briar. "You can see he's still enjoying himself. He only pleaded not guilty so that all those people would have to be reminded what they went through."

"We can't be sure of that," Foulsham protested.

"More worried about him than about his victims, are you?" the tobacconist demanded, and the optician intervened. "I know it seems incredible that anyone could enjoy doing what he did," she said to Foulsham, "but that creature's not like us."

Foulsham would have liked to be convinced of that. After all, if Fishwick weren't insane, mustn't that mean anyone was capable of such behavior? "I think he pleaded guilty when he realized that everyone was going to hear all those things about him he wanted to keep secret," he said. "I think he thought that if he pleaded guilty the psychiatrists wouldn't be called."

The eleven stared at him. "You think too much," the tobacconist said.

The hairdresser broke the awkward silence by clearing her throat. "I never thought I'd say this, but I wish they'd bring back hanging just for him."

"That's the Christmas present he deserves," said the veterinarian who had crumpled the evidence.

The foreman of the jury, a bank manager, proposed that it was time to discuss what they'd learned at the trial. "Personally, I don't mind where they lock him up so long as they throw away the key."

His suggestion didn't satisfy most of the jurors. The prosecuting counsel had questioned the significance of the psychiatric evidence, and the judge had hinted broadly in his summing-up that it was inconclusive. It took all the jurors apart from Foulsham less than half an hour to dismiss the notion that Fishwick might have been unable to distinguish right from wrong, and then they gazed expectantly at Foulsham, who had a disconcerting sense that Fishwick was awaiting his decision too. "I don't suppose it matters where they lock him up," he began, and got no further; the rest of the jury responded with cheers and applause, which sounded ironic to him.

Five minutes later they'd agreed to recommend a life sentence for each of Fishwick's crimes. "That should keep him out of mischief," the bank manager exulted.

As the jury filed into the courtroom Fishwick leaned forward to scrutinize their faces. His own was blank. The foreman stood up to announce the verdict, and Foulsham was suddenly grateful to have that done on his behalf. He hoped Fishwick would be put away for good. When the judge confirmed six consecutive life sentences, Foulsham released a breath which he hadn't been aware of holding. Fishwick had shaken his head when asked if he had anything to say before sentence was passed, and his face seemed to lose its definition as he listened to the judge's pronouncement. His gaze trailed across the jury as he was led out of the dock.

Once Foulsham was out of the building, in the crowded streets above which glowing Santas had been strung up, he didn't feel as liberated as he'd hoped. Presumably that would happen when sleep had caught up with him. Just now he was uncomfortably aware how all the mannequins in the store windows had been twisted into posing. Whenever shoppers turned from gazing into a window he thought they were emerging from the display. As he dodged through the shopping precinct, trying to avoid shoppers rendered angular by packages, families mined with small children, clumps of onlookers surrounding the open suitcases of street traders, he felt as if the maze of bodies were crippling his progress.

Foulsham's had obviously been thriving in his absence. The shop was full of people buying Christmas cards and rolled-up posters and framed prints. "Are you glad it's over?" Annette asked him. "He won't ever be let out, will he?"

"Was he as horrible as the papers made out?" Jackie was eager to know.

"I can't say. I didn't see them," Foulsham admitted, experiencing a surge of panic as Jackie produced a pile of tabloids from under the counter. "I'd rather forget," he said hastily.

"You don't need to read about it, Mr. Foulsham, you lived through it," Annette said. "You look as though Christmas can't come too soon for you."

"If I oversleep tomorrow I'll be in on Monday," Foulsham promised, and trudged out of the shop.

All the taxis were taken, and so he had to wait almost half an hour for a bus. If he hadn't been so exhausted he might have walked home. As the bus labored uphill he clung to the dangling strap which was looped around his wrist and stared at a grimacing rubber clown whose limbs were struggling to unbend from the bag into which they'd been forced. Bodies swayed against him like meat in a butcher's lorry, until he was afraid of being trapped out of reach of the doors when the bus came to his stop.

As he climbed his street, where frost glittered as if the tarmac were reflecting the sky, he heard children singing carols in the distance or on television. He let himself into the house on the brow of the hill, and the poodles in the ground-floor flat began to yap as though he were a stranger. They continued barking while he sorted through the mail which had accumulated on the hall table: bills, advertisements, Christmas cards from people he hadn't heard from since last year. "Only me, Mrs. Hutton," he called as he heard her and her stick plodding through her rooms towards the clamor. Jingling his keys as further proof of his identity, and feeling unexpectedly like a jailer, he hurried upstairs and unlocked his door.

Landscapes greeted him. Two large framed paintings flanked the window of the main room: a cliff baring strata of ancient stone above a deserted beach, fields spiky with hedgerows and tufted with sheep below a horizon where a spire poked at fat clouds as though to pop them; beyond the window, the glow of streetlamps streamed downhill into a pool of light miles wide from which pairs of headlight beams were flocking. The pleasure and the sense of all-embracing calm which he habitually experienced on coming home seemed to be standing back from him. He dumped his suitcase in the bedroom and hung up his coat, then he took the radio into the kitchen.

He didn't feel like eating much. He finished off a slice of toast laden with baked beans, and wondered whether Fishwick had eaten yet, and what his meal might be. As soon as he'd sluiced plate and fork he made for his armchair with the radio. Before long, however, he'd had enough of the jazz age. Usually the dance music of that era roused his nostalgia for innocence, not least because the music was older than he was, but just now it seemed too good to be true. So did the views on the wall and beyond the window, and the programs on the television—the redemption of a cartoon Scrooge, commercials chortling "Ho ho ho," an appeal on behalf of people who would be on their own at Christmas, a choir reiterating "Let nothing you display," the syntax of which he couldn't grasp. As his mind fumbled with it, his eyelids drooped. He nodded as though agreeing with himself that he had better switch off the television, and then he was asleep.

Fishwick wakened him. Agony flared through his right leg. As he lurched out of the chair, trying to blink away the blur which coated his eyes, he was afraid the leg would fail him. He collapsed back into the chair, thrusting the leg in front of him, digging his fingers into the calf in an attempt to massage away the cramp. When at last he was able to bend the leg without having to grit his teeth, he set about recalling what had invaded his sleep.

The nine o'clock news had been ending. It must have been a newsreader who had spoken Fishwick's name. Foulsham hadn't been fully awake, after all; no wonder he'd imagined that the voice sounded like the murderer's. Perhaps it had been the hint of amusement which his imagination had seized upon, though would a newsreader have sounded amused? He switched off the television and waited for the news on the local radio station, twinges in his leg ensuring that he stayed awake.

He'd forgotten that there was no ten o'clock news. He attempted to phone the radio station, but five minutes of hanging on brought him only a message like an old record on which the needle had stuck, advising him to try later. By eleven he'd hobbled to bed. The newsreader raced through accounts of violence and drunken driving, then rustled her script. "Some news just in," she said. "Police report that convicted murderer Desmond Fishwick has taken his own life while in custody. Full details in our next bulletin."

That would be at midnight. Foulsham tried to stay awake, not least because he didn't understand how, if the local station had only just received the news, the national network could have broadcast it more than ninety minutes earlier. But when midnight came he was asleep. He wakened in the early hours and heard voices gabbling beside him, insomniacs trying to assert themselves on a phone-in program before the presenter cut them short. Foulsham switched off the radio and imagined the city riddled with cells in which people lay or paced, listening to the babble of their own caged obsessions. At least one of them—Fishwick—had put himself out of his misery. Foulsham massaged his leg until the ache relented sufficiently to let sleep overtake him.

The morning newscast said that Fishwick had killed himself last night, but little else. The tabloids were less reticent, Foulsham discovered once he'd dressed and hurried to the newsagent's. MANIAC'S BLOODY SUICIDE. SAVAGE KILLER SAVAGES HIMSELF. HE BIT OFF MORE THAN HE COULD CHEW. Fishwick had gnawed the veins out of his arms and died from loss of blood.

He must have been insane to do that to himself, Foulsham thought, clutching his heavy collar shut against a vicious wind as he limped downhill. While bathing he'd been tempted to take the day off, but now he didn't want to be alone with the images which the news had planted in him. Everyone around him on the bus seemed to be reading one or other of the tabloids which displayed Fishwick's face on the front page like posters for the suicide, and he felt as though all the paper eyes were watching him. Once he was off the bus he stuffed his newspaper into the nearest bin.

Annette and Jackie met him with smiles which looked encouraging yet guarded, and he knew they'd heard about the death. The shop was already full of customers buying last-minute cards and presents for people they'd almost forgotten, and it was late morning before the staff had time for a talk. Foulsham braced himself for the onslaught of questions and comments, only to find that Jackie and Annette were avoiding the subject of Fishwick, waiting for him to raise it so that they would know how he felt, not suspecting that he didn't know himself. He tried to lose himself in the business of the shop, to prove to them that they needn't be so careful of him; he'd never realized how much their teasing and joking meant to him. But they hardly spoke to him until the last customer had departed, and then he sensed that they'd discussed what to say to him. "Don't you let it matter to you, Mr. Foulsham. He didn't," Annette said.

"Don't you dare let it spoil your evening," Jackie told him.

She was referring to the staff's annual dinner. While he hadn't quite forgotten about it, he seemed to have gained an impression that it hadn't much to do with him. He locked the shop and headed for home to get changed. After twenty minutes of waiting in a bus queue whose disgruntled mutters felt like flies bumbling mindlessly around him he walked home, the climb aggravating his limp.

He put on his dress shirt and bow tie and slipped his dark suit out of the bag in which it had been hanging since its January visit to the cleaners. As soon as he was dressed he went out again, away from the sounds of Mrs. Hutton's three-legged trudge and of the dogs, which hadn't stopped barking since he had entered the house. Nor did he care for the way Mrs. Hutton had opened her door and peered at him with a suspiciousness which hadn't entirely vanished when she saw him.

He was at the restaurant half an hour before the rest of the party. He sat at the bar, sipping a Scotch and then another, thinking of people who must do so every night in preference to sitting alone at home, though might some of them be trying to avoid doing something worse? He was glad when his party arrived, Annette and her husband, Jackie and her new boyfriend, even though Annette's greeting as he stood up disconcerted him. "Are you all right, Mr. Foulsham?" she said, and he felt unpleasantly wary until he realized that she must be referring to his limp.

By the time the turkey arrived at the table the party had opened a third bottle of wine and the conversation had floated loose. "What was he like, Mr. Foulsham," Jackie's boyfriend said, "the feller you put away?"

Annette coughed delicately. "Mr. Foulsham may not want to talk about it."

"It's all right, Annette. Perhaps I should. He was—" Foulsham said, and trailed off, wishing that he'd taken advantage of the refuge she was offering. "Maybe he was just someone whose mind gave way."

"I hope you've no regrets," Annette's husband said. "You should be proud."

"Of what?"

"Of stopping the killing. He won't kill anyone else."

Foulsham couldn't argue with that, and yet he felt uneasy, especially when Jackie's boyfriend continued to interrogate him. If Fishwick didn't matter, as Annette had insisted when Foulsham was closing the shop, why was everyone so interested in hearing about him? He felt as though they were resurrecting the murderer, in Foulsham's mind if nowhere else. He tried to describe Fishwick, and retailed as much of his own experience of the trial as he judged they could stomach. All that he left unsaid seemed to gather in his mind, especially the thought of Fishwick extracting the veins from his arms.

Annette and her husband gave him a lift home. He meant to invite them up for coffee and brandy, but the poodles started yapping the moment he climbed out of the car. "Me again, Mrs. Hutton," he slurred as he hauled himself along the banister. He switched on the light in his main room and gazed at the landscapes on the wall, but his mind couldn't grasp them. He brushed his teeth and drank as much water as he could take, then he huddled under the blankets, willing the poodles to shut up.

He didn't sleep for long. He kept wakening with a stale rusty taste in his mouth. He'd drunk too much, that was why he felt so hot and sticky and closed in. When he eased himself out of bed and tiptoed to the bathroom the dogs began to bark. He rinsed out his mouth but was unable to determine if the water which he spat into the sink was discolored. He crept out of the bathroom with a glass of water in each hand and crawled shivering into bed, trying not to grind his teeth as pictures which he would have given a good deal not to see rushed at him out of the dark.

In the morning he felt as though he hadn't slept at all. He lay in the creeping sunlight, too exhausted either to sleep or to get up, until he heard the year's sole Sunday delivery sprawl on the doormat. He washed and dressed gingerly, cursing the poodles, whose yapping felt like knives emerging from his skull, and stumbled down to the hall.

He lined up the new cards on his mantelpiece, where there was just enough room for them. Last year he'd had to stick cards onto a length of parcel tape and hang them from the cornice. This year cards from businesses outnumbered those from friends, unless tomorrow restored the balance. He was signing cards in response to some of the Sunday delivery when he heard Mrs. Hutton and the poodles leave the house.

He limped to the window and looked down on her. The two leashes were bunched in her left hand, her right was clenched on her stick. She was leaning backward as the dogs ran her downhill, and he had never seen her look so crippled. He turned away, unsure why he found the spectacle disturbing. Perhaps he should catch up on his sleep while the dogs weren't there to trouble it, except that if he slept now he might be guaranteeing himself another restless night. The prospect of being alone in the early hours and unable to sleep made him so nervous that he grabbed the phone before he had thought who he could ask to visit.

Nobody had time for him today. Of the people ranked on the mantelpiece, two weren't at home, two were fluttery with festive preparations, one was about to drive several hundred miles to collect his parents, one was almost incoherent with a hangover. All of them invited Foulsham to visit them over Christmas, most of them sounding sincere, but that wouldn't take care of Sunday. He put on his overcoat and gloves and hurried downhill by a route designed to avoid Mrs. Hutton, and bought his Sunday paper on the way to a pub lunch.

The Bloody Mary wasn't quite the remedy he was hoping for. The sight of the liquid discomforted him, and so did the scraping of the ice cubes against his teeth. Nor was he altogether happy with his lunch; the leg of chicken put him in mind of the process of severing it from the body. When he'd eaten as much as he could hold down, he fled.

The papery sky was smudged with darker clouds, images too nearly erased to be distinguishable. Its light seemed to permeate the city, reducing its fabric to little more than cardboard. He felt more present than anything around him, a sensation which he didn't relish. He closed his eyes until he thought of someone to visit, a couple who'd lived in the house next to his and whose Christmas card invited him to drop in whenever he was passing their new address.

A double-decker bus on which he was the only passenger carried him across town and deposited him at the edge of the new suburb. The streets of squat houses which looked squashed by their tall roofs were deserted, presumably cleared by the Christmas television shows he glimpsed through windows, and his isolation made him feel watched. He limped into the suburb, glancing at the street names.

He hadn't realised the suburb was so extensive. At the end of almost an hour of limping and occasionally resting, he still hadn't found the address. The couple weren't on the phone, or he would have tried to contact them. He might have abandoned the quest if he hadn't felt convinced that he was about to come face to face with the name which, he had to admit, had slipped his mind. He hobbled across an intersection and then across its twin, where a glance to the left halted him. Was that the street he was looking for? Certainly the name seemed familiar. He strolled along the pavement, trying to conceal his limp, and stopped outside a house.

Though he recognized the number, it hadn't been on the card. His gaze crawled up the side of the house and came to rest on the window set into the roof. At once he knew that he'd heard the address read aloud in the courtroom. It was where Fishwick had lived.

As Foulsham gazed fascinated at the small high window he imagined Fishwick gloating over the sketches he'd brought home, knowing that the widow from whom he rented the bed-sitter was downstairs and unaware of his secret. He came to himself with a shudder, and stumbled away, almost falling. He was so anxious to put the city between himself and Fishwick's room that he couldn't bear to wait for one of the infrequent Sunday buses. By the time he reached home he was gritting his teeth so as not to scream at the ache in his leg. "Shut up," he snarled at the alarmed poodles, "or I'll—" and stumbled upstairs.

The lamps of the city were springing alight. Usually he enjoyed the spectacle, but now he felt compelled to look for Fishwick's window among the distant roofs. Though he couldn't locate it, he was certain that the windows were mutually visible. How often might Fishwick have gazed across the city towards him? Foulsham searched for tasks to distract himself—cleaned the oven, dusted the furniture and the tops of the picture-frames, polished all his shoes, lined up the tins on the kitchen shelves in alphabetical order. When he could no longer ignore the barking which his every movement provoked, he went downstairs and rapped on Mrs. Hutton's door.

She seemed reluctant to face him. Eventually he heard her shooing the poodles into her kitchen before she came to peer out at him. "Been having a good time, have we?" she demanded.

"It's the season," he said without an inkling of why he should need to justify himself. "Am I bothering your pets somehow?"

"Maybe they don't recognize your walk since you did whatever you did to yourself."

"It happened while I was asleep." He'd meant to engage her in conversation so that she would feel bound to invite him in—he was hoping that would give the dogs a chance to grow used to him again—but he couldn't pursue his intentions when she was so openly hostile, apparently because she felt entitled to the only limp in the building. "Happy Christmas to you and yours," he flung at her, and hobbled back to his floor.

He wrote out his Christmas card list in case he had overlooked anyone, only to discover that he couldn't recall some of the names to which he had already addressed cards. When he began doodling, slashing at the page so as to sketch stick-figures whose agonised contortions felt like a revenge he was taking, he turned the sheet over and tried to read a book. The yapping distracted him, as did the sound of Mrs. Hutton's limp; he was sure she was exaggerating it to lay claim to the gait or to mock him. He switched on the radio and searched the wavebands, coming to rest at a choir which was wishing the listener a Merry Christmas. He turned up the volume to blot out the noise from below, until Mrs. Hutton thumped on her ceiling and the yapping of the poodles began to lurch repetitively at him as they leaped, trying to reach the enemy she was identifying with her stick.

Even his bed was no refuge. He felt as though the window on the far side of the city were an eye spying on him out of the dark, reminding him of all that he was trying not to think of before he risked sleep. During the night he found himself surrounded by capering figures which seemed determined to show him how much life was left in them—how vigorously, if unconventionally, they could dance. He managed to struggle awake at last, and lay afraid to move until the rusty taste like a memory of blood had faded from his mouth.

He couldn't go on like this. In the morning he was so tired that he felt as if he were washing someone else's face and hands. He thought he could feel his nerves swarming. He bared his teeth at the yapping of the dogs and tried to recapture a thought he'd glimpsed while lying absolutely still, afraid to move, in the hours before dawn. What had almost occurred to him about Fishwick's death?

The yapping receded as he limped downhill. On the bus a woman eyed him as if she suspected him of feigning the limp in a vain attempt to persuade her to give up her seat. The city streets seemed full of people who were staring at him, though he failed to catch them in the act. When Jackie and Annette converged on the shop as he arrived he prayed they wouldn't mention his limp. They gazed at his face instead, making him feel they were trying to ignore his leg. "We can cope, Mr. Foulsham," Annette said, "if you want to start your Christmas early."

"You deserve it," Jackie added.

What were they trying to do to him? They'd reminded him how often he might be on his own during the next few days, a prospect which filled him with dread. How could he ease his mind in the time left to him? "You'll have to put up with another day of me," he told them as he unlocked the door.

Their concern for him made him feel as if his every move were being observed. Even the Christmas Eve crowds failed to occupy his mind, especially once Annette took advantage of a lull in the day's business to approach him. "We thought we'd give you your present now in case you want to change your mind about going home."

"That's thoughtful of you. Thank you both," he said and retreated into the office, wondering if they were doing their best to get rid of him because something about him was playing on their nerves. He used the phone to order them a bouquet each, a present which he gave them every Christmas but which this year he'd almost forgotten, and then he picked at the parcel until he was able to see what it was.

It was a book of detective stories. He couldn't imagine what had led them to conclude that it was an appropriate present, but it did seem to have a message for him. He gazed at the exposed spine and realized what any detective would have established days ago. Hearing Fishwick's name in the night had been the start of his troubles, yet he hadn't ascertained the time of Fishwick's death.

He phoned the radio station and was put through to the newsroom. A reporter gave him all the information which the police had released. Foulsham thanked her dully and called the local newspaper, hoping they might contradict her somehow, but of course they confirmed what she'd told him. Fishwick had died just before nine-thirty on the night when his name had wakened Foulsham, and the media hadn't been informed until almost an hour later.

He sat at his bare desk, his cindery eyes glaring at

nothing, then he stumbled out of the cell of an office. The sounds and the heat of the shop seemed to rush at him and recede in waves on which the faces of Annette and Jackie and the customers were floating. He felt isolated, singled out—felt as he had throughout the trial.

Yet if he couldn't be certain that he had been singled out then, why should he let himself feel that way now without trying to prove himself wrong? "I think I will go early after all," he told Jackie and Annette.

Some of the shops were already closing. The streets were almost blocked with people who seemed simultaneously distant from him and too close, their insect eyes and neon faces shining. When at last he reached the alley between two office buildings near the courts, he thought he was too late. But though the shop was locked, he was just in time to catch the hairdresser. As she emerged from a back room, adjusting the strap of a shoulder-bag stuffed with presents, he tapped on the glass of the door.

She shook her head and pointed to the sign which hung against the glass. Didn't she recognize him? His reflection seemed clear enough to him, like a photograph of himself holding the sign at his chest, even if the placard looked more real than he did. "Foulsham," he shouted, his voice echoing from the close walls. "I was behind you on the jury. Can I have a word?"

"What about?"

He grimaced and mimed glancing both ways along the alley, and she stepped forward, halting as far from the door as the door was tall. "Well?"

"I don't want to shout."

She hesitated and then came to the door. He felt unexpectedly powerful, the winner of a game they had been playing. "I remember you now," she said as she unbolted the door. "You're the one who claimed to be sharing the thoughts of that monster."

She stepped back as an icy wind cut through the alley, and he felt as though the weather was on his side, almost an extension of himself. "Well, spit it out," she said as he closed the door behind him.

She was ranging about the shop, checking that the electric helmets which made him think of some outdated mental treatment were switched off, opening and closing cabinets in which blades glinted, peering beneath the chairs which put him in mind of a death cell. "Can you remember exactly when you heard what happened?" he said.

She picked up a tuft of bluish hair and dropped it in a pedal bin. "What did?"

"He killed himself."

"Oh, that? I thought you meant something important." The bin snapped shut like a trap. "I heard about it on the news. I really can't say when."

"Heard about it, though, not read it."

"That's what I said. Why should it matter to you?"

He couldn't miss her emphasis on the last word, and he felt that both her contempt and the question had wakened something in him. He'd thought he wanted to reassure himself that he hadn't been alone in sensing Fishwick's death, but suddenly he felt altogether more purposeful. "Because it's part of us," he said.

"It's no part of me, I assure you. And I don't think I was the only member of the jury who thought you were too concerned with that fiend for your own good."

An unfamiliar expression took hold of Foulsham's face. "Who else did?"

"If I were you, Mr. Whatever-your-name-is, I'd seek help, and quick. You'll have to excuse me. I'm not about to let that monster spoil my Christmas." She pursed her lips and said, "I'm off to meet some normal people."

Either she thought she'd said too much or his expression and his stillness were unnerving her. "Please leave," she said more shrilly. "Leave now or I'll call the police."

She might have been heading for the door so as to open it for him. He only wanted to stay until he'd grasped why he was there. The sight of her striding to the door reminded him that speed was the one advantage she had over him. Pure instinct came to his aid, and all at once he seemed capable of anything. He saw himself opening the nearest cabinet, he felt his finger and thumb slip through the chilly rings of the handles of the scissors, and lunging at her was the completion of these movements. Even then he thought he meant only to drive her away from the door, but he was reckoning without his limp. As he floundered towards her he lost his balance, and the points of the scissors entered her right leg behind the knee.

She gave an outraged scream and tried to hobble to the door, the scissors wagging in the patch of flesh and blood revealed by the growing hole in the leg of her patterned tights. The next moment she let out a wail so despairing that he almost felt sorry for her, and fell to her knees, well out of reach of the door. As she craned her head over her shoulder to see how badly she was injured, her eyes were the eyes of an animal caught in a trap. She extended one shaky hand to pull out the scissors, but he was too quick for her. "Let me," he said, taking hold of her thin wrist.

He thought he was going to withdraw the scissors, but as soon as his finger and thumb were through the rings he experienced an overwhelming surge of power which reminded him of how he'd felt as the verdict of the jury was announced. He leaned on the scissors and exerted all the strength he could, and after a while the blades closed with a sound which, though muffled, seemed intensely satisfying.

Either the shock or her struggles and shrieks appeared to have exhausted her. He had time to lower the blinds over the door and windows and to put on one of the plastic aprons which she and her staff must wear. When she saw him returning with the scissors, however, she tried to fight him off while shoving herself with her uninjured leg towards the door. Since he didn't like her watching him—it was his turn to watch—he stopped her doing so, and screaming. She continued moving for some time after he would have expected her to be incapable of movement, though she obviously didn't realize that she was retreating from the door. By the time she finally subsided he had to admit that the game had grown messy and even a little dull.

He washed his hands until they were clean as a baby's, then he parceled up the apron and the scissors in the wrapping which had contained his present. He let himself out of the shop and limped towards the bus stops, the book under one arm, the tools of his secret under the other. It wasn't until passersby smiled in response to him that he realized what his expression was, though it didn't feel like his own smile, any more than he felt personally involved in the incident at the hairdresser's. Even the memory of all the jurors' names didn't feel like his. At least, he thought, he wouldn't be alone over Christmas, and in future he would try to be less hasty. After all, he and whoever he visited next would have more to discuss.

The Child Killer

Steve Rasnic Tem

All the mommas cry when the Sackman comes.

It was the neighborhood fairytale, the nursery rhyme, the cautionary fable meant to scare the children just enough that they wouldn't stray too far, talk to strangers, or cross the wrong borders. He'd been hearing the stories for forty years, from the beginning of it all. And at one time the image of the large man (but not tall, not fat) with the huge, sure hands, walking the night streets with the voluminous gray sack across his back—a sack that sighed and cried, wriggled and shook as if there were small animals inside—had an almost romantic appeal. He felt flattered, and in fact the image hadn't been that far from the truth.

All the mommas cry when the Sackman comes around. Back in the beginning, people minded their own business. Sackman. Like some sort of superhero. Now if people saw you with a sack like that they'd call the police. Even as all the mommas used the Sackman to scare their kiddies out of misbehavior.

Now his hands shook, the way the children shook

while he told them their special, their final bedtime stories.

When he'd started it had been back after the war, and a sack wasn't all that unusual to see. Sometimes a sack was all a man had to carry what was important to him. And surely children were the most important things of all. Children were a comfort. Children were our future.

And he was the man whose task it was to murder the future.

Better get in before the Sackman comes. Don't touch that if you don't want the Sackman comin' round here! Better be good tonight or the old Sackman may just up and take you for his dinner!

Back then, as now, what was important was the children he found. And no matter how good parents were, a few children confounded the purpose of these scary old cautionary tales. A few children were even more daring and reckless upon hearing of the Sackman's activities. A few children were seemingly eager to fill his sack.

These were not *bad* children. The Sackman had a hard time thinking of any of them as bad. Most often he thought it was, in fact, the best children who came into his sack, the ones with their heads all full of fairytales and visions of the future.

The Sackman would send them all back to heaven if he could.

This was impossible, of course, especially at his present age. Even if he recruited and shared his mission with thousands of like-minded others—and surely they were out there, others cognizant of the need for such drastic measures—he couldn't send them all back. He knew it was impossible because they all needed a song or a story to send them on their way, much as small children about to fall into dreamland need a story to send them on their way, and he knew he would never be able to trust anyone else with such a grave responsibility.

The little girl with the red dress was once again in his park. She always wore the red dress and he had come to assume that she must have little else to wear. The dress had torn lace in the back and had faded almost to pink in the seat area. She always came to the park unsupervised. Sometimes her face was dirty, or bruised. He wondered, in part because of these things, if she understood yet that adults were monsters.

He would be very surprised if she had such an understanding. One of the stellar charms of children was that they could be so trusting. This quality never failed to move him. They could be lied to, cheated, and abused by half the adults of their acquaintance, and still the little angels continued to put their trust in these grown-up monsters.

"Where's your mother, dear?" he asked her again. She looked up at him solemnly, but said nothing. He patted her shoulder. He noticed with some inner disturbance that his hand trembled again. "Ah, at least someone has taught you not to speak to strangers. That's an important thing to remember, dear." He looked around and saw that no one else was around. He looked back down at her. "But I'm no stranger. You see, I'm just the grandfather you've never met, the kindly old man you've always dreamed about." Her eyes grew wider. "I can see that dream in your eyes right now, dear. I can see every little thing you're thinking. I *know* about little girls and little boys, you see."

Then he took her hand and she held on tightly, letting him know once and for all time that she was at last ready to go with him. They left the park hand-in-hand, in no particular hurry. He had been wearing makeup on all his trips to this park in another town, and he had been watching the child for weeks. Her calmness, her peace with him would allay all suspicions. Anyone who did see them together would assume he was an older relative taking the child to the park. If they wondered about anything it would be why the old man didn't buy the child a new dress. Obviously no one cared about this child. No one but the Sackman.

She slid easily into the front passenger seat of his ancient, dark-blue Buick. She was too short to see over the dashboard, but appeared fascinated by the old gauges beneath their highly-polished glass. He made sure she buckled the seat belt he had had installed. His hands shook again (*small animals in his sack*) when the car wouldn't start, then calmed when the engine coughed into rough activity. He smiled down at the little girl. It warmed his old heart when she smiled back.

The drive back to his own home town was a long one, but the little girl sat through the trip patiently. At least someone had taught her manners. Now and then she would comment politely on the beauty of the drive. He had not lived in the actual town itself for many years, preferring the relative obscurity and safety of the mountains and lakes beyond. The old Buick struggled its way up the steep incline of the initial part of the drive, then relaxed as the highway leveled a few miles from his home. He had no idea how much longer the Buick could manage these trips. He supposed that once it failed his career as the Sackman would be finished.

Not once on this long trip did this little girl ask where they were going. He took this to be clear evidence of a long pattern of deprivations. Normally he would have had to trot out any one of a dozen different fantasies in order to placate the little darling. Depending on the perceived needs, they were visiting long-lost parents or friends, conducting a secret mission for the government, aiding a dying or injured relative, or visiting a castle, space ship, or miscellaneous wonderland. But the little girl asked no questions, so he was careful not to provide any answers.

When they finally arrived she jumped out and ran toward the house. "It's like a cave!" she exclaimed, and indeed it was. More than half of the house had been built into a hollow carved into the mountainside.

Here comes the Sackman, sweetheart, he thought as he followed her to the undersized front door. As always he had to stoop with the key in his trembling fist in order to let them inside.

"Wait here while I get the light," he said softly to the darkness. He reached overhead for the cord to the bulb. That was when she ran away into the shadows of his mountain home.

He was too startled to speak, reduced to gripping and ungripping the cotton light cord as if in a spasm. The bulb flickered into yellow dimness.

"Where? Are you!" he finally sputtered in rage. There was no answer from the shadows of his cave.

He waited by the door for a time, listening carefully the way the Sackman was supposed to listen—the Sackman who all the mommas said could detect a small child's heartbeat amongst all the other heartbeats in the deep dark woods—but he heard nothing. He felt suddenly exhausted, as if all the bright red blood had run out of him, and he was compelled to collapse into the overstuffed chair by the door—placed there years before for exactly these attacks of sudden fatigue. He could remember placing the chair here himself one day after a young boy of seven had run him practically to tatters in the surrounding woods. He could remember, too, how he had felt when he'd finally caught the boy (who, also tired, could only look up at the Sackman with eyes the size of quarters), and telling the boy about the lands that lay beyond dreams, the countries where children had no bodies that puked and stank but instead traveled within beams of pure white light, had placed his huge rough hand over the small boy's face and with only the tiniest of disturbances—a cough and a squirm as if the lad were stirring within a bad dream—had sent him swiftly into that wondrous land.

But the Sackman could not remember when he had grown so old.

"Little one!" he called, after catching his breath enough to say it softly, tenderly. "Come back to see your old grandpa, honey. We'll play hide-and-go-seek later. I promise." There was a distant giggle back in the dark far-off rooms of his house, but nothing more. The Sackman bit into his lower lip until the blood spurted, and then he began to suck. He closed his eyes and stared at red circles in the darkness. When he at last opened them again the giggles had started again. It had been a very long time since a giggle had been heard in his house.

To the casual observer the Sackman's front room was furnished unremarkably—the more obvious mementoes of all his children were displayed in the back rooms of the house, the chambers down under the cool mountainside, the shadowed places where the little girl in the red dress now laughed and hid.

"Are you Little Red Riding Hood? Is that who you've decided to be, my sweet?" Then the Sackman howled his best wolf howl, an old wolf certainly, but without a doubt a huge, snarling horrific wolf it was. For the Sackman had had much practice over the years playing the part of the wolf.

There was no answer and the Sackman laughed as loudly as he had howled, and felt young again.

Then the Sackman sucked some more of his own

salty blood, smiled and looked around his front room, and saw:

A large pot he'd once upended over a small girl, four or five years but small for her age, the smallest child he'd ever had in his home. (Although not the smallest he'd ever sent back to heaven. Back during the fifties he'd sent back a half-dozen babies who'd been sleeping in bassinets and on blankets in the park. All that had been required was something to distract the mothers. There'd been time for only the briefest of bedtime stories, but babies required very little, being half dream and parental anticipation already.) He'd kept her in that pot until she'd been quite convinced he was going to cook her, so that she was almost relieved when finally it was his hands that sent her on her way.

A worn-out sofa with oversized cushions. For three full days he'd once lain on that sofa, taking his meals there, even relieving himself into a hole in the worn-out upholstery when he couldn't hold it any longer. A visitor would have seen a smelly, sickly old man lying there, perhaps breathing his last. A visitor never would have guessed a skinny ten-year-old boy lay underneath those cushions, the life squeezing out of his semi-conscious body an hour at a time.

A tall kitchen trash can over in the corner once contained twin six-year-olds tied together, face-to-face. He'd used both his huge hands to send them on their way, at the same time, providing them with a joint fairytale, a shared dream, making sure that they might look into each other's eyes as they began their long journey back. Now he could not remember if they had been boys or girls.

The fireplace along a side wall appeared much too large for the room, but otherwise was unremarkable in every way. It didn't even sport a rudimentary mantel. But more than once it had contained giant logs of newspaper wrapped in wire, each with a small child completely hidden inside. He would never have considered burning a precious child, although he had been content to let them think so. It was all part of his game, and their personalized fairytale.

The Sackman had no illusions about what an outsider might think if he or she (some matronly social worker, going house to house on behalf of children's welfare) stumbled onto his doings, or witnessed any of the games he played with the children. He had given up hope for understanding many years ago, although he was convinced there were hundreds of people like him in the world who might appreciate his mission. Who understood that children were lied to, made to anticipate an adulthood full of promise and dream, when all the time the promises and dreams ended with the onset of puberty. The life of an adult was made putrid by constant disappointments and betrayals. Only a child, a mere eyeblink out of heaven's embrace, could glimpse glory. But after the development of the sexual organs and the accompanying desires it was as if they had been blinded, never to see the brilliant light of heaven again.

The Sackman loved children, and envied them. So what better way might he show that love than to send them back to heaven where they belonged, where they would truly want to go if they only had the understanding ironically wasted on adults?

From the Sackman's under-the-mountain rooms, where much more obvious secrets and mementoes of his career were kept, came the sound of footsteps and giggles and can't-catch-mes. Surely it was time for this particular child's game to end, and her final fairytale to begin.

* * *

The Sackman's eyes were old, but they were still the eyes of the Sackman. *Who sees everything, child, so just you watch out! Don't let him catch you out tonight!* He could still see clearly where this one little girl had been.

One of the giant clothes closets off the east hallway had been opened up, and decades of children's dresses and shorts, pants and socks and shirts and underwear had spilled out, some of it vomit- or blood- or other-stained, all of it precious reminders of the children he had known and loved into heaven. He stopped for a moment and tried to pick some of these up, trying to match pieces of outfits, trying to match clothing with vague, frightened, then peacefully sleeping little faces, but it was an impossible task. There were too many dead children spilt here, too many tiny ghosts struggling into these scattered outfits every morning. With tears washing his face he cast them aside and called "Darling!" and "Sweetheart!" and even "Grandchild!", careful to keep the growing rage out of his voice, but all he heard was the distant laughter, the small feet running from room to room, crashing through all the doors of his life.

"Baby!" he shouted, kicking the piles of torn little body parts aside. "Baby, come here!" and pounded his feet into the floor to make a Giant's footsteps guaranteed to terrify even the bravest Jack.

He could hear her somewhere just ahead of him now, racing in and out of the numerous dimly-lit or dark rooms that spread far under the mountainside.

In one room numerous toys, furred in greasy dust so that they appeared half-animal, half-appliance, had been removed from their storage shelves and scattered about the floor. The hands that had once played with these played with toys of pure light now. But it still angered him that they'd been touched, perhaps even damaged, without his permission. "Nice little girls *ask* before playing with another's things!" he shouted into the darkness. But the darkness continued to run and cast its laughter back at the Sackman.

He inhaled deeply of the cold, musty air of these back rooms, these storage chambers of his past, this air redolent of ten thousand children's screams, children's fear sweat, breath stink, and blood. He felt the air lengthening his stride, putting the power back into his huge hands. With each inhalation, with each new insult from this anonymous little girl, he felt as if his mass and muscle were increasing, his old man's fatigue draining away, until by the time he reached the farthest, deepest rooms, he'd become convinced that he was the Sackman of forty years ago, the terror of children and their parents for three states around.

The doors to wall cabinets had been thrown open, countless pairs of small children's glasses spilled out onto the hard gray rock floors. Some were shattered, some had their frames bent and twisted. He gathered them up by the handfuls and piled them on a nearby table alongside two miniature prosthetic arms, a prosthetic leg, and several cigar boxes full of dental appliances. One pair of glasses had snagged on his black coat sleeve—he picked it off and examined it, recalling how he'd always been amazed by these prescription lenses for children, how small they were, as if fitted for dolls or ventriloquist dummies. He tried to wedge the glasses over his own eyes, and his eyes seemed larger than the lenses themselves *(The Sackman has great big saucers for eyes. He can see you wherever you go. He always knows what you're doing.)* From beneath the small lenses he could feel the darkness pushing down in a spiraling rush, a huge face suddenly looming over him, greasy lips parting to show dancing teeth as the Sackman began his recital of the final fairytale.

He jerked the glasses off and threw them across the room. When he turned, he could hear the footsteps in an adjacent room. Far too many footsteps.

At the next room he opened the heavy door *(heavy as stone the door to his home)* and was greeted by a shower of children's shoes: high-tops, sneakers, black patent leathers, flip-flops, leather sandals, Buster Browns, Oxfords, Minnie Mouse slippers, skates, tap shoes—as they fell from upended shelves and splintered apple crates. He screamed a not very Sackman-like scream as the shoes tumbled over his head and shoulders, soles slapping a staccato as if in footless dance. Yet even as he screamed he could still hear the high hysterical giggles of sung accompaniment gradually fading into the rooms beyond.

The Sackman kicked his way through the knee-high piles of shoes into the disarray of the next room (crude children's drawings of knifings, stranglings, and decapitations littering the floor like gigantic leaves), and then the next (piles of naked dolls, dark bruises and red tears painted on their faces), and the next (volumes of candid photographs of dead children, taken immediately before and after their last moments in this loathsome world, ripped and torn and tossed up into the cold drafts like confetti).

"Enough! Enough!" he cried, feeling uncomfortably like a timid schoolmaster who's lost control of his class. "It's *fairytale time*! You like fairytales don't you?"

"Oh yes oh yes," she murmured from not so far away.

He turned his head and staggered in fatigue, suddenly feeling old again. He was alarmed to find that he could not quite catch his breath. "Just let me . . . let me catch my breath . . . please . . ."

"No! I want my storyyyyyyy!" The little girl appeared at the end of the hall swathed in sheets stained maroon

from dried blood *(she's been in my private bedroom!)* and started running toward him. Startled, the Sackman lost his balance and fell to the floor. As her laughter reached for an ever higher pitch he lifted his huge, child-killer hands to protect his face.

She pulled a round, flat object—larger than a dinner plate—out of the bloody sheet and threw it at him much in the manner of a frisbee. He recognized it as a trophy he had made for himself many years ago. It broke into pieces on his arms, cutting and *(gnawing)* into his tender old flesh. He groped for the pieces on the floor and came up with handfuls of his children's precious baby teeth which had been glued onto the trophy as decoration, and finally the larger pieces—part of what had once been a beautiful lily glued together from thousands of such teeth.

"You little *bitch*!" He scrambled to his feet and lunged toward her ghostly form. She backed away and backed away, tittering and chuckling, the snot running from her nose as she grew more hysterical. He almost had her within his grasp when she turned and ran. He lunged again, pulled the rotting sheet from her body, and crashed through the next door, huge splinters piercing his face, ramming through the loose flesh on his arms, hammering through knuckles and the webbing by each thumb, working themselves deep into his belly as if conscious and determinedly murderous.

They were in his secret bedroom *(my heart!)*. The little girl in the tattered red dress jumped up and down on his bed, picking up the old blood-stained covers and tossing them into the far corners of the room. *Oh, she's found my secret heart!*

"Can't catch me now can't catch me now . . ." she chanted breathlessly. The Sackman could see that she had smeared herself with the rancid fluids of corruption from his bottle collection underneath the bed (even he would not have done such a thing—for him it was always enough just to know they were there beneath his reclining form). She stuck out her tongue demonically.

He tried to get up off the floor but each movement brought the sharp splinters deeper into his body. He knew she had done real damage to him because he had a vague sensation of soft, secret things tearing away inside him. But strangely enough all his rage had fled him. He felt too old for such anger. His mission, as always, was most important now. "Child . . . sweet child," he implored weakly. "It is time for your story. Surely you want your story? Hurry! While I still have the strength . . ."

"I love stories," she said quietly, but not looking at him. Instead she looked around at his bedroom. She was the only person besides himself ever to be in his bedroom.

"All children love stories," he replied. "Especially bedtime stories." But still she wouldn't look at him, intent on the walls of his bedroom, walls decorated with all the collages of his universe he had constructed over the years:

Along the bottoms of the walls were countless pictures of children, but with heads, arms, legs removed, eyes cut from their sockets, genitalia snipped and glued to their foreheads, ears and eyes glued over small, immature breasts, tongues affixed to the bottoms of tiny feet. The children were stacked and piled until they made a terrible weight at the bottom of each collage, where sometimes the paper was cut, and passages were made to other collages which were even more crowded with segmented children. Brown and red offal and old excrement had been smeared in and out of these segments for this was the world, this was the everyday ground human beings walked on, slept on, rutted and conducted their commerce on.

Arranged at eye level were various upright figures: roaches and mayflies and lizards and centipedes and dark birds. These were built from shapes outlined in charcoal, cut out, then arranged to construct the desired form, or sometimes they were photographs of world leaders—Stalin, Reagan, Thatcher, De Gaulle—with bits cut away until the hidden creature had been uncovered. Each held a knife or an axe or a sack or a pair of scissors, for these were the harvesters. Here and there their barbed legs or wings reached down into the collages below to snare a child and free it from its own corporeal filth.

But above eye level, further than a child could reach on his or her own, was heaven, where the walls had been scrubbed until they were practically no color at all. There the Sackman had pasted small bits of paper. And on each piece of paper was scribbled the final words of a child he had personally harvested, liberated, discorporated, sent back. All the *no please momma stop daddy yes I'll be good your eyes why your hands can't why Why WHYs,* and prayers far more obscure than he had ever heard.

"You're a *bad* man," the little girl said, and grinned. A stare into the brilliance of the little girl's grin and the Sackman felt bathed in ice.

"No. No, honey. I'm the very *best* of men. You'll understand that after I've told you your story."

Then he grabbed her by one scuffed tennis shoe and began pulling her off the bed and into his bloody, splintered embrace. The little girl squealed as if it were a game. The Sackman began to relax, because it *was* a game, the most important game she would ever play.

"This is a story about a little girl in a red dress," he whispered from bloody lips.

"And you're making it lots more redder," she said moistly into his ear.

"Who never wanted to grow up," he continued.

"I wouldn't want to be like you!" She giggled.

"Stop interrupting," he said firmly, and she snuggled closer to him, soaking herself completely in the blood seeping from his enormous lap. "Now that might sound strange to some people, not wanting to grow up, but this little girl was very smart, you see . . ."

"*Very* smart," she interrupted, but he ignored her.

". . . because she'd known lots of grownups in her time, and she'd learned what awful beasts grownups could be. They'd forgotten what it had been like to be a child, how very hard it had been, and it was this absent-mindedness that had turned all the grownups into scaly, putrid monsters!"

"Really?" the little girl asked, wide-eyed.

"Really."

"So what did she do?" She seemed genuinely interested.

He'd never had a child so relaxed in his arms before, despite all that had happened. Perhaps this would be the one child who really understood. Perhaps she would go easily, with no need for a struggle. He stretched his fingers and spread his huge hands *(watch out! watch out!).* He brought his fingers closer to her neck *(when he comes),* closer to her tiny, grape-shaped eyes *(when the Sackman comes).*

"What did she do, you ask? Why, she visited the Sackman, of course."

"That was *stupid!"* she squealed, and rammed a long splinter of wood up through his belly until it found the Sackman's chest.

As the Sackman felt himself falling into bits and pieces, his legs tumbling one way, his arms and belly another, he tried to think of the word he'd want the little girl to write down for pasting into his Sackman heaven.

She let him pull her closer. He could see her leaning over his lips with an anxious expression on her face, ready to hear and record.

He closed his eyes and opened his mouth, and felt her eager fingers tearing at his tongue.

THE LICK OF TIME

JONATHAN CARROLL

Before leaving her apartment, Erin turned on the new answering machine. Several nights before, sitting down with the instructions and a glass of wine, she'd waded through a long list of what-to-do's to make the expensive, high-tech-looking thing work. She was tired of missing telephone calls. People complained all the time about not being able to reach her. Now, having gotten the new job with the theatre group, it was more important than ever to know what the last few hours had said to her.

Suspicious of any machine that would suddenly rid you of a problem so completely, she'd stayed home Saturday night just to see if the gadget worked correctly each time.

The phone would ring three times, then a click and her girlish voice said, "Hello. This is 335-9063. Sorry no one's home, but if you'll leave a name and number, I'll get back to you as soon as I can. Wait for the beep. Thanks."

She heard Bob's voice. "Hey, you finally got a machine. Thank the Lord! This is your beloved brother. Call me when you're in."

"Erin? I hate these machines. Call Lucia."

"Hi, 'I just called to say I love you—' Don't forget Gary's party."

So many calls! Did she talk to that many people every day and never realize it? She replayed the messages a number of times that first night, listening carefully to the way voices inevitably changed when people realized they were talking to a tape and not her. They lost heart, is how it sounded. Here they were calling, prepared for some human give and take, but all they got was a zippy, taped Erin saying she had no time for them now, any of them, but might later.

That first night, she responded out loud to the messages as she'd really like to have done. To her pushy, demanding brother, she told him to buzz off and leave her alone. Her mother usually called to scold about something, so she told Mom's recorded voice to back off and say something nice for a change. "Why don't we just have a *chat,* Mom? No finger-pointing or trouble. I won't pull your chain if you don't pull mine." It was fun talking to her machine for a while, but then she stopped, having realized how rarely she told her family the truth. She had never told Bob to buzz off, or her mother to stop bullying. It made her feel sad and cowardly to know she would never say these things directly to them.

Sighing, she got up from the couch and in a kind of unconscious benediction, put a hand on the machine as if to tell it she believed in its powers—she'd trust it now.

A nice extra was the thing came with a remote control unit which allowed her to call in from outside and get messages.

At lunchtime she went to a phonebooth and gave it a try. How disconcerting to hear yourself answer the telephone! Like listening to your voice for the first time on a tape recorder. But she smiled the strangeness away and, holding the little remote box to the receiver, pressed the button. The tape stopped immediately. She heard a slight whirring sound, and then there they were: Calls from Weber Gregston and Wyatt Leonard. What a marvelous thing to have! In her theatre group they were doing scenes from *Death of a Salesman.* In one, a man tells Willy Loman how wonderful it is to have a tape recorder—everyone should get one. Stepping out of the phone booth with the messages from her machine, she felt like saying the same thing—everyone should have one of these gizmos.

The real not-so-secret reason for her machine was a new friend named Will Morgan. He was short and good-looking and gave Erin the feeling they could have something special if they worked on it hard enough. He was a landscape architect from Duluth who, on their second date, shyly confided he designed children's playgrounds for a hobby. How she wanted him after that! The image of this man hunched over a drawing board late at night puzzling over the perfect swing or sandbox for kids made her long to hold and take care of him and at least be his friend for years. It was plain there was a chance all of these things could happen, but only if she didn't push or demand, her two great failings.

Erin was born impatient and it had grown worse the older she got. Waiting for anything was agony—the mail, the line at the grocery store to move, for herself to decide. She tried to go into stores knowing what she wanted so there'd be no wait. She made detailed, beautifully spaced lists. Bit her tongue or looked away when friends were late or took too long. Always early for meetings, always the first one out, she was capable and efficient but not very successful. Erin made too many people nervous with her acute punctuality and grim faces if they happened to arrive for a drink at 5:10 instead of 5:00. One lover cruelly said she was incapable of being anally retentive because she already had so many clocks up her ass that there was no more room.

So far, Will Morgan arrived when he said he would and once even beat her to a rendezvous in front of Indochine. The only really unusual thing about him was he liked to talk on the telephone at all hours. He'd call at eleven and ask if she were watching the movie on the late show. Or at seven on a Saturday morning to see if she was in the mood to go for a walk later. Initially, she assumed the man just liked to use the telephone, but he won even more of her heart when he said he *hated* it, but liked talking to her and hearing her voice.

Will called so frequently, she was constantly afraid of missing something important he might want to tell her. Now, however, that worry was resolved with the arrival of her answering machine. He was even a little bolder talking to it than to her. He was the one who'd sung the first bars of "I Just Called to Say I Love You," although normally that wasn't his style. His sweet slight Midwestern accent singing the familiar words made her resolve to keep that first tape and not erase it.

At lunchtime that first day she checked it again and once more in the middle of the afternoon when her group was taking a coffee break. And why not? That's what the damned thing was for!

Yet with her impatience, she didn't want to get into the habit of calling it five times a day when she was out. *That* would be pathetic, but Erin could already feel the urge to do something screwy like that: Being in two places at one time was a real temptation for her. Always knowing what was going on in her two lives.

Everything was fine for a couple of weeks, but then one afternoon after a particularly hard day at work when it felt like the whole cast was in a bad mood, she did something a little strange but cute at the same time. Erin wasn't exactly embarrassed, but not proud either. It wasn't the sort of thing she'd tell another.

She had a favorite phone booth on 64th Street she often used to call the machine. It was relatively clean, despite a mysterious smell of bananas that was always there. It wasn't raining outside but looked and felt like it. Feeling damp and unclean after a day of tiresome arguments and tempers that had flared and fizzled like half-wet matches, she hoped for a nice message from Will. The night before, they'd had a tiff that grew till it bordered on a real fight about something so dumb and . . . dumb was the only word for it. It was her fault, but she wanted him to say it was his. It was a test. If he did that, she'd know he cared just that much more. Taking the blame to keep the peace was a significant act in the beginning of a relationship: I love you. It's my fault. Can we forget about it now?

But there was no nice call from him. In fact, there were no calls at all, which gave her an instant terrible cramp in her stomach, as happened when she was frightened. Not Will. Please do not let him go away.

Hanging up, she looked at the shiny black telephone and then dug some more coins out of her purse. Sliding one into the slot, she dialed her own number. It rang three times. Then there was her voice doing her little *shtick* to whoever was listening. After it finished, she waited for the 'peep'; then said in her own voice, "Erin, this is Will. I just called to say I love you. Everything is okay. It was my fault completely."

She hung up with a fast bang and leaned her head against the phone.

* * *

At home, the apartment was warm and cozy and as soul-lifting as a hot bath, which she also had. Only after she'd fixed a fast dinner and watched the seven o'clock news did she check for messages. He'd called! And not her silly little nonsense, but the *real* Will Morgan had called and said "Hi, it's me. I think we'd better talk. I hope you're not angry. I am not." Then, almost as a surprise because she was so happy to hear his voice, came her . . . him. She smiled it away and felt a brief embarrassment, but it'd been good therapy at the time and she dismissed it with that justification.

Will took her to the Plaza for drinks and told her he was going to Saru in a month. Where was that? In the Middle East. How long would he be there? Probably years. He'd learned only this week about the project, a once-in-a-lifetime opportunity, and that's why he was so unpleasant with her the last time they'd been together—he was confused. He loved her, that was for sure, but didn't know if they should get married now, "or what."

Would she be interested in going to a place as weird as Saru for a few years? She'd have to cover herself completely in typical Muslim style and women weren't allowed to work there. Actually they weren't allowed to do much of anything in Saru, outside of having babies. He smiled when he said that. And that "c'est la vie" smile, more than anything, made her dislike him. Dislike him enough to say she didn't think marriage would be such a great idea for them. His smile stayed where it was and didn't change into anything else—remorse, bitterness, surprise. That was how she remembered his face forever after. That smile. That mysterious, shitty smile.

* * *

The rest of the evening, what little there was of it, went to hell fast. The last time they "saw" each other, she was giving him her back as she strode off after telling him how damned selfish and presumptuous he was to even . . . Didn't he once think perhaps she'd like to have been consulted about being married or going to Sabu?

"Saru," he corrected her, with that same unfair smile.

She was off.

Twenty blocks later she stomped into a telephone booth and called herself up. As soon as the voice came on the other end, she started speaking. "You were right, Erin. He's a big shit. Believe me, he's just a big selfish macho shit."

But all that was captured on the tape when she played it back was a beep and the word "shit." In her anger she'd spoken too fast, too soon.

How do these things happen? How do we go mad in small ways and calmly work the madness into our everyday like exercises or whole grain toast at breakfast?

Little by little, Erin began calling herself in earnest. There is no other way to express it. She called when she was sad, she called when she'd forgotten something. She called because she felt like it. She changed the recorded message after a while just so she'd hear other words on the line before she began talking.

If anyone had eavesdropped, they'd have heard a very normal woman telling someone things that weren't especially interesting or informative.

Women love to chat. It is in their nature, particularly with other women. If someone had eavesdropped on Erin Jennings' half of the conversation, they'd have heard a nice-looking woman chatting away. Big deal. On the other hand, if they'd known who she was chatting *with,* they'd have walked fast in the opposite direction.

She called and talked about men (naturally a lot about Will who hadn't even sent a letter from that end of the earth), her job, how she should have stood up to her mother at lunch last week. She spoke until the second beep came which meant her time on the tape was over. Sometimes she hung up immediately, sometimes she said "See ya." Once even "Wait! I'll call you back." But that was only a joke.

She learned to get everything off her chest in thirty seconds, which was as much time as the tape allowed before it beeped. In the comic strip "Peanuts" Lucy has the booth with a sign saying "Psychiatric Help 5 cents." A telephone call cost more, but Erin looked at "Peanuts" differently after discovering this new way of using her answering machine.

It became her friend and silent confidante; it soon knew her darkest secrets. She read an article in a magazine about a service where you could call in and confess anything. Why would anyone want to do *that*? It was too much like going to confession at church and telling an anonymous priest what you'd been up to. Erin didn't want that—she wanted a sympathetic ear and soul that would hear her out and either commiserate or side with her right down the line. If she phoned a confession line, who was to say some listener might not laugh at her sadness, or smirk at a feeling that arose from the depths of her heart? The only person who listened to her confessions, screams, admissions, properly was Erin Jennings and that was exactly as she wanted it.

To crown the pleasure, one day she did something very uncharacteristic which nevertheless helped enormously. Late at night there was a show on the radio where a well-known psychologist answered calls from listeners about their problems. One time Erin steeled her courage and called the number that was repeated three or four times an hour.

"Hi. You're on 'Night Ear.' What can I do for you?"

"Dr. Knight, this is . . . well, it doesn't matter who I am. Listen, I've been doing this kind of strange thing lately? I guess I kind of want to hear whether you think it's crazy or not."

"Tell me and we'll see."

"Well, I just got this telephone answering machine? And sometimes . . . sometimes I call *myself* on it and leave messages? You know, like if I had a bad day, I call from a booth and tell it—tell myself to cheer up? Or I pretend I'm someone else and leave a nice message or something . . ." Her lips, which were very dry, kept moving soundlessly, but she was scared to say anything more, thinking she'd already sounded crazy enough.

"Wow! That's one of *the* most innovative and imaginative uses for those damned machines I ever heard of. It's wonderful, whoever you are. I'm going to tell some people I know to do exactly what you've been doing.

"Are you listening out there, Night Ears? Because if you've got one of these machines I think our caller has come up with one hell of a good idea. It's a cheap and supportive way of giving yourself a lift exactly when you need it. Give yourself a call and say 'You're okay.' or 'What you did was right. *They* were wrong, not you.' "

Doctor Knight went on and on about how creative and useful Erin's idea was. Nine other people called in to say the same thing. At least half an hour of the show that night was call-ins elaborating and expanding on the uses to which one could put their answering machines. All because of Erin. She felt smart and helpful. More importantly, she felt absolved.

* * *

She got a postcard of a nondescript modern airport. When she turned it over, the printing at the top said "International Airport of the Republic of Saru." For an instant, she had to think what was "Saru." But as she thought, her eyes traveled down the card and she recognized Will Morgan's handwriting.

"It is actually a nice place, but I miss talking to you on the phone. I miss a lot about you and I." There was an address and an underlined (three times) request that she write.

She made a suggestion to the director of her theatre group about a possible way to block a scene they were doing. He grabbed her by the shoulders, kissed her, and said that was the first smart thing anyone, including himself, had said all day.

We are as unprepared for a run of good luck as we are for the bad we are always half-expecting. One nice thing after another happened to Erin for a few weeks yet she never grew blasé about any of them. Each came as a delightful surprise.

She traced the luck back more or less to the time she called the radio station. That made her wonder if she were somehow being rewarded for sharing her answering machine secret with the world. How many people in the city were feeling better about themselves or their lives because of her little trick?

Ironically, she hadn't used the machine much for that purpose in recent days because life had been going so well for her, but she knew it was there if and when she needed it.

She needed it the day she was almost raped. It was raining, she was in Greenwich Village waiting in a doorway for a taxi to drive by. Suddenly the door behind her opened and she felt someone grab and pull her backward. She kicked and screamed and never even saw the man's face before he got scared and ran off up the staircase.

Erin went directly to the police to report the attack. But they were obviously uninterested in her story and after dutifully writing down the details, did little to calm or comfort her. The bastards! All the stories she'd heard about the callous indifference of the New York police were true. She hadn't done anything but was attacked. Worse, like a good citizen, she reported it but got nothing more than the line "We'll look into it, lady, but we're pretty busy around here. Your rapist's probably in White Plains by now."

Stamping out of the police station, she went to the nearest booth, but before she got the door closed she was crying. Fear and helplessness and other things combined to turn her inside out and it was a long time before she could put a coin in the box and call her number.

She didn't wait for her message to end before she started gasping out what had happened in the last hour. While she spoke, she dug in her purse for another coin because she knew there was so much to say about the outrage and its aftermath that she would need to call a couple of times because of the damned beep limit on her message tape.

"—and then he grabbed me by my hair and punched me in the chest—" It felt so good to talk to someone who'd care and understand. When she played it back hours later, she would relive all of these terrible moments, but that was the point—she would know exactly what it had been like and so would be the most sympathetic person in the world to the poor victim.

"—I tried to push him away, but—"

"Who cares?" Quiet, steady, her voice came out of the other end.

She jerked the receiver from her ear, then pressed it back. "What did you say?"

"I said who cares? He tried to rape you. Maybe it would have been good. Maybe you should have let him do you."

"Who is this?"

"This is Erin Jennings. Why are you asking? You keep wanting to talk, but you never think maybe you don't want to hear. Or not *all* of you wants to hear.

"It's boring, Erin. *You're* boring. Not all of you, but most. Every time you call up it's to whine and cry 'poor little me.' Never 'Are you okay?' Or 'Isn't life great? Look at all the good things that have been happening lately.' Did you ever call to talk about that in your life? To congratulate us about the good luck? The good things? Not once.

"You're like the man who calls the woman once a month so he can screw her and then he forgets her for another thirty days.

"It's so utterly rude and selfish. No wonder Will left for the desert. Maybe you *should* have let that guy fuck you today. Then you'd have had an idea of how it feels to be used.

"Don't call here again—there won't be anyone home. You don't deserve a twenty-four-hour listener to your pathetic little life. Call your mother! Call your *brother*!"

The line went dead after she heard her own voice on the other end laugh a moment in an entirely new, nasty way. A frightening way. She looked at the receiver, another coin in hand, but was too afraid to drop it in. What if she dialed but no one answered? What if she dialed and someone *did*?

THE EDGE

RICHARD CHRISTIAN MATHESON

Peter yawned.

How long had it been? How many hours since he hadn't been bored out of his mind? He listened to the music squirting through the armrest, up the rubber tube, into his head. Stared out the window. Thought about his life. How it had all started.

The turbulence was fading and he sighed; too bad.

Clouds tumbled by and he drifted backwards. Thirty-five years . . .

The doctor had ensnared his doughy head in forceps and told Peter's mother to breathe rapidly; bear down. The struggle of Peter slithering from between his mother's thighs continued for hours. Then, inexplicably, stopped.

The doctor said he'd never seen anything like it. He told her Peter had suddenly stopped fighting expulsion into the world and cooperated with the rhythmic kneading of his mother's womb for "no reason."

Peter watched lights on the big steel wing blink.

"No reason." Absurd. He knew better. Though it was over forty years ago, he could remember the precise second of his birth when he'd decided to stop fighting. It was no mystery to him. The whole thing had simply become predictable.

Infant years were no improvement. His mother and father would hold him in their arms and coo, but Peter could remember the sense of well-being lasting only a short while. After that, it became drab and he responded to keep his parents from feeling bad.

But it had been the same story: it just wasn't fun after a while. It was dull. Rewards were over in a moment; their capture hopeless.

As a boy, the tendency eased somewhat. Peter was popular, and after school always had a swarm of children trailing behind, wanting to play.

But he only went along with it.

Things didn't hold his attention for any length of time. He didn't really understand it. It wasn't as if he were overly intelligent or preoccupied. It was something more fundamental. He just got bored a lot.

His mother and father became briefly concerned when he took unusual interest in the misfortunes of others. For Peter, it was the only thing that secretly seemed to reverse his descents into the inert.

When his parents would take him to the movies, he would sit transfixed during the violent parts, eyes recording every blast and bloodstain. He would stop eating his popcorn at every scream. It hypnotized him.

Ultimately, his parents passed it off as a meaningless phase.

"After all," his father was prone to say, in Peter's defense, "violence is part of being human."

Peter's mother would nod in agreement, though Peter didn't feel one way or the other. He just knew he liked watching pain: the only thing that seemed to lift him from his feelings of ennui.

By the time he was in high school, he was on constant look-out for anything physically abusing. He was in attendance at every football game and sat as close to the front line as possible; the best view of the violence. He could could hear as flesh collided, helmets and bodies battling. He could see players when they lay on the torn ground, holding broken bodies, faces in agony.

He loved every second and stared expectantly with each hike of the pigskin, watching for injured players. He would look intently at their hands which would tighten in pain and clench ruined flesh.

Blood would soak grass, making it look wounded, and Peter would watch, rapt. The sufferers were carried to the sidelines or rushed into ambulances and once they were removed, Peter always wanted to leave. The game, without injuries, was of no interest.

On his sixteenth birthday, he became concerned for himself and confessed his aberrant perspective to his father. He told him everything bored him except violence and pain.

His father laughed, saying pain was America's national pastime. He told Peter not to worry and Peter went to the pool outside his parents' condominium, did a few laps and tanned on the hot cement. He felt lucky and watched in fascination when a man slipped on the decking and fell into the water.

Blood ribboned from the man's head and he thrashed for air as Peter dashed to the pool edge to help. But instead, he just watched. The man struggled in a pinkish swirl and gulped down water. As he looked up at Peter, eyes pleading, Peter perched, stared back. As much as Peter tried to fight it, he was consumed by excitement; pulse racing, shivers bugling through him.

As others pumped water from the man's lungs, Peter licked his bottom lip, transfixed. There was no denying it: much as good taste dictated against such obsessions, watching things brutal, violent and painful was his favorite activity.

By the time he'd finished high school, he was regularly attending savage films, live prize fights, and wrestling matches. He obsessively scanned news for gruesome crimes; disasters. It made life palatable. By watching or reading about pain and suffering, Peter could go on; remain reasonably interested.

But in time, feelings of boredom erupted more frequently. The passage of time rendered even live violence dull. His problem was getting worse.

He visited a psychiatrist and was told mental release through vicarious imaginings was healthy. The doctor asked Peter if he'd ever done anything violent. Peter said no. The doctor said in that case he was just experiencing repressed anger. Peter saw him twice more, never went back.

The psychiatrist didn't understand.

No one did.

Peter knew it wasn't just imagination. It was something else; something bad. But he couldn't trace it to anything. He'd had a nice upbringing. And it happened when he'd first exited the birth canal. He knew that wasn't normal. Newborn babies didn't get bored. The malaise was inescapable and indeed, even as he thought about the condition, he became bored. He tried to think about people starving to death in India but it didn't help.

He felt lost.

By his twenty-fifth birthday, even human bloodshed no longer helped. He'd hoped something stronger might aid his outlook and headed one weekend to Mexico.

In a crowded bullring, he watched a huge black bull with lances buried in its shoulder struggle against horrid pain for an hour. It helped a little. But it was feeding a hunger with a biteful.

Then, on the drive home, stuck in border traffic, it happened. A VW had smashed into a Greyhound filled with commuters and exploded into flames.

As the screaming passengers watched the VW driver burning to death, Peter watched with pleased relief. He opened his window and leaned out to see the driver's flesh browning in gasoline flames and listen to his dying screams. Peter watched as a patrol car pulled up and police tried to pry the driver from the tiny car. He watched as people yelled at each other to do something. He watched Spanish- and English-speaking adults cover the susceptible eyes of children, close to the nightmare. He heard yelling and screaming and watched it all with undivided attention.

For Peter, it was spectacular.

He was thrilled and found his emotions honestly moved. Before him was life's fragility. Existence at its most extreme. He knew at that moment what life was about.

The edge.

He knew from then on, if it wasn't the real thing, it was no good. Organized sports, movies and memorized horrors wouldn't satisfy. He needed the real article. And if he got enough of it, he knew he'd never have to be bored again. Life was filled with war, misery, mutilation, disfiguring accidents, and other catastrophes ideally suited to his needs.

He'd finally found the reason to go on.

Within a week, he'd seen his fourth car accident. At night, he'd drive onto freeways and busy stretches of road, going back and forth for hours.

Looking; hunting for horror.

One night, he saw a good one. A family of four was

trying to escape an overturned station wagon. Their wretched screams were breathtaking. Peter had watched as emergency workers used blowtorches, crowbars and metal-cutting saws. They worked furiously as the family convulsed and pleaded.

It interested him. For a while. But he eventually grew sluggish and drove away. Car accidents were becoming passé; the listlessness of life was engulfing him again.

On the drive home, the only way he could rescue himself from apathy was to envision a campus murder he'd read about in the paper. As he imagined a knife slicing a coed's face and torso, he perked up and enjoyed the ride home.

But it was too good to be true and soon over.

By the weekend, nothing interested him. He'd decided to take a trip, thinking it would slow the sense of his insides sinking. He began to realize true boredom was slow death. Probably worse.

Peter was stirred from thoughts by the stewardess serving dinner. As the 747 bounced through mountains of cloud, hungry passengers gobbled chicken and lasagna. Peter ate without interest. The stewardess gathered the trays and Peter looked out his little window, watching the sun slowly flatten; a tired eye.

A film began and he watched credits roll. It was a comedy and he yawned. Laughter rose. He felt torpid; uninvolved. Nothing compelled him. Stagnation stabbed every cell. He tried to stir himself, remembering an account he'd read of an old woman who'd swallowed Drāno. But it was useless.

Then, it happened.

A roar. Ripping sheet metal. A sharp tilt of the carrier's angle. An engine had failed; exploded. Horror-stricken passengers yanked their headsets off as the jet plunged through blackness.

As it fell, flames dragged behind and hands clutched desperately. Screams lurched like guttural beings. Faces twisted.

The jet dropped faster, and as the ground neared, passengers embraced in terror.

Peter remained in his seat, peering out the window at the burning wing and onrushing community below.

He smiled.

This was going to be good.

How Would You Like It?

Lawrence Block

I suppose it really started for me when I saw the man whipping his horse. He was a hansom cab driver, dressed up like the chimney sweep in *Mary Poppins* with a top hat and a cutaway tailcoat, and I saw him on Central Park South, where the horse-drawn rigs queue up waiting for tourists who want a ride in the park. His horse was a swaybacked old gelding with a noble face, and it did something to me to see the way that driver used the whip. He didn't have to hit the horse like that.

I found a policeman and started to tell him about it, but it was clear he didn't want to hear it. He explained to me that I would have to go to the stationhouse and file a complaint, and he said it in such a way as to discourage me from bothering. I don't really blame the cop. With crack dealers on every block and crimes against people and property at an all-time high and climbing, I suppose crimes against animals have to receive low priority.

But I couldn't forget about it.

I had already had my consciousness raised on the subject of animal rights. There was a campaign a few years ago to stop one of the cosmetic companies from testing their products on rabbits. They were blinding thousands of innocent rabbits every year, not with the goal of curing cancer but just because it was the cheapest way to safety-test their mascara and eye liner.

I would have liked to sit down with the head of that company. "How would you like it?" I would have asked him. "How would you like having chemicals painted on your eyes to make you blind?"

All I did was sign a petition, like millions of other Americans, and I understand that it worked, that the company has gone out of the business of blinding bunnies. Sometimes, when we all get together, we can make a difference.

Sometimes we can make a difference all by ourselves.

Which brings me back to the subject of the horse and his driver. I found myself returning to Central Park South over the next several days and keeping tabs on that fellow. I thought perhaps I had just caught him on a bad day, but it became clear that it was standard procedure for him to use the whip that way. I went up to him and said something finally, and he turned positively red with anger. I thought for a moment he was going to use the whip on me, and I frankly would have liked to see him try it, but he only turned his anger on the poor horse, whipping him more brutally than ever and looking at me as if daring me to do something about it.

I just walked away.

That afternoon I went to a shop in Greenwich Village where they sell extremely odd paraphernalia to what I can only suppose are extremely odd people. They have handcuffs and studded wrist bands and all sorts of curious leather goods. Sadie Mae's Leather Goods, they call themselves. You get the picture.

I bought a ten-foot whip of plaited bullhide, and I

took it back to Central Park South with me. I waited in the shadows until that driver finished for the day, and I followed him home.

You can kill a man with a whip. Take my word for it.

Well, I have to tell you that I never expected to do anything like that again. I can't say I felt bad about what I'd done. The brute only got what he deserved. But I didn't think of myself as the champion of all the abused animals of New York. I was just someone who had seen his duty and had done it. It wasn't pleasant, flogging a man to death with a bullwhip, but I have to admit there was something almost shamefully exhilarating about it.

A week later, and just around the corner from my own apartment, I saw a man kicking his dog.

It was a sweet dog, too, a little beagle as cute as Snoopy. You couldn't imagine he might have done anything to justify such abuse. Some dogs have a mean streak, but there's never any real meanness in a hound. And this awful man was hauling off and savaging the animal with vicious kicks.

Why do something like that? Why have a dog in the first place if you don't feel kindly toward it? I said something to that effect, and the man told me to mind my own business.

Well, I tried to put it out of my mind, but it seemed as though I couldn't go for a walk without running into the fellow, and he always seemed to be walking the little beagle. He didn't kick him all the time—you'd kill a dog in short order if you did that regularly. But he was always cruel to the animal, yanking hard on the chain, cursing with genuine malice, and making it very clear that he hated it.

And then I saw him kick it again. Actually it wasn't the kick that did it for me, it was the way the poor dog cringed when the man drew back his foot. It made it so clear that he was used to this sort of treatment, that he knew what to expect.

So I went to a shoe store on Broadway in the teens where they have a good line of work shoes, and I bought a pair of steel-toed boots of the kind construction workers wear. I was wearing them the next time I saw my neighbor walking his dog, and I followed him home and rang his bell.

It would have been quicker and easier, I'm sure, if I'd had some training in karate. But even an untrained kick has a lot of authority to it when you're wearing steel-toed footwear. A couple of kicks in his legs and he fell down and couldn't get up, and a couple of kicks in the ribs took the fight out of him, and a couple of kicks in the head made it absolutely certain he would never harm another of God's helpless creatures.

It's cruelty that bothers me, cruelty and wanton indifference to another creature's pain. Some people are thoughtless, but when the inhumanity of their actions is pointed out to them they're able to understand and are willing to change.

For example, a young woman in my building had a mixed-breed dog that barked all day in her absence. She didn't know this because the dog never started barking until she'd left for work. When I explained that the poor fellow couldn't bear to be alone, that it made him horribly anxious, she went to the animal shelter and adopted the cutest little part-Sheltie to keep him company. You never hear a peep out of either of those dogs now, and it does me good to see them on the street when she walks them, both of them obviously happy and well cared for.

And another time I met a man carrying a litter of

newborn kittens in a sack. He was on his way to the river and intended to drown them, not out of cruelty but because he thought it was the most humane way to dispose of kittens he could not provide a home for. I explained to him that it was cruel to the mother cat to take her kittens away before she'd weaned them, and that when the time came he could simply take the unwanted kittens to the animal shelter; if they failed to find homes for them, at least their deaths would be easy and painless. More to the point, I told him where he could get his mother cat spayed inexpensively, so that he would not have to deal with this sad business again.

He was grateful. You see, he wasn't a cruel man, not by any means. He just didn't know any better.

Other people just don't want to learn.

Just yesterday, for example, I was in the hardware store over on Second Avenue. A well-dressed young woman was selecting rolls of flypaper and those awful Roach Motel devices.

"Excuse me," I said, "but are you certain you want to purchase those items? They aren't even very efficient, and you wind up spending a lot of money to kill very few insects."

She was looking at me oddly, the way you look at a crank, and I should have known I was just wasting my breath. But something made me go on.

"With the Roach Motels," I said, "they don't really kill the creatures at all, you know. They just immobilize them. Their feet are stuck, and they stand in place wiggling their antennae until I suppose they starve to death. I mean, how would you like it?"

"You're kidding," she said. "Right?"

"I'm just pointing out that the product you've selected is neither efficient nor humane," I said.

"So?" she said. "I mean, they're cockroaches. If they

don't like it let them stay the hell out of my apartment." She shook her head, impatient. "I can't believe I'm having this conversation. My place is swarming with roaches and I run into a nut who's worried about hurting their feelings."

I wasn't worried about any such thing. And I didn't care if she killed roaches. I understand the necessity of that sort of thing. I just don't see the need for cruelty. But I knew better than to say anything more to her. It's useful to talk to some people. With others, it's like trying to blow out a lightbulb.

So I picked up a half-dozen tubes of Super Glue and followed her home.

The Moment the Face Falls

Chet Williamson

Rebirth, Paul Kenyon thought. Re-frigging-birth. One call on the phone that hadn't rung casually in days, warmly in weeks, importantly in years, and suddenly Kenyon's apartment didn't look at all like a four-hundred-dollar-a-month rat hole, but like the home of a man the industry still wanted.

"Yes," he said as he looked at the framed clippings, yellow with age, that hung over his desk.

"Yes," he said louder as his gaze fell on the poster for *Trail Dust,* Jimmy Stewart tight-lipped behind his six-shooter, Dan Duryea in the background, clutching a rifle with wicked intent, Jeanne Crain with one hand-tinted glove on Jimmy's narrow shoulder, and those magic words in small print at the bottom, "Written by Dennis Collins and Paul Kenyon."

And *"Yes,"* he said for the third time as he looked at the cover of the June 1954 *Screen Stars,* from which he and Clare DuPont, his first wife, waved gaily at fans and photographers, two nominees running the gauntlet to where those priceless, golden statuettes would be doled out.

Kenyon stood up and walked across the small room that held everything he owned. He looked at the pulp magazines, the digests, the paperbacks that began in the late fifties and ended just last year. The earliest had his name on the spines, but the later ones, the ones that all looked and read the same, had "Brent Stock" in letters much smaller than the word, *Gunman,* the appellation of a series hero with a name as simple as his motivations.

Paul Kenyon had been Brent Stock for books number 21 through 47, and number 48, *Bloody Gun,* was in the typewriter now. Four books a year at four grand each was a living, though not much of one. Enough for rent and food and booze, enough to see some movies to keep up with what was hot, thinking that one day his agent would place a script again, and writing, always writing.

But, he thought as he looked at the piles of pulp, no more of this shit. One call had changed all that.

The caller's name was Richard Dunne, and he was an independent producer funded by Paramount. He sounded sharp and savvy, and best of all he wanted Kenyon, actually *wanted* him.

"It's an unpublished novel," he had said on the phone. "Simon and Schuster's gonna do it, contemporary western, *The Big Chill* married to *Lonesome Dove,* got that scope, got the characters. It's the greatest thing I've ever read."

"But . . . why did you call me?"

"Because ever since I was a kid and saw that movie you wrote for Jimmy Stewart—the one Anthony Mann directed—hell, it just knocked me out. The script, well Christ, it's incredible, but I didn't realize until I was grown up the script made that movie. You were nominated for it, right?"

"Yes, I—"

"Shoulda won. Shoulda won hands-down. What won that year anyway?"

"From Here to Eternity."

"Shit. That screenplay was all *over* the place. Never focused, too many characters. *That* Oscar rode in on the others' coattails. Goddam sweeps. Anyway, you're the guy I want. It's a done deal, Costner and Julia Roberts are a go, and Jim Cameron's just about locked to direct. Now don't tell me to call your agent, I'll do that, we don't have to talk money, money's the least of the worries, but I want to *meet* you first, meet the guy who's given me so damn much pleasure over the years. Okay?"

"Well . . . well, *sure."*

"Great. Lunch at Nicky Blair's. Today. One. Meet you right at the door."

"Uh . . . sure. Okay. One. At the door."

When he hung up, Kenyon thought it might be a dream, but he was awake. Then he thought maybe he was drunk and had imagined it all, but his hangover told him otherwise. Finally he thought it might be a joke one of his ex-wives was playing, but since he hadn't had any contact with the three Norns for six years, he dismissed that as well.

No, it was for real. Somebody remembered. The good work he did nearly forty years before was finally paying off, and what a long, strange trip it had been.

Western movies had started dying when they got big on TV. He had tried to make the transition, but the weekly pressures had been too much for him. And now that he had finally learned to write to deadline, TV westerns were deader than Duke Wayne. His whole career had been a study in frustration. Until now.

Jesus, Costner and Julia Roberts and James Cameron, things were cooking, dammit, cooking. He could pay off his bills, even get back on top again. He thought about calling his agent, but he knew that even if he got through it would be the old *Sorry, babe, money's on the other line, I'll call you right back,* and he never did.

Well, maybe he wouldn't cut Lou in on this one. Maybe he'd find another agent to handle this deal and just let Lou fuck himself. Maybe he'd do that.

But now he had to dress. Had to look good. Had to look like a successful writer that only a wonderful film opportunity could lure out of the ivory towers of fiction. He chose a dark blue suit with broad shoulders, an off-white shirt, and a bold patterned tie. Looking at himself in the chipped mirror on the closet door, he thought the illusion was satisfactory. He didn't look like a drunk, and toothpaste and mouthwash assured that he didn't smell like one.

He knew who Dunne was right away. He wore a standard producer's uniform—small, round tortoise-shell glasses, a gray Italian-cut jacket, brown campaign shirt, pants so loose they resembled garment bags, and a belt whose array of studs and mesh even Gene Autry in his heyday would have found ostentatious.

Kenyon figured he must have been as easily recognizable, for a smile creased Dunne's clean-shaven face, and he came up to Kenyon, said, "Paul, right?" and pumped the older man's hand. The man was younger than Kenyon had thought he would be, probably in his early thirties. His hair was blond and cut short, and he ran his hand through it once, then gestured to the door. "Let's go."

Inside, Dunne gave his name, and they were shown to a table near the back. "I like privacy, you know?" Dunne said by way of explanation. "I'm past that 'gotta be seen' crap. Besides, I want to talk to you without anybody interrupting us."

They sat, and Dunne set the box he was carrying on

the floor. Kenyon guessed that it contained the manuscript of the novel. Dunne ordered a Saratoga water, then said to Kenyon, "Have something stronger if you want," but Kenyon just smiled tightly and asked for coffee.

When they were alone, Dunne leaned forward. "Damn, it's a pleasure to meet you, Paul. You're really one hell of a screenwriter. What you been doing with yourself?"

Kenyon shrugged. He had known the question would come up. "Semi-retirement. I've done a few recent films, but nothing big. Not many westerns anymore."

"Shame to waste your talent in retirement."

"Semi," Kenyon repeated, smiling. "I do the occasional novel."

"Really? I haven't seen anything by you."

"Oh, pseudonymously. I keep Paul Kenyon for film work."

Dunne grinned, then winked. "Say no more. So. I'm really excited about working with you, my friend. Now, I'm a hands-on guy, so I hope that won't bother you. I'm good with story, like to see a nice tight arc, and this novel moves around a little too much."

"From Here to Eternity," Kenyon said.

Dunne laughed. "Yeah! Yeah, that's how it goes all right, from here to eternity. I wanta bring it back *here,* to earth, concentrate on the main characters, zero in, you know?" He reached down and picked up the box, then passed it to Kenyon. "This is it. Guy's first book, long mother, thousand pages in manuscript. High six-figure advance, you read about it?" Kenyon shook his head. "Guaranteed bestseller. My best D-girl nailed it. She suggested Bob Towne, but when I read it I said fuck him, I know who this is right for if I can find him. So I got your name out of that *Films of Jimmy Stewart* book, and you're still in the Guild, so here we are."

With his thumb Kenyon started to slit the tape that held on the box cover, but Dunne held up a hand. "Ah, read it later. You're gonna skim a thousand pages before lunch?"

The waiter brought the drinks, and Dunne raised his glass of Saratoga. "Here's to a profitable relationship, huh?"

"Here's to it," Kenyon said, feeling foolish, but lifting his coffee cup anyway, clinking it against the glass.

After they both sipped, Dunne shook his head. "I can't believe I got you here. That movie of yours just stayed with me, you know? When I was a kid, I used to play that I was Jimmy Stewart, and the bad guy had me and that old prospector pinned down from the cliff? And one of my friends would climb a tree and be Robert Ryan, and I'd sneak up on the other side, and . . ."

Dunne rattled on, but Kenyon didn't hear it. All he heard was a rushing sound, as if all the blood in his body had suddenly surged into his ears. He didn't feel the smooth ceramic of the cup in his fingers. All he felt was a terrible mixture of cold and heat that clamped a fist around his chest and squeezed.

The world had fallen out from under him. Old prospector? Robert Ryan? They weren't in *Trail Dust.*

But Kenyon knew what film they *were* in.

"Greatness," Dunne was saying. "Absolute joy. They don't tell *stories* like that anymore." He shook his head, still looking at Kenyon, smiling at him, and took another drink of water.

"The . . ." Kenyon began, but his throat was too dry, and he cleared it, then sipped his coffee, wishing it was bourbon. "I think you . . . uh . . ." He stopped and started again, slowly. "The movie. The movie of mine. What, uh, what was the movie?"

Dunne pressed his eyebrows together and grinned,

as though Kenyon was putting him on. "Whatta you talking about? *Your* movie, Paul—Jimmy Stewart, Anthony Mann, Oscar nomination, hell, you know what movie."

The words didn't want to come, but Kenyon forced them out. *"The Naked Spur."*

Dunne shrugged and laughed. "Well, yeah, *sure, The Naked Spur."*

Kenyon looked down at the surface of the coffee. The dark liquid caught the light and reflected red, like blood. When he spoke again, the words were very quiet and controlled. "I . . . didn't write *The Naked Spur.* I did *Trail Dust.* With Mann and Stewart. They were both with Mann and Stewart."

He looked up at Dunne, whose smile was still there, but mixed with puzzlement. "*Trail Dust*?" Dunne said, and Kenyon nodded. "*Trail Dust.* Ah. Ah." It sounded as if Dunne was cooing to a baby. "Who, uh, else was in that?"

"Dan Duryea. Jeanne Crain." Nobodies now. Long forgottens. Has-beens, like me, Kenyon thought.

Dunne frowned. Then a tongue came out and licked his lower lip, and he shook his head again. It was probably, Kenyon thought, as mortified as Dunne ever allowed himself to look.

"Jesus," Dunne breathed, his eyes never leaving Kenyon's face. "Jesus, I feel like *such* an asshole."

"It's okay," Kenyon said, trying to smile, thinking that maybe, just maybe this didn't have to be a wash. "Did you ever see *Trail Dust*?"

"Don't think so. Seen most of Mann's stuff, but not that one. On video?" Kenyon nodded. "I'll have to check it out."

"If you liked *The Naked Spur,* you'd like *Trail Dust."*

"Yeah. Probably would."

The waiter came to the table and asked if they were ready to order. Dunne smiled and said, "Might as well eat, since we're here," then deferred to Kenyon, who, having no appetite, asked for a salad. Dunne ordered lemon chicken.

When the waiter left, Dunne chuckled and waved a hand in the air. "Well, this has to be one of the most awkward moments I've ever had. My apologies, Paul."

"Oh, that's . . . all right. It's easy to confuse two films so much alike."

"Uh-huh. Oh, could I have the . . . uh . . ." Kenyon handed over the manuscript box, and Dunne smiled. "Thanks. Wouldn't want to forget it."

Neither spoke until the food came, but halfway through his chicken, Dunne asked, very casually, "By the way, do you know if the screenwriter for that *Naked Spur* thing is still around?"

Kenyon didn't.

After the meal was over, Dunne paid and offered to drive Kenyon home. Kenyon accepted with a nod, and they climbed into a dark blue Testarossa. When they got near Kenyon's apartment, Kenyon asked Dunne to pull over and let him off at the corner. Dunne apologized again, and added, "Listen, I'm gonna get this *Trail Dust,* and if anything comes up I think you'd be right for, I'll definitely be in touch. Hey, it's just a matter of time. But good meeting you, Paul. Take care."

"Thanks," Kenyon said, and began to shuffle away.

Dunne sat and watched him go. He thought he understood why Kenyon had wanted off at that corner. There was a bar up the street.

When he saw Kenyon enter its doors, Dunne pulled the Testarossa out into traffic, and drove over to West Hollywood, where he dropped the car off at a rental agency, paid the fee, and got into his own 1986 Ford Escort. He drove a few blocks to the small apartment he shared with an actress, parked the car, climbed the stairs. The door was unlocked, which meant that she was home.

"Where were you?" she asked, not looking up from a script she was studying. "Bob called."

Bob was Dunne's agent. "Yeah?"

"The studio turned down your script."

"I know." He tossed the manuscript box full of empty sheets of paper on the couch.

"You *know*?" She looked up now, saw how he was dressed.

"I ran into one of their D-girls jogging this morning."

"Oh Christ . . ."

"What?"

"Christ, you did it again, didn't you?"

"Come on, Greta—"

"We can't *afford* it, Rick! A goddam Jag again? Or a Mercedes this time? And where'd you go for lunch? Morton's? La Dome?"

"Nicky Blair's."

"Nicky . . . Christ, you're a sick fucker sometimes, you know that?"

"I need this, Greta."

"Need it? Need to fuck people that way?"

"How I stay sane, baby. We all have ways to deal with disappointment. Now matter how bad things get, I know that there are people worse off than me."

"And that makes it okay."

"Yeah, that makes it so I can keep going. So I can crank out another flying-glass script and maybe someday Schwarzenegger or Bruce Willis will drive their cars through the windows *I* made up. I *need* this. I need to know that at least I'm not at the bottom."

She looked at him for a long time, enraged, and he wondered again why she didn't leave him. But she didn't, and that was enough. Finally she turned away angrily, concentrated on her script again.

"You ought to see it," he said softly.

She didn't say a word.

"When I start filling in details, when it starts to dawn on them that hey, that's not *me* you're talking about, and finally when they're sure, when they know, when their face falls so far you swear you can hear their jaw hit the table like in a Tex Avery cartoon."

She kept reading her script, turned a page with a sharp snap of paper.

"It's not as good as selling a script," he said, "but it's better than a lot of things. It's better than coming."

He didn't wait to watch her cry. Instead he went into the bedroom, walked to the desk, sat down, turned on his computer, and brought up the word processing program from the hard disk. He retrieved the file named COMEBACK, and the list came up on the monitor, white letters on a blue background.

The list was long. There were hundreds of names of writers, performers, directors, all of whom had seen little work since the first time the gods had blessed them, then left them behind for fresher faces, newer talents. Paul Kenyon's name was at the top, along with the words, "TRAIL DUST/1953/J.Stewart/A.Mann/AAN." He blocked the line and moved it down to the bottom of the list, thinking that by the time he came to him again, Kenyon would be ready once more. Hope springs eternal in the town of dreams, Dunne thought, and so does despair and humiliation.

Then he closed COMEBACK, and opened the file of a spec screenplay he had nearly finished. He felt like working now. The disappointment was gone. He was whole again, ready to write.

A little while later he thought of the two names Kenyon had mentioned, Dan Duryea and Jeanne Crain. He hadn't heard about either of them in a very long time, and wondered if they were still alive. He would have to check. If they were, they just might be interested in a comeback.

JUDGMENT

ED GORMAN

The man had been standing here for twenty minutes, just after dusk, just after the rain began. The drops were silver in the dirty light of the street lamp. It was chill enough, this late April, to tint the man's cheeks a winter red and make his nose run.

Dressed as he was in a dark cap and dark topcoat and dark slacks, the man was nearly invisible in the gloom. Not that he had to worry much about being seen. This part of the city was being torn down, hundred-year-old houses leveled and many of the rest boarded up. Only a few people lived here anymore, and most of them were the homeless who huddled in the corners of empty houses shivering against the cold in their rags and gloves with missing fingers, drinking cheap wine that was as bitter as lighter fluid.

The house the man stared at was boarded up, but on the second floor you could see a faint light between the boards over the windows. At one time the place had been a respectable two-story white frame house. Husbands and wives and kids and dreams had lived here, but no longer. Now just a man named McLennan walked its floors.

A car went by, the sort of car you'd expect to see in this neighborhood, a big old dinosaur a dozen years old with a smashed windshield and cancerous rust everywhere and a rumbling muffler in bad need of replacement and three teenagers in the front seat giggling behind pot and beer.

Nicholas Ryan stepped out of the light till the car got past and then he walked quickly through the dirty puddles in the middle of the street.

Rain spraying his face, Ryan hurried onto the lawn of the house and then moved in the shadows along the side of the place. Two or three times he felt his foot slide into dogshit and once he crushed the ragged neck of a broken beer bottle. The once-white siding was now covered with rust stains, as if it were bleeding.

Ryan took the stairs leading up the side of the house. Whipping wind covered any noise he made.

When he reached the top step, he put his head close to the torn screen door and listened. He heard nothing. McLennan was an alcoholic who started drinking right after he got off his factory job. He was usually passed out by now. That's what Ryan was counting on, anyway.

The door was easy to push open, the inside lock hanging at an angle just as Ryan remembered.

A minute later, he stood inside.

During the last of its years, the house had been rented out as two large apartments, upstairs and downstairs. Ryan just hoped the downstairs looked better than this.

The upstairs consisted of a single large room plus a bathroom and a tiny room for storage. The furniture had all come from Goodwill, sprung purple couch and wobbly blond coffee table and any number of knickknacks that were embarrassing to behold, not least the hula-girl lamp on one of the end tables. The faded floral wallpaper was peeling, and ran with the same sort of stain as the white siding.

The floor was an obstacle course of empty beer cans, pizza cardboards, dirty socks, dirty underwear, gigantic dust balls, steel-toed workshoes, and endless empty gnarled-up cigarette packages.

If only I could count on him getting lung cancer, Ryan noted ruefully.

But the smell was worst of all. It was the smell of mildew and age and dust and dirt and shit and piss and sweat; and the smell of perversion. Ryan could think of no other way to characterize it. This large squalid room reeked of a decadence that almost made him vomit. He wanted to get out of here as soon as he could.

Richard McLennan had the ancient Motorola TV console and the purple couch and the overstuffed armchair with the filthy orange slipcovers and the blond coffee table arranged so that it all fit together like a tiny living room. He could sit in the chair with his feet on the coffee table guzzling beer after beer and watching the black and white 21″ Motorola TV screen.

Next to the chair was a cardboard box, and Ryan knew right away that this was what he was looking for. The proof he needed.

Before seating himself and going through the box, he walked over to the far east corner of the room where the single bed was pushed up against the wall and where McLennan lay snoring. Above the bed was a cheap plastic crucifix, Christ dying endlessly. A crucifix did not belong in such a room. Ryan wanted to tear it from the wall.

Ryan stood above the bed and looked down at the man. He was really pretty nondescript, McLennan. Fleshy but not fat; unpleasant-looking (always needed a shave and a haircut) but not ugly; middle-aged but not really aged. Now, lying among sheets that hadn't been washed or straightened out in a long time, McLennan slept with a brown quart bottle of beer clutched in his right hand. The beer had spilled on the bed. McLennan lay face-up, his snoring a wet ugly sound.

Ryan, assuming McLennan wasn't going to wake up, went back to the chair. He sat on the edge of it and picked up the cardboard box.

The first picture was a Polaroid color shot. It showed a girl approximately six years old standing completely naked and staring at the camera. She had some kind of dog collar around her neck. In the right of the photo you could see a whip dangling. It looked like a long black terrible snake. The little girl's expression was blank. She had probably been drugged.

The next photograph he found was of a little boy and a dog and—

Sickened, Ryan tossed the photo back into the box and set the box back down. There would be hundreds of such photographs in the box, every sort of little boy and girl, every imaginable configuration and position and perversion and—

Ryan put his face in his hands and began drawing deep, deep breaths. He wanted to smell clean, fresh air. It would be good to stand outside again in the chill night. Be reinvigorated. Redeemed. This place and all it represented was beginning to overpower him. Over there in the west corner was where the photo of the little girl and the whips had been taken. He tried not to think of what had become of her after McLennan was done with her. What had happened to any of the children.

He went straight over to the bed now and took out the Walther and fitted the silencer to it and then put the weapon right against the center of McLennan's forehead.

Ryan said, "Wake up."

After a time, the snoring spluttered to a stop and McLennan's sad frantic brown eyes showed themselves.

He was still drunk—his rank breath overwhelming even from this distance—but not so drunk that he didn't understand immediately what was going on.

"Hey!" he said. "What the hell's happening here?"

He tried to jump up from bed. Ryan kept the muzzle of the Walther tight against his forehead.

"You didn't stop the way you promised, did you?" Ryan said.

"Hey, what the hell're you doing here? You think I don't know who you are and what you are?"

"You promised me, McLennan. You promised me you'd stop or get help."

"You can't do this. You're a—"

But before he could get the word out, Ryan killed him. A single bullet straight into the brain.

A small gelatinous embryo was borne out the back of McLennan's head. He jerked and jumped as if he'd been electrocuted and then he lay quite still. The air smelled of the gunshot and blood and of McLennan shitting his pants.

Ryan raised his hand and made the sign of the cross and then said some words in Latin. He still preferred Latin.

Before he left he dumped the cardboard box in the sink and took lighter fluid and burned all the photographs.

"Bless me Father for I have sinned. It's been three weeks since my last confession."

"Go on. Confess your sins."

"I killed a man tonight, Father."

There was a long silence in the darkness of the

confessional. In the shadows on the other side of the curtain the old priest sighed. On the air was the sweet scent of incense. It was nearly nine o'clock on a Saturday night. The church was empty except for a lone old lady who knelt beneath her bright ethnic headscarf far ahead at the communion rail.

The old priest sighed again. "It's you, isn't it, Father Ryan?"

"Yes, Father, it is."

"This is the third time you've confessed to me in a year."

"Yes, Father."

"Yet you continue to kill people."

"Only those who won't help themselves or seek help from others. The man I killed tonight confessed to me once a month that he had molested children. I told him to stop, I told him where he could find psychiatric help. But he did nothing to help himself." He paused. "We've taken the vow of silence, Father. I couldn't turn him in. I stopped him the only way I could—before he hurt any other children."

"And the two others you killed?"

"An arsonist who set several fires that killed people, and a rapist who mutilated his victims afterward."

"And you could find no other way to stop them, Father Ryan?"

"No other way. Otherwise they would continue to kill people."

In the vast shadows of the church, the old woman at the communion rail coughed. The sound reminded Ryan of a gunshot.

"Are you sorry for your sins, Father Ryan?"

"I want to be sorry, Father."

"Then pray with me that you never again do such a thing."

"Yes, Father."

"Pray with me now, Father Ryan. Pray harder than you ever have in your life, Father Ryan."

"Yes, Father. I will. I promise. Harder than I ever have in my life."

Three weeks later, the man came back to Father Ryan. Late on a Saturday night. Father Ryan in his confessional. Only a few people left kneeling before the flickering green and yellow and blue votive candles.

Father Ryan recognized the voice immediately.

"Forgive me, Father, for I have sinned."

"Go on. Tell me your sins."

A pause. "My daughter, Father. She's ten and I—"

"Yes?"

"I force her to have sex with me."

"I see." Trying to control his anger, Father Ryan said, "You've been here before."

"Yes, Father."

"Confessing the same sin."

"Yes, Father."

"And I've told you about the psychology clinic over on Third Avenue by the railroad tracks."

"Yes, Father."

"How it's free and confidential."

"Yes, Father."

"Have you gone there yet?"

"No, Father."

"But in the meantime, you've molested your daughter again?"

"Yes, Father."

Father Ryan said nothing. "Are you going to go to the clinic?"

"Yes, Father."

"You absolutely promise me?"

"Yes, Father."

Father Ryan heard the rest of the man's sins and then gave him his penance.

When he left, the man sounded quite sorry about what he'd done.

Father Ryan had to hurry. Slip out the side door to the parking lot and catch a glimpse of the man and the car he was driving.

Father Ryan stood in the shadows of the church door watching a nice-looking man in a three-piece suit get into a small sports car. Father Ryan, who had a good memory for figures, noted the man's license number.

Sadly, turning back to the interior of his church, Father Ryan knew that he would soon enough be using the man's license number as he set about investigating the man just as he'd first investigated McLennan and the two others.

Father Ryan, alone in the church now, went to the communion rail and prayed long into the night.

REALITY FUNCTION

J. N. WILLIAMSON

"Civilisation has separated us from our deep, instinctive will to live, eroded our 'reality function.' . . . We are highly vulnerable."

—Colin Wilson, *C. G. Jung: Lord of the Underworld*

(With particular thanks to my wife and in-house editor, Mary T. Williamson)

If a single and singular knack—one exceptional attribute—set Matthew Miliken apart from all the other teachers he had ever known and also made him clearly superior to them, he felt sure he knew what it was.

Mr. Miliken had always remembered just what it was like to be a high school underclassman, and he treated his own pupils accordingly.

What was it like? It was like being a motherless transfer student from a small county school to a big-city institution, the last eligible pledge to the one fraternity that posed an indifferent invitation, the rawest recruit on the military base, and the newest, lowliest member of the English Department at Salinger High School rolled into one. Matthew Miliken had been all those people, he recalled exactly what it had been like each time, and he treated his own students accordingly.

Just the same way he'd been treated, only worse. More subtly the past seven years he'd served as department head, but definitely, decidedly, worse.

Seven years of cleverly weeding out the great unwashed from a department that had threatened to become a benevolent protective society for sheerly titular teachers—people whose copycat appearances implied the worship of some modish, hirsute god frozen forever midway in puberty! Seven years of wielding a scythe with the skill of a neurosurgeon to prune the department of intellectual kudzu and lay bare the brilliant brain gleaming with naked purity at its throbbing center—*his,* eager to take full charge of the responsibility for Salinger's pseudo-students of English! Seven—count 'em!—seven years to make that fool Cross accept his own definition of the word *faculty.* For it was not primarily "a teaching staff," but the other two definitions Webster supplied: The specialized power of a living organism, and an authorization. In short, an empowerment.

Seven, the central, the operative, magic number in Miliken's life. That many years he had been obliged to suffer the inadequacies of his pupils without retaliation. *Twice* seven years ago, he hadn't been so subtle, so skilled at laying plans with infinite attention to detail—and he'd been summarily discharged from his prior post for disciplining some idiot of a youth. Exactly what had transpired had tended until recently to escape Mr. Miliken's memory. Lately, however, he'd started anew to toy with multiples of his favorite number, to recollect the exquisite pleasures of what he'd done to the ignoramus of a boy before several other instructors stopped him, and to feel the stirrings of old delight, the embryonic yen anew. Three times seven years into his past he'd been obliged to deal with his army sergeant, during target practice. Not that long a period before the sergeant's accident, he had also needed to get the high-and-mighty fraternity president off his back, but Welch had survived—albeit without taking his diploma. *Four* times seven years ago, when he was a transfer student, the boys who harassed Matthew Miliken had not been so fortunate.

And at age seven, Mother had been the origin of young Matthew's awakening to the fine efficacy of the number seven in his life.

Now it was seven minutes past three P.M., exactly.

Alone in his classroom except for nearly thirty young people who were pretending to focus their attention on a scene from *Romeo and Juliet,* Mr. Miliken lofted his hands from his desk, expressionlessly regarded the life lines of his palms, and extended his ten fingers into the air. He left the five of his left hand up, then tucked the ring and baby finger of the right hand beneath a prehensile thumb. The result provided him with mild enjoyment and so, after gazing with boredom above the fingertips at his pupils' lowered faces, he surrendered to the impulse to smile.

Surely now it was time again. All of them were alive. And so far as Mr. Miliken knew from casually tracking the obituaries—anything deeper would have been compulsive—every student who'd passed through Salinger High's department of English for the previous seven years was still alive.

None had died in the manner of his drill sergeant or the unfeeling boys who had taunted the young Matthew, nor had any died the way Mother and his predecessor as department head had perished—which was the death of preference, where Mr. Miliken was concerned. None of the thick-headed, inconsistent, easily-distracted, unruly and obstinate little gland-dominated cretins had died in any way at all!

His was the patience of Job—no, of a god.

It was time.

Now it was a case of wise choice, particularly if they

were to end their space-devouring existences the way that he considered cleverest, most fulfilling, and safest. Selecting half a dozen to die would be egregious; overbearing. Five would bring the closest scrutiny regardless of *how* they exited life, and he could not be certain he still possessed the psychic endurance for the task; one was well to admit the inroads of temporal attrition.

Four then? Awkward. Pastimes of this inventive magnitude demanded the concentration of a chess master. Four was also, according to the ancients, a number of totality; completion. In spite of middle age, Mr. Miliken was trim, watched his diet, never smoked. Twice-seven years from the present, he'd only be fifty-six; *three* times seven—bringing him to age sixty-three—why, with moderation and prudence, his little forays into extracurricular intellectual adventure would not have to end even then!

Well, then . . . three. Not all bad. An appealing number. He shifted in his chair. One-two-*three;* there were no obvious flaws to it no matter how Mr. Miliken examined it. *Three.* Dropping his left hand, he freed the ring finger of the right in order to allow it to join the adjacent middle and the index digits. Head cocked, he studied the finger trio for a moment, noting that the longer middle gave the structure a nice pyramidal look. Very well! For now, for the present purposes, three of them would be ideal. Not perfect. Ideal.

Do I see the hands of any volunteers? he wondered. His round, brown eyes like chocolate tarts rolled from face to face, his rare smile a marvel of instructional eagerness to be of help.

From somewhere in the room, a voice—young, female, bell-like in its purity, its clarity! "Mr. Miliken?"

His telepathic powers hadn't abandoned him! "Yes?" he cried, scanning juvenile faces as all of them looked up.

He realized distantly that he didn't know any of them well enough to identify their voices.

The fair-skinned teenager was in third-row-left, three back. Mr. Miliken didn't fail to resonate to the perfection of the repeated number. And he did know her; she was the athletic person, possibly track. He'd seen her jogging on the streets often enough to recognize her profile. Unlike most, that was her best side, but she was so alert, so inquisitive, that she always managed to stare back, full face. He peered down into his open roll book. "Yes, *Ms.* Auel?" Megan Auel, and he'd been sure to address her in the idiotic modern idiom.

"I wanted to be sure I understood," Megan began—

"Stand; rise!" he urged her with an evangelist's gesture.

"—What Juliet means here," she finished, rising. Pretty only as an echo of earlier childhood or as a foretaste of what might lie beyond her high school years as a sprinter, Megan had rather close-cropped hair hopelessly lost between a light brown and a blond hue that came out best—like Megan herself—when she ran in sunlight. Her proudest moment had occurred when her coach, Marva Smith-Coles, told her she had less extra body fat than any other athlete Marva'd ever coached. "It says, 'I have an ill-divining soul! Methinks I see thee, now thou art below, As one dead in the bottom of a tomb . . .' " Morgan met Mr. Miliken's stare. "She doesn't really see him that way. Right?"

He asked back, "What do you think?"

Megan flushed. "Well, I think she was sorta psychic, maybe." Her tousled head came forward in a sudden, soundless laugh of rueful embarrassment. "I mean, this is *Shakespeare*—so what do I know?"

"Well," said, "*I* think you may be quite correct. Besides, the Bard wrote for an audience no better informed than this class will be, if I have *my* way about it!"

Laughter rippled, Megan sat, and Matthew Miliken turned his head toward the one student he'd definitely had in mind upon reaching today's important decision. "Lyall," he said softly, "why don't you rise and read Romeo's response to the fair Juliet's visionary apprehension?"

Lyall Dorris stood with an expression of doom on a face that was almost as round as it was long. If his teacher's question had not been rhetorical, Lyall could have answered, "Because I stammer so badly it's nearly impossible to say good morning." Or, "I'm sick of how you call on me three or four times every class, practically inviting other boys to make fun of me." Lacking freedom or facility, he gripped the thin volume of Shakespeare so tightly in his hands that one page gave way beneath his pressing thumb, and an audible ripping noise drew giggles from the students close to—staring up at—Lyall.

" 'A-And t-trust m-m-m-me, l-l-l-l-love,' " he read aloud bravely, " 'in m-my eye s-so d-d-do y-y-y-y-you—' "

"Thank you, Lyall," Miliken said, and the boy seemed to disappear as he plumped down into his chair. "I want to see you, briefly. After class."

This wasn't the first time. "M-My b-b-b-b—"

"Your *bus,*" Mr. Miliken finished it, unable to resist raising his gaze to the heavens, "won't leave before I'm through with you. I plan to do most of the talking." Amid chuckles and without the need to read from the book, he completed Romeo's lines: ". . . 'So do you: Dry sorrow drinks our blood.' Mr. Stillings." He recognized an upthrown arm. "You have an observation for us?"

Fifteen-year-old Kenneth Stillings, a year or better the junior of the others, his hand wiggling from the wrist. He who had skipped grades, Mr. Miliken reflected, and might never know love because he was so enchanted with his own IQ. *One, two, three,* he told himself. *Megan, Lyall, and Kenneth—volunteers all.*

"Megan omitted one of fair Juliet's lines." This Kenneth, short and small. Ludicrously, sexlessly small. People today failed entirely to grasp the purpose of education. No student should be allowed to dispense with a year of schooling as if he were discarding a disposable can. This child had missed so much, and now he'd be missing so much *more.* "If I may rectify the omission?" Kenneth's unfeeling Delft eyes glazed with memory and knowledge. " 'Either my eyesight fails or thou look'st pale.' Thank you, Mr. Miliken." He lowered himself with almost proprietorial aplomb to his own chair.

"To *rectify,* Mr. Stillings," the teacher said as he stood away from the desk, "is to correct, to put right." He smoothed down his buttoned, brown suit coat. Afoot, he looked tall to most Salinger students and knew it. Once he'd yearned to own six suits of exactly this color because it was just the shade of his eyebrows, but he had only found one other. He wore one or the other suit seven days a week and the dry-cleaner's people addressed him, without authority, by his first name. "By definition, an omission is an absence, a nothingness. I think the correct word you were questing for was 'supply.' "

Kenneth, both feet on the floor only when he leaned forward in his chair or rose, returned a two-inch-long smile. It was the most harmonious blend of adoration and envy approximating hatred Mr. Miliken had seen on the human face. "Thank you, sir."

Footsteps were moving in the halls and soon the buzzer would sound. "Mr. Stillings, am I correct that you're attending biology club after school?"

"Yes, Mr. Miliken." This was the final class of the day and only Lyall, who'd been kept after, and small Kenneth were not rising to rush for the door. "Is there something you would like me to do, sir?"

Miliken nodded absently. Megan Auel was hurrying out without a sidelong glance in his direction and even his nimble mind hadn't yet devised a reason to delay her. Those facts cemented her status as No. 3. *"I think she will be rul'd In all respects by me,"* Capulet's speech played in Miliken's memory. Appropriating it, he added another: *"Well, we were born to die."*

"Yes, there is, Kenneth," he told Stillings. He pretended to appear uncertain. "Your father . . . isn't home a great deal these days?"

Kenneth did a credible imitation of a small statue. Something decorative, more ornamental than statuesque. When the child's lips formed assent, Mr. Miliken recalled small-boy *objets* in garden fountains, cascading water from tiny penises.

"Your mother frets over you, I know," Miliken continued. "Stop by here and I'll drive you home. I think a little heart-to-heart is in order."

"Did I do something wrong?"

Mr. Miliken liked reading student files from time to time. Learning about the families, the intimate problems pupils confessed to their counselors. Kenneth's mother had gotten religion, his father had not. He'd gotten interests away from home, both from his wife and son. Little Kenneth's record of straight-A final marks had been no more compelling to him than his wife's born-again status, and neither parent was capable, it seemed clear to the teacher, of appreciating an offspring who was a boy genius. Now that it occurred to Mr. Miliken, nobody was. "You possess a hunger for knowledge, Stillings. It is knowledge I mean to offer you—more than you're likely to get from a room filled with cretins whose truly best hope is that they *will* be . . . born again. Four-twenty, then?"

When the child nodded and rushed off to his club, Mr. Miliken turned his attentions to the stammering Lyall with a surge in his intestines that he hadn't known for five-six-*seven* years. The warmth that only came when the major decisions of life were made, the preliminary steps taken, and it became possible to stare down at a pupil from his full height—and eventually discern a *number* beginning to take form on his forehead, just over the brow line.

Often, Miliken had wondered if superior men of the past had shared with him the special gift, this exciting evidence of psychic contact being made between his dynamic intelligence and the scared-mouse section of his chosen victims' lesser brains. Though his reading was catholic, though he had searched for the record of another man with the power to detect the succession of identifying numerals starting to illumine the sloping foreheads, one by one—like bull's-eyes—he'd had to accept the glorious isolation inherent in the likelihood that he was the only one.

He bore up well under it, however.

He approached Lyall arms akimbo, noticing for the first time how like a chipmunk he looked. "Mr. Dorris, d'you know why I asked you to stay after?"

You hate me, Lyall thought. He concentrated, brow furrowing. "Same r-reason a-as t-t-the other t-t-times?"

Mr. Miliken beamed. "I like that. I really do." Big nod. "As stalls go, it's clever. Relatively speaking." Of late, he had refound the delight of arousing hope in student bosoms, then dashing it. Perhaps he'd sensed at an unconscious level that today's decision might be reached and then primed the pump that was pudgy, stuttering Lyall Dorris.

But until that instant, he had not imagined it was conceivable to begin driving three students to kill themselves—Mr. Miliken's favorite, foolproof preference of method—that very afternoon!

Not that the girl or the brainy upstart, Stillings, would be easy tasks. He couldn't even be sure that he could make the Dorris boy do it. That was the thrill, however, and probably why *he* possessed the gift of psychic contact while other superior men lacked it—because Matthew Miliken settled for nothing less than *genuine challenges!*

Additionally, he was not one to grow obsessive over his pastimes. If he failed to motivate any of the three pupils to destroy themselves—

He was perfectly willing to destroy them himself!

"I didn't keep you after school for the same reason, Lyall," he said. "I have given up on you, you see." He shrugged his well-pressed jacket shoulders. "Repeatedly, I've tried to stop your stammering. Over and over I've called on you in class, to read. I've sat here on my own time and listened numerous times to your butchering of some of the best works of fiction in our language. Yet *you,* boy"—skillfully, he lifted a single fine brow—"refused even to carry my recommendations of assistance home to your father!"

Once, in a mood of foresightful wisdom, he had in fact scrawled a note to the elder Dorris in which he stated baldly how consuming Lyall's problem was, emphasizing how disruptive he was in class, stressing that Lyall might "require considerably more than what a speech therapist can provide." He'd added a tactful fillip implying an absence of "social courage," then photocopied the note—believing with all the certainty he had that Lyall would *not* take it to Lieutenant Steve Dorris of the homicide department, a police officer decorated for bravery. He still owned the photocopy and relished knowing that he was obliged to motivate the boy to end his existence rather than taking matters into his own hands. Had the senior Dorris toiled as a clerk or maintenance man, there'd have been literally no challenge to his first student designation.

"Lyall . . . son . . . you're here now so that, without others overhearing, you may learn how hopeless your situation is. I feel I owe you the truth—a commodity of immense scarcity in our time and one almost never conveyed from parent to child. Do you follow me?"

A definite, incipiently terrified bob of the head.

"Life is not what once it was, lad. The infirm are everywhere; recall what you've seen on television. Appeals for funds, for people with spare time to care for the abused or homeless and to serve as surrogate this or that. Doubtlessly you have, yourself, felt pity . . . compassion . . . for those whose very limbs will not work properly."

Lyall nodded slowly.

"Listen to me," Mr. Miliken said, eyes smoldering. "There is not enough money to go around, there aren't enough people with leisure time, to deal with the needs of those like yourself. In the distant past, when the United States was full of small towns, people knew one another, *cared* for one another." Mr. Miliken pinched the trousers of his brown pants, sat in the chair nearest—opposite—Lyall. "Even when a youngster was totally *incapable* of speech, his family or friends looked after him. *No more.*"

The child felt his mouth drop open. He needed to argue, say something; but what he might say was unthinkably rude to an adult, and mired in complexity. His heartbeat hadn't accelerated but fallen so quiet he wondered if he was alive.

"Here are the facts I promised," continued Mr. Miliken, appearing to muster the manliness needed for unutterable truths. "These days, the living bestow honor on those whose nerves are firm. Steady, unflagging. Do not, please, misunderstand. I'm not saying that a youngster must be a genius, or live heroically—like your father, for example—or even have all the answers."

"N-N-No?"

Miliken put out an arm to place one hand gently on Lyall's. "But the *appearance* of those attributes—the very *look* of absolute preparedness, insight or insiders' knowledge—of wit, a flair for repartee, vast social charm—is what wins out." He saw that the light of horror in the teenager's eyes needed a bit more support. "Always."

"Alll-w-w-ways?"

"They are basic, Lyall, invaluable not just to success—but to survival itself." He made himself pause to let everything sink in. Seeing the lips unadorned even by the possibility of a beard begin to part, he said with his own lips, *Always.*

And then he counted *one, two, three,* and laid out the rest of it. "Lyall, it is only the haunting dead who could exhibit compassion for your plight. Well, there are your *parents;* but the city's finest are notoriously underpaid, aren't they?"

"The d-d-d-d-d-d-*dead*?"

"D'you go to films of fright, boy? Do you?"

His eyes just went on saying "the dead." Like neon lights.

"I know they're called 'horror movies,' but I think of them as tales about quivering, trembling, gutless fools who survive merely for the enjoyment of powerful entities—who always know *their* minds! Helpless imbeciles who run to ground, *high* ground, trapping themselves." Mr. Miliken tilted back his head as if laughing in recollection. "Dying there is the only thing they *ever* do right, isn't it? And if they *can* succeed in speaking, as the unconquerable foe deliberately mounts the steps, the next thing a movie-goer hears is—a *stammer*!"

Lyall's hand beneath Miliken's spasmed as he tried instinctively to jerk it away, but it stayed put.

"You know, that's what make such pictures work, boy." Mr. Miliken leaned more weight on the plump hand. "That moment of amusement and derision shared with the audience when the pathetic, squirming victim *must take* decisive action—or at least, come up with a convincing argument for *why* he should go on living!"

The child pulled harder but the hand was pinned.

"D'you recall the next part, the *last* part, Lyall?" Miliken's fine brows rose and fell, alternately. "It's when the doomed victim—usually a young person these days—finally gets his mouth open. And while his silly eyes practically ex*plode* from his head, he looks straight into the camera to defend himself with the immortal—'B-b-b-b-b-*b-but*!' "

Mr. Miliken abruptly sat up. Arms folded, he laughed noiselessly.

Hand tugged free, Lyall fell off his chair. Pale, he got to his feet with sweat flooding from the temples and fled the classroom with both hands pressed to his mouth. From somewhere up the corridor, he howled.

Mr. Miliken stopped laughing. Simple satisfaction with a job well done was enough, and the boy genius, Kenneth Stillings, would arrive soon for his ride home.

And even before the teacher had made more than a start on the papers he began grading a moment after Lyall's exit, the small and dark-haired image of Salinger

High's straight-A's-always pupil was waiting expectantly in the doorway.

Ms. Megan Auel's test paper was next on the pile and Mr. Miliken just glanced at it before inscribing a red-penciled D at the top of the page, then rising.

One-two-three—but not necessarily in that order. "How are things at biology club, Mr. Stillings?"

"Skeletal," Kenneth said. He knew the quip wasn't original with him, but he remembered to add a smile to it.

"Clever boy," Mr. Miliken said. He clapped him on the shoulder and made a show of activity as he loped around him, out into the corridor. "Come along. Your mother will be expecting you." Waving his arm, he rushed ahead.

"I didn't make up that joke, sir." The voice in Mr. Miliken's wake, in common with the rest of the fifteen-year-old, was small. "I heard a football player say it."

Miliken looked back, noticing Kenneth's pullover and remembering too late his car coat in the teachers' cloakroom. Precipitate action was always his potential downfall. "You really do have the most singular fondness for facts."

Kenneth was nearly running to keep pace. "What else is there to depend on, sir?"

They were in the lot behind the building, Mr. Miliken craning his neck in search of his car. He shivered as much from excitement and anticipation as from the winter that wouldn't quite go away. *" 'O, thou art deceived,' "* he murmured. "Mercutio, I think." He saw his four-year-old brown-for-his-eyebrows car gleaming with near-twilight glory and strode blithely toward it. "I want to discuss that subject on your ride home. Hop in."

Kenneth opened the passenger door and did so.

Hopping, at his height, was the only way to enter a full-sized automobile. "What subject, sir?"

"Reality," Miliken replied. He turned his key in the ignition, waited until the small boy was in. "The reality function, to be precise."

"Oh," Kenneth said noncommittally. The way he looked at someone grown-up with his particularly amazing blue eyes—as veiled by a protective covering of solid fact as an addict's by drugs—might have daunted a lesser man than Miliken. "Is this about religion, sir? Because Mother—"

"It is not," Mr. Miliken said flatly. "Religion is about truth. I want to talk with you about facts." *That should hold him,* he thought, pausing with the car in the street to learn the boy's address. What was needed now was demonstrating to Stillings that he, himself, possessed superior knowledge or was smarter; preferably both. From studying the student files he knew not only that the father was usually absent and that the mother was attempting to replace him with churchly matters, but that Kenneth had a weakness: He'd gotten a B+ on a recent weekly exam. In sex education. A psychiatrist wasn't required to know that the father's dalliances combined with the emotional flareups of the mother had bewildered a child of somewhat protracted puberty. One who'd do anything to keep his straight-A record intact—

And who was in urgent if unknowing need of a father figure.

To Miliken, the pretty consistency of reliable data seemed nothing more challenging now than a ledge for an egghead to perch upon till it could be made to crumble. Once it did—when small Mr. S. was adequately overpowered by information *beyond his ken*—he would fear what was massing on the ledge with him so much that jumping became preferable . . .

"I said that I hope to add to your store of knowledge some information that is unavailable at the school library." He looked straight ahead, calmly setting the stage. "You see, Mr. Stillings . . . Kenneth . . . I think you've developed a habit of taking too much for granted. 'Rectify' as an all-purpose term, for example. What do you know"—he drew in a breath—"about the atom?"

"I guess I couldn't actually make an A-bomb," Kenneth answered. "But atomic energy isn't a big *secret* anymore." A shrug.

"All right." He glanced toward the boy. "Then I take it you would not experience much sense of challenge were I to ask you to . . . *show me* an atom."

Kenneth glanced back, alerted. An apostrophe formed between his brows. "If the conditions were right—"

"If you and I stood in *sight* of a nuclear reactor," Mr. Miliken interposed, "*could* I see an atom—utilizing *any* equipment you wish? One, single atom?"

"Well, sure," the child said with a laugh. "Of course!"

Mr. Miliken's delight was just marginally concealed. "*Wrong!* No one has *ever* seen an atom!" Fingertips danced on the wheel. "*No one,* Mr. Stillings. So it goes without saying that subatomic particles such as neutrons have never been seen. An entire science—the citadel of fact—is based solely upon the *invisible*!"

The mark between Kenneth's furrowing brows was a quotation mark.

"Words must be defined by an object's constancy, by determining its boundaries. But Kenneth—*Kenny*—particles come and go, like *ghosts.* While scientists *predict* they are there, physicists cannot say that any given particle will weigh such-and-such or even how long it will be around!"

"Like *ghosts*?"

"Ghosts." Miliken turned to nod and quite nearly lost control of his car.

The number "2" glowed prominently on young Stillings' forehead like a gold star.

In spite of it, the teacher had managed before they stopped in front of Kenneth's house to touch on a number of allied topics—the impossibility of comprehending how gravity worked or evolving a theory to explain black holes to every astronomer's satisfaction—and to shatter much of the boy's faith in reality as he knew it.

"I swore by the inconstant moon, I guess," Kenneth joked, getting out. His gaze swept to a second-floor window where a curtain was held back by a feminine hand. Looking again at his teacher, his striking eyes were as red-rimmed as if he had been reading.

"Think of Romeo, not Juliet," suggested Mr. Miliken. " 'O, Will I set up my everlasting rest; And shake the yoke of inauspicious stars From this world-wearied flesh.' " He gunned his engine. The numeral on Kenneth's face shimmered in fading daylight. "We continue our discussion before and *after* class tomorrow."

A blink. "I don't know . . ."

"Your sex education teacher told me your record of consecutive A's is in jeopardy." He saw the boy blink again, crimson. "You require the guidance of a mature man . . . *Ken.*" And his tires wailed as he sped swiftly off.

One, *then* two (the challenge grew as the numbers ascended) and, finally, three. The increase was predictable, just what made it fulfilling enough to stop after No. 3—pause, actually—and wait another seven years without succumbing to his periodic impatience.

This third choice, though—Mr. Miliken had to concentrate to bring the name "Megan Auel" to his conscious thoughts—demanded clear-headed reflection. They were different, females. Stronger in a certain way.

Fewer were suicides, which explained in part why more of them were dealt with violently. *Ms.* Auel gave every indication, also, of being that rare bird, a well-adjusted teenager, even a *happy* one. He turned the car up a street that would return him to Salinger, smiling at his sudden thought: Normal teenagers were mixed up, out of place, grew easily depressed. Since that made this child *abnormal* by psychiatric definition, his attentiveness to her might be viewed as the tender ministrations of a concerned citizen doing his social duty! That made Matthew Miliken a bit of a healer!

An hour of poring through her school records and personal file persuaded Mr. Miliken that he knew the girl well enough to devise a basic plan.

Megan Auel's assets were her potential liabilities. Having been a fourth child and, she felt, an unwanted one—the data coaxed from pupils by psychological profile was *wonderful*—she had kept to herself and become the shyest of children until the occurrence of puberty. Discovering athletics in general and running in particular seemed to have been a revelation and brought her out of herself. A silly, admiring note scribbled by Coach Smith-Coles claimed she was the best female athlete in Salinger High School history.

But those probing tests that evaluated the intelligence also showed the sixteen-year-old capable of earning far better grades; for the most part, Megan was inclined to settle for B's or high C's—and that was where Mr. Miliken found his opening.

However gifted or skilled, *no* athlete was allowed to participate on a team without achieving a certain (and absurdly low!) grade level. Young people wildly exaggerated the importance of matters. Sometimes they killed themselves because someone with muscles and pimples or a padded bra would not go out with them—and

Megan's running was the *sole* activity that brought her a sense of identity, of worth!

It was also the one activity Matthew Miliken could deny her and drive the child to despair, ultimately to suicide! Why, his intuitive mind had already guided his hand to affix a D to her most recent paper. Unread!

A problem was that the overall grade average couldn't be sufficiently reduced by one teacher's mark. The realization caused Mr. Miliken to frown and ponder until the solution surged into his consciousness with the radiant suddenness of the numerals rising to his selections' foreheads: Any F would get Megan suspended from team practice for the day, and an F final would get her thrown off the team—so he'd *flunk her!*

But he wouldn't lower her present grade from a D. No; Ms. Auel needed to feel fear and tension and not be pushed to the principal's office with a claim that he was being unjust. She had to see *herself* fail—and Miliken knew just how to accomplish it!

Tomorrow, in class, Megan would leave the starting blocks in her greatest race, and her last. Which was, Mr. Miliken promised himself as he graded the rest of the papers, retrieved his coat and walked without stealth to the darkened parking lot, just where the musclebound little female cretin would finish: *Dead last.*

Alone in his apartment, he spent a relaxing evening, retired for the night without giving a thought to any of his school activities (the healthy man compartmentalized his affairs), and awakened the next day fully rested, bothered neither by dream nor nightmare.

But he had been awakened by his telephone jangling, not by his clock-radio.

He answered with his mind functioning at noontime proficiency. "Miliken."

"Matthew, I think I have some terrible news."

"Well, Simon," he told the newest and youngest man in English, "I should think it either is or isn't." He stretched his long back, caught a glimpse of the calendar on a wall round the corner from his kitchenette. He always drew a slash through the day's date with a red crayon before departing for school, and today's date was the 7th. *Auspicious,* he noted, paying closer attention to the caller.

"It is terrible. Tragic." Simon Fontaine lowered his voice as if one might wish to keep what followed secret. "He's a pupil of yours, I think. Lyall Dorris?" Simon paused for a reaction, got none. "He shot himself. Just heard about it on the news." A second pause. "With his father's gun."

Mr. Miliken pursed his lips. He looked forward to going into his bathroom to see the number "7" appear in each of his mirrored eyes. The numeral, black, shiny as pitch, would not linger long. "Thank you for notifying me," he added, remembering his etiquette.

"Kid had just seen a horror flick," Simon blathered. "Wonder if that had anything to do with it. What do you think, Matthew?"

"I think it was probably his stammer." He lifted the arm that was free above his head, yawned. "The poor boy."

Then he had twenty-four satisfying minutes to spend in his morning ablutions, with the added feature. His ride to Salinger was uneventful, the day spent largely in listening to whispers and horrified gasps from faculty and student body alike. The sounds served as a delightful counterpoint to Mr. Miliken's private ruminations until, just before afternoon class began, little Kenneth Stillings obediently arrived on time.

"I looked up some of the stuff you mentioned." Standing on the side of the desk opposite to his teacher,

Kenneth's size and sober face made Mr. Miliken think of history, of boy sopranos whose voices were so pure they were said to have been castrated before puberty, turned for all their lives into adorable songbirds. The old customs . . . "You were right," Kenneth said.

"I was."

Kenneth frowned. "It was kind of hard even to check out some of it."

"Why do you imagine that was, Mr. Stillings?"

A troubled sigh. "I guess some experts don't like to admit it when . . ." He let his voice trail away.

The teacher linked his fingers. "—When reality escapes them. They have no further reason to exist." His elongated thumbs circled one another slowly.

"I don't think I passed the quiz in Ms. Rathman's class today. I sort of knew the answers, but I c-couldn't put them down."

"The sex education class." He saw Kenneth falter, stare down. "You were embarrassed, weren't you?"

Kenneth reddened, wasn't far from tears. "Mother doesn't want me to take that class 'cause I'm too young, or shouldn't hear about things . . . that way. Or—"

"Kenny." Miliken spoke quietly, gently. "We're *men* here." The hard glaze over the blue eyes started to melt. "Son," he added, "I understand."

The teenager checked the door to make sure no other pupils had entered. "You do?"

It took an effort made possible only by unstinting practice, but Mr. Miliken bestowed on him the sweetest smile Kenneth had seen on a man's face. "Yes, I do." He held the boy's gaze as he would have held the world's most precious and fragile jewel. "Ken, for some, sexuality is merely an annoyance; perturbation. Are you aware that for some males—healthy, dare I say it, normal males?—the idea of animalistically pursuing a female is abhorrent. And do you know why?" A wait for the head shake. "Because, boy, it is an interference in the cool intellectual activities of life—the superior life."

"Well," Kenneth whispered, "I can see that."

"*You* can," Miliken cried, "of course!" He was at his most affably authoritarian and paternal. "History is full of outstanding men who learned ways to *subdue* what the great unwashed call the 'natural' drives." A delicate pause. "Such techniques might be a bit advanced for you at present—not that you'd find a word about them in the school library!"

Footsteps shuffled outside in the corridor. Kenneth went round the desk to Mr. Miliken, leaned down. "What if y-you've begun having . . . a *little* of those drives? Not *much,"* he said, cheeks red again, "but what if—"

"Later," Mr. Miliken said as the others began to file in. His gaze touched the arriving Megan Auel. He hid a frosty smile behind a reassuring clap on Kenneth's arm. "Don't fret, Ken. We'll work together on this problem as long as it takes!"

He waited until his students were seated and asked for a moment of silence to "honor your poor classmate, Lyall." While heads were bowed, he finished ironing out details in his foolproof plan for the female athlete. When it occurred to Mr. Miliken to pass out the graded papers from yesterday's test, to worry and fluster Megan, he was out of his chair, giving them to a pupil named Martin to pass back, like a shot.

Watching Megan's expression change, he knew he had done the right thing.

Rising, he went round to the front of his desk, sat lightly on it, and explained that he intended to try something "a little different today." He stressed that their marks for that period would depend upon the "performance" of those he called on. There was only one pupil among them, he knew, who could cope well with the assignment, and he did not plan to call on Kenneth Stillings.

"Without opening your books," he began, "I want the pupils whose names I call to tell all of us the story of *Romeo and Juliet.*"

The classroom fell utterly still.

"Is it an unreasonable request?" he inquired. "I don't believe so. We've read many scenes aloud. Surely the majority of you have been adequately intrigued by one of the greatest dramatists to leaf through the rest of the play without my prompting." He smiled sunnily, especially upon Ms. Auel. With her training schedule, she was not likely to have read more than the assigned passages. He'd call on her last; let her stew. And the way she slipped yesterday's paper surreptitiously into a notebook suggested how much she surely hoped he would not call her name. "We begin at the beginning—Act I, Scene I; a public place—with"—he paused dramatically before choosing Martin, who had dispersed the papers for him—*"you."*

It was—all of it—a predictable disaster. With an eye on the classroom clock, Mr. Miliken corrected outrageous guesses, supplied names, occasionally described whole scenes, and steadily worked his way round the room to Megan Auel. Despite Kenneth Stillings' periodically wildly-waving arm, he pretended not to see him.

At last, as they limped their way into Act V—the churchyard scene—Miliken stood away from his desk, faced Megan Auel. " 'Ah, dear Juliet,' " he intoned with unblinking eyes, " 'Why art thou so fair? Shall I believe That unsubstantial death is amorous; And that the lean abhorred monster keeps Thee here in dark to be his paramour?' Tell us, my dear, what Romeo clutches in his hand, what he does with it, then be good enough to summarize the remainder of the play."

Since her successes in track, she had come to believe that everyone actually liked her a little. Now she sensed animosity and it made her feel the way she had as an unwanted child. Megan said, "Well, he had poison, and he takes it."

"Does he share it with Juliet?"

She hesitated. Megan knew both star-cross'd lovers died so the teacher must be asking her a leading question. "I think. Yes, he must have."

"So *wronnngg*," Mr. Miliken moaned. "She drew Romeo's dagger and killed herself with it, that 'true and faithful Juliet' as Montague expressed it." He sounded as if the exhaustion they were inflicting on him was too much to bear. "Go on."

"Go on?" Megan repeated, stunned. "They're dead. Isn't that it?"

It was not, and Matthew Miliken was obliged to display his own acting skill in order to seem as let down as he did. "Prior to that question, Ms. Auel," he said with apparent misery, "I was considering a D for the woeful work we've seen today." He returned to the chair behind his desk just as the buzzer ended the class. "Today's class grade is—an F."

The athlete was facing him across the desk by the time he was sitting. "I don't think that's fair to the kids you didn't call on." She nodded at Kenneth, who was waiting behind her. "It's not their fault. Please don't do that to them."

Mr. Miliken pretended to think hard about what she had said. "You have a point even if it's just possible you're *more* concerned because your D yesterday has descended to today's F." He smiled and pulled his grade book nearer. "Very well, I'll record an F only for you who so pitifully tried to tell the story. I suppose that means you will not be allowed to practice with your team until you bring the mark up?" His smile became a smirk. "Perhaps you'll do better next week and use your free time to become better acquainted with the Bard."

"Sir," Megan began. But her eyes filled with tears. She could not trust herself to speak. So she rushed out of the room silently and left Kenneth with Miliken.

"That was nice of you, not giving the rest of us an F," the boy said.

"I strive, always, to be a reasonable man," Mr. Miliken said modestly. He got unhurriedly to his feet. "What would you say to another ride home?"

The child grinned. "I'd say thanks," he said. And that was done.

A block or two away from Salinger, Mr. Miliken reprised the theme of his earlier topic. "You asked me, I believe, what could be done if certain passionate drives were only starting to shake a man's equilibrium. Like subatomic particles, they come and go—and may be successfully diverted."

"It is a real problem sometimes," Kenneth confessed. "I would never mention it to Mother. And Dad—well, he just isn't around much."

"How sad for you." Obviously, Mr. Miliken thought, Kenneth was well into puberty; obviously, Rathman's class had explained what was happening to his body but not to his mind. Miliken sighed, recalled his own early longings. It was just about then that he had started to become the man he was today. "I told you that certain techniques could prove to be somewhat advanced. However, some of the older students—that football player you mentioned, for example—might know what I was referring to." He shrugged. "Don't make too much of it . . . or too little."

"Sir?"

Miliken stared at Kenneth's puzzled face and said what he meant: "The primary obligation of the superior male is to let nothing stand in the way of his basic plans."

"Nothing?"

"Nothing."

"So I ought to go ahead and just—"

The teacher shook his head. "Not so long as *anyone or anything* is there, to free you of the impediment. Reduce tension, so you can return to your chosen course as soon as possible." He was firing the warhead of his design for the teenager. It all depended on his reading of Kenneth. He felt sure the parents had done their part, whether they'd meant to or not, by loading him with the requisite guilt. "A superior man has focus, maintains his course. If he has not *sought* the disease of either human dreams or desires, it is his duty to cure himself of both in order to focus on his own mandated objectives."

"You said 'anyone,' Mr. Miliken?" The glowing "2" was back in the center of his forehead as if the skin were inflamed. "And *anything?*"

Appearing not to hear, Mr. Miliken took his lengthiest pause. "D'you like animals, Mr. Stillings?" He basked from head to toe in the warmth of the red numeral. "Do you have any *pets,* Kenny?"

And that, he thought as the child got out in front of his house, was every bit that he could do. A living seed, planted in a timely manner, grew—and ideas were such seeds. How long it took for the crop to reach the state of harvesting was impossible to gauge. But he was sure to give little, troubled Kenneth his phone number at home "in case you have need of me."

He paid his respects to Lyall Dorris in the morning at the mortuary. Because the casket was closed, he did not view the remains. He did introduce himself to Police

Lieutenant Dorris and the sedated mother. No, he hadn't known Lyall was so unhappy; yes, it could be hard to understand children these days; blah-blah-blah. Then he inspected the floral wreath he'd ordered during the lunch hour the day before and left his signature in the keepsake register with a flourish.

That turned out to be Mr. Miliken's happiest moment until the evening.

Megan Auel didn't attend his class. That was highly peculiar, since he'd have sworn he saw her out jogging on her familiar route on his way to the funeral home. In the principal's office, the only fact he elicited from Mr. Cross's secretary was that she'd actually been in school. Mystifying. She wasn't ill, old Cross didn't care that she had cut his class, and the secretary refused to say more.

Wondering what was going on or being kept from him left Mr. Miliken with so much neurotic tension for the remainder of the afternoon and evening that, when small Mr. Stillings phoned just before midnight, he almost shouted at him.

Kenneth did not seem to notice. "Dad was here," he said. "They're getting a divorce." As he paused, Mr. Miliken swallowed a Medipren. But the child wasn't waiting for sympathy. "I called one of the older guys and he knew what you were talking about. I got some pictures; other stuff." Their connection was remarkably clear and it sounded, now, as if Kenneth was whispering in his ear. "I asked a girl to go out, see, but I don't have a driver's license so—well, I'm feeling a lot of tension. I want to get back on course."

Miliken's heart began to pound heavily. He thought he knew what Kenneth meant but needed to make sure. "The 'stuff,' " he said. "Does it include a—*rope?*"

"Sure. You have to have one, or just the right sort of

belt. Sir, thanks for talking to me about not letting dumb things stand in my way."

"The superior male won't permit it." It was delicate, now; maybe the brat wanted to be talked out of it.

"Well, that's what I want to be. Not like my father. More like you." He swallowed hard, sounded reassured. For a moment white sound was between them. Then, like that, " 'Bye." And he'd hung up.

"Well, well," said Mr. Miliken, smiling. He walked down a short hallway to his bath, closed and bolted the door after him. His head was ever so much better. He undressed, then took the chair he almost kept in the room and turned it to face the mirror and basin. Sitting, he folded his arms, crossed his legs, and waited. He was very good at it. He believed honestly that he could wait until hell froze over.

It only took him until one A.M. to see the informative black 7 gleaming in the pupils of his eyes.

Sleeping blissfully that night, he was quite prepared to project astonishment and grief when Simon Fontaine and Mr. Cross both phoned to report the sad news about Kenneth Stillings having hanged himself.

But only old Cross had heard the horrifying detail that Stillings had been found naked from the waist down in his closet, the victim of an auto-erotic experience. "Photographs, strewn at his feet," Cross said raspily, midway between a kind of furious sadness and disgust. "Was the boy a troublemaker?"

"My, no." Miliken stretched his arm to draw a red mark through the new day's date. Another red-letter one. "He was perhaps the most gifted pupil I've had."

"Well, your afternoon kids are becoming very odd," Cross droned. "Megan Auel, the sprinter, has asked for a transfer to Simon Fontaine's class."

The crayon fell from his fingers. "Why?" The bitch!

He'd counted off numbers one and two with an efficiency that surprised even him; now a *female athlete* was threatening the overall plan! And all three of them were *volunteers!* "You didn't authorize the transfer?"

"Sure. No reason not to." No *reason?* "That kid is some runner, and athletes are sensitive these days. Well, there's no rule against it till after semester finals."

Mr. Miliken hung up as soon as Cross again mentioned his sadness about Stillings. *Not in* your *rules, maybe!* he thought. How could he get to Auel now? She was enrolled in no other classes of his; he couldn't stop her in the school corridors and *stab* her!

Seven *years* he'd been the soul of patience, awaited the proper signs, even eschewed the impulse to pick five or six of them. He'd *let* them put up their own hands, then proceeded discreetly, juggling the trio of cretins as if they were eggs. One was followed by two, two by three—teenagers today couldn't follow the simplest arithmetical progression!

Livid, he snatched up the dropped crayon, broke it in two (S.O.P. for dropped crayons), then tore open another box and drew out the red one. He canceled out the day's date so violently that the tip broke off. Furious now, he threw the rest of the crayons at his wastebasket and missed, spilling them onto the floor.

Abruptly, the need to buy another box or, when tomorrow came, of pinching the tip of the replacement crayon between thumb and index was an outrage! Megan Auel *had* to be punished, soon! He had even been prevented from going to the bathroom to see the sevens shine from his eyes again! Well, he'd already perceived her to be happy, therefore abnormal; now he had the insight to see her as a lesbian—who else could have stalled his plans by merely transferring from one class to another?

But she had not reckoned (he reminded himself with yet another flash of uncanny inspiration) on his perfect willingness to *help* fulfill their commitments! Colliding with the jut-out of the wall and his kitchenette counter, he read the time shown on the clock and drew in a satisfying, quick breath:

He knew the hours when *Ms.* Auel went jogging and the course she followed—and right *now,* she would be leaving home to do her exercises before the school day began!

Throwing on his suit coat, leaving it unbuttoned for the first time in years, he went looking for her. In general, that would be Archer Road because it led to the school. But he'd have to hurry in order to get close enough for him to see the "3" on her forehead *just as he ran her down.*

The morning was so overcast and threatening he thought not of *Romeo,* and Verona, but *Macbeth* and Scotland. The world was awry, nature askew, helpless to permit spring because of the ignorance and immorality of today's teenagers. Well, *he* did not lie down and allow the cretins to clamber over him. The Matthew Milikens—the superior men—knew ways to cope with the brats! *He* would not be pushed around or conned by them!

He whipped the brow-matching automobile round a corner with his thumbs folded so tightly round the steering wheel—and so far—that they almost touched. He squinted narrowly through the wet windshield, turned the wipers on. Archer had little traffic flow since the installation of the nearby freeway. These days, the two-lane road was used primarily by other time-wasting joggers or those motorists obliged to cross Archer to wend their way out of or into the bleak older neighborhoods. Mr. Miliken raised his left index finger and two fingers of his right hand from the wheel just long enough to note and count them. *I've even triumphed over mathematics,* he realized, beaming. *For the first time in history one plus one equals three!*

Rather more than a block ahead, a slender form jogged at the side of the road. A *familiar,* a *female* form. Moving in the direction he was headed, he realized; away from him.

Not nearly fast enough to stay *so,* Mr. Miliken thought.

The total realization of that brought a rising thrill. This young athlete had acquired a reputation—become a Salinger High superstar—because she imagined, doubtlessly, that she could outrun anyone. Well, they'd see about *that!*

But there was no rush, no hurry at all, dear *Ms.* Auel. Indeed, there was pre*cise*ly as much time as Matthew Miliken cared to give Megan before he drove his car *right up her back.* With the windows rolled down then, to hear the small bones of her spine crack and crunch!

"*A*-one, *a*-two," he sang and, without accelerating in the least, tooted his horn. But Auel was carrying one of the modern radios and she couldn't hear him yet. Well, she *would* know he was there! Perhaps he would just eeease up behind her, take the whole process *slooowwwly,* permit her fear to build. Then—at the last conceivable second—*Ms.* Auel would finally see him and learn who was *teacher,* who was *superior!*

Suddenly, he was practically on *top* of her! Mr. Miliken had to tap his brake to keep from ending it too fast! Leaning angrily on the horn, he kept the heel of his hand there until the blast might have awakened the dead.

Megan peered over her shoulder without haste and motioned for him to pass.

His brown brows rose, descended, repeated the exercise several times before he grasped what was happening.

The little bitch imagined she was being pursued by boys from the track team who enjoyed teasing the female athletes. And the noise slamming into her ear from the Walkman was deafening her!

Irked because his next thrill had been thwarted and because he did not like being confused with anyone else, Mr. Miliken allowed his car to pull again within feet of Megan. It occurred to him briefly to go *ahead,* to *do* it—take no remote chance of letting her escape her assigned numerical position. Then he realized he was not going fast enough at all to be *sure* the car killed her, and had no choice but to cut the wheel to his left and sweep around her.

Yet what happened that instant brought the sunshine back to his cheeks.

Megan *looked directly at him,* and *recognized him,* and the surprise on her face appeared to be matched by a *discernible rise of fear!*

"Three lit-tle words," he sang a snatch of the old melody, his heart tom-tomming accompaniment. When was the last time a number had stared back with a suspicion of his intentions? Exciting! Well, he had only to find somewhere to turn in, make a U, drive back and make one more, then he'd be right on the bitch's heels again. This time, he'd build up enough speed during his approach to plow Ms. Megan Auel into the concrete!

Matching action to plan, he spotted a driveway and whipped his car into it at reckless speeds, backed out joltingly, and roared down Archer Road with his eyes rolling from left to right in search of the sprinter. He could thank his stars another vehicle hadn't hit him when he backed out; now he'd rein in the impulse to rush—

proceed in a truly systematic manner in order to fulfill the mission.

And as for those "three lit-tle words," they simply meant *I'll kill you!*

—*There* she was! Mr. Miliken's heart soared. Clearly, she thought he had driven on—probably to school—that she'd been wrong in believing there was menace in the horn blast and his abrupt materialization. She was simply jogging along Archer Road at an easy pace, as oblivious to danger—to him—as they'd all been over the years. *Idiots!* he thought, his well-trained memory providing the apt lines from the tragedy he taught so well: "Doth she not think me an old murderer, Now I have stain'd the childhood of our joy . . . ?" But when he had sped by and looked in his rearview mirror, she still had not caught on, hadn't even *noticed* his car returning on the other side of the road, now disappearing over a ridge!

So he made the second U, then stared at Megan's peaceful form effortlessly drifting along the road. Rain was coming down more heavily, slanting across the windshield; yet *Ms.* Auel hadn't even increased her speed. She was volunteering again! Transmission in neutral, Matthew Miliken raced his car engine, imagined for a moment he was making his own thunder. " 'Three words, dear Juliet,' " he paraphrased, and slipped the transmission into *Drive.* "One . . . two . . . *three!*"

His automobile peeled powerfully away. All he needed to remember now was to focus his attention on the girl's face at the point of contact so he wouldn't miss seeing the 3 come to throbbing life on her fair forehead. Afterward, when she lay crushed beneath his wheels, he could tilt his rearview mirror down in order to watch his eyes change. Knowing her body was ruined and dead under the car at the instant he saw the black sevens shine like light from the center of the earth might make it go on glowing well into the seven years he'd wait before making his *next* selections.

He began hammering his horn with his balled fist as soon as he was able to make out her close-cropped, light-brown hair. "*Look* at me," he willed her—*"look at me!"*

Hearing the born blare above the music from her radio, Megan did look back, eyes widening in a terror of understanding.

But she looked forward again too soon for Mr. Miliken to glimpse her forehead, then *seemed to fly*—ran so *fast* that he, in sudden panic not to let her escape, let his foot slip off the accelerator. And before he could have counted three, an astounding *gap* lay between them. Worse, Megan seemed to be looking for somewhere she might *run off the road!* That would force him to stop, chase her *on foot*—and there was no way in hell he could catch her that way!

Entirely unprepared for such a swift reaction, he hadn't moved the car forward an inch when the athlete next glanced back. She was the length of a football field ahead of him!

Damn them *all,* he thought, damn *all the brats!* Fingers and prehensile thumbs tight on the wheel, dizzyingly frustrated, his brown brows working furiously, he drove his foot into the accelerator and floored it.

"One-two-*three,*" he muttered, *"Onetwothree,"* in a combined prayer and chant. It wasn't possible for her to outrun a car, it was unthinkable for a pupil to destroy his pastime, his world! Through the drenching rainfall he watched the car narrow the distance quickly between them, thought of it as *devouring* the gap. It was *time,* he was *empowered,* he was a *god!* Almost there, nearly to completion! *Look at me,* he ordered her mentally, hurling the thought-command after her—*LOOK at ME!*

Incredibly, she *did*—and seemed to stumble. She broke stride just as she hazarded a swift, desperate glance over her shoulder—and he was *seven yards* behind her, *six* yards, *five, four, THREE* . . .

And for a flash it was as if she had *vanished* from Matthew Miliken's sight—because she had jumped a ditch and dashed into the woods! Compelled to crush her, he spun the steering wheel in the direction she seemed to have gone—

And the car rammed headfirst into the ditch, jammed there momentarily on end, then flipped into the air. Not achieving much height, it came down on its top like a titan's fist slamming into the earth, its tires spinning as if possessed by an idiot's desire to continue the chase.

Through a torrent of blood that he took dimly for red rain, Mr. Miliken saw the upside-down feet of the young woman who would never be third approaching, hesitantly. *"As one dead in the bottom of a tomb,"* he remembered; was that why she wasn't seeing if she could help?

Then, when Megan finally did lean down and peer through the shattered windshield, he observed that she was wearing a school jersey under her unzipped warmup jacket. The number "7" was sewn into it in vivid crimson.

Because of the way his neck and spine were broken, leaving his fingers clutching the wheel, it was too difficult for Mr. Miliken to decide if the number was a sign or not, perhaps even a benediction. And when he strove to speak, he wasn't able to enunciate more than the beginning letter of the word, *help.* Despite all his will power, the only other thing he could manage was to stare at her, stupidly, his brown eyes virtually popping from his head.

Telepathy, he thought, seeking an apt line and, finding it, projecting it mentally with everything he had: *"A greater power than we can contradict hath thwarted our intents."* He hurled the words from his scared-mouse brain to her shocked but well-ordered mind. Now, at least, she would know he was still alive!

Megan Auel stepped well back from the brown car before it burst into flame, and, just before the fire got to him, Mr. Miliken was fairly sure she had nodded.

SACRIFICE

KATHLEEN BUCKLEY

WIRE KILLER CLAIMS 6TH VICTIM.

T*he world's a hell of a place,* John Henderson thought, tossing the morning paper into the waste basket. He heard his son's steps in the corridor. Killing for safety, money, or even revenge, he could understand, sure. But strangling women with barbed wire: that was crazy.

"Brian!" Henderson called, as his son passed his office door, jacket slung over one shoulder. "Take a walk with me before lunch." It was not a request. Henderson conducted a semi-automatic inventory of the material on his desk, and decided none of it was incriminating. No, confidential. Old habits die slow. Anybody was welcome to search his office.

Brian leaned against the corridor wall, waiting. Brian never questioned him. Which was strange, because his son was smart and had a mind of his own.

Brian had turned out fine. It was too bad it took until the third grade to find the right school. The first five had been no good. The teachers and other kids had had it in for Brian because Henderson had money or because someone had started a rumor he had mob connections or maybe just because Brian was handsome and smart. Once they'd found the proper environment for him, he'd done fine. Didn't have to defend himself from the little punks in the public schools. And there had been no more accusations like the one from that little subnormal. But the jerk's mother had told the teacher and principal her kid was a liar and hurt himself to get attention. It had cost Henderson five thousand. But what's money? He'd wanted Brian to have all the advantages. Still . . .

In spite of Henderson's best intentions, and almost by accident, Brian made his bones when he was sixteen. The boy had come home late one Friday night and told him that some punk had tried to mug him, and he'd hit the turkey harder than he meant to. Actually, he'd happened to have a wrench. The only thing was . . .

The only thing was, he had the body in the car.

"Why didn't you leave it where it was?"

Brian gave him a look from those Siamese-cat blue eyes. "My car might have been seen. I thought a police investigation might be embarrassing for you. For Mom and Marguerite." They went out to the garage together. Brian's mother and little sister were safely asleep.

The body was in the trunk. "It looks like you worked him over pretty good," Henderson observed. The face was pulped and those gobbets of gray stuff had been brains.

"If I'd left him alive, he might have come after me."

The guy had been alive when Brian put him in the trunk, Henderson thought. If he'd been dead, there wouldn't be so much blood.

Well, maybe Brian had panicked. He'd led a sheltered life.

"Dad?" His voice sounded like a little boy's. "What am I going to do?"

"Go to bed and forget about it. Give me your car

keys. Don't think about it again. Brian? Is the wrench in there?"

"Uh-huh. On the right side." Brian started to reach into the reeking mess. Henderson caught his arm. "Make sure there's nothing on your clothes. Then go to bed."

After Brian went upstairs, Henderson called a man he trusted. Lou brought a box of heavy trash bags, a gallon of peroxide and a shop vacuum. The corpse was gone before daylight; Brian had not spoken of it again until he graduated from college.

Yes, the kid had turned out well. He was good-looking, too, with the mahogany hair and sapphire eyes he'd inherited from his mother. He had his father's height and features, though his lips were fuller and his face less sharp. He would look good on a campaign poster.

They walked out through the reception area, and Henderson congratulated himself again on having chosen the right decorator. The offices of Henderson Enterprises oozed affluence. Personally, he thought the lithographs on the walls were ugly, but his wife (whose family and money went back almost to the Revolution) approved, so they must be all right. Henderson's old man had operated out of a garage with pin-up calendars for decoration. Life was damned good.

In a year or so, Brian should marry a nice girl with good connections, then maybe run for city council. After that, it should be easy enough to get him elected to some position in state government. And then . . .

Leaving the lobby-level line-up of espresso bar, executive toy store, gourmet popcorn stand and trendy café, they walked a block down to the waterfront. During the summer, it was a popular tourist attraction, with a variety of shops and food stands. There was also a small park with benches, a piece of cement artwork, and excellent views of the harbor. On a windy April day it was deserted: a good place for a private chat. Henderson positioned himself against the rail, the wind in his face, and gazed at a Japanese freighter anchored at a grain elevator—the something-or-other *Maru*.

"This girl of yours," he began.

"Tracy?" Brian inquired casually. "Look, there's another freighter coming in. I wonder what she's carrying."

"Yes, Tracy—unless you've got another girlfriend."

Brian glanced at him with a slight, mildly surprised smile. "No," he said.

"How much does she know?"

Brian shrugged. "She knows I'm handsome, fun and horny. She knows I can afford to take her to Fiji and Bermuda."

"I'm not saying you have to dump her," Henderson said carefully. "Have your fun—but remember that's all it is. And make sure she doesn't know more than you think."

"Don't worry, Dad."

Henderson wished he could take the advice. "She's not your class. No money, no connections—" No brains. Fortunately, Brian had a streak of calculation and a fine appreciation of his own interests. "You know your mother and I want the best for you."

"Sure, Dad, I know. See you back at the office." With another of those smiles, he turned and walked away.

Henderson watched his son striding across Water Street toward his favorite lunch place. Shoji, an ultratrendy renovated warehouse, catered to the young with looks and bucks, and served nothing but teriyaki. John had not developed such cosmopolitan tastes until his thirties. When he was Brian's age, chop suey and fortune cookies had been the Yellow Peril. On impulse, Henderson hailed a cab and asked to be taken to Alfredo's 402.

Alfredo's was conservative, dim and expensive, and the waiters remembered your name. Henderson preferred its stodgy elegance to the flashy, short-lived dives Brian patronized. Kids grew up so fast now, and all of them, even the ones with money, dressed like hoods or whores. It was just a fad, he guessed. He sure didn't feel any nostalgia for the old days.

The day after Brian's graduation, he'd told his son, "I want you to work with each of the businesses for a while. You can start with JH Properties—get a feel for property management. Then you can move on to Henderson Enterprises. Then maybe . . ."

"I don't think I'd like that. Ever since that time with the mugger, I've been thinking. You have connections with the local Syndicate, don't you, Dad?"

Henderson had taken a long drink of gin and tonic. He had intended to explain things to Brian after his son had been in the business for a while—but he disliked being pushed. "I guess you've heard stories about your grandfather. Maybe he sounds kind of . . . kind of exciting. What Marguerite would call 'romantic.' Well, it's all a load of crap. I don't do business the way he did. And I'm not going to die with my guts spilling on the sidewalk, like him, or get gang-raped in the pen, like my brother. And you damned well aren't."

Brian nodded knowingly. "I understand why you don't want to talk about it." He punched the 'Power On' button on the radio and tuned in to a rock station. Loud. "So what do I do in the outfit?"

"You'll begin as Frank's administrative assistant," Henderson replied, and added dryly, "Nobody says 'outfit' here. That's a Midwest word."

"Pushing paper?" Brian demanded. "Any nerd can do that. Where's the excitement?"

"I'm in business, Brian. No fun and games, just hard work."

"I'm too young to have a middle-aged job, Dad. If I can't get an interesting job with one of your companies, you could pull some strings to get me a field job with the CIA. Then maybe I'll come into the business later."

Deliberately, Henderson mixed another drink. "You want to get into trouble?"

Brian grinned. "I just want to have some fun before I settle down—"

"I've been working most of my life to get us to where we are," Henderson interrupted. "I set things up so you'd have it better than I did—" *Got out of the strong-arm rackets after Jimmy died and into legitimate business. More or less. Got as far away as he could from the stuff that leads to police lineups.* "Now you want to play games. Other kids want to be rock stars or help the hungry. What's wrong with you?"

"Heredity," Brian replied with a sly grin. Henderson had to laugh. Maybe Brian took after his grandfather. *The old man always told me I was soft. But I'm not soft enough to let Brian screw up his future. And Marguerite's.*

"You'll start as Frank's assistant. That had better be enough excitement for you."

"It's nice to see you, dear," Ann was saying to their son. Henderson knew that she meant it was nice he had not brought his girlfriend to dinner. Not that Ann disliked Tracy; she just did not think she was good enough for Brian. It was kind of funny: there was something nice and old-fashioned about the girl, even if she was playing house. Brian would have to be tactful about paying her off, to avoid hurting her feelings.

"I didn't think Tracy would be comfortable here,"

Brian was saying, "so I told her I was going out on business."

"What kind of business?" Henderson asked when Ann and Marguerite were both out of the room.

"What?"

"What kind of business did you tell Tracy was taking you out on a Friday night?"

Brian laughed. "She thinks I work for the National Security Agency, so she doesn't expect to keep tabs on me."

"And she believes that?"

"Sure."

Marguerite came down the stairs, slipping on her neon-green jacket.

"Going somewhere, sweetheart?"

"Only to Amber's, dad."

That was only six blocks, and the neighborhood was exclusive, with no through streets. Henderson was going to give his permission when Ann came out of the dining room with doom on her face.

"I'll give you a ride," she stated in her no-argument voice. "And I'll expect Amber's family to give you a ride home. If they can't, call us."

"Nobody's been killed in this part of town," Marguerite objected, with fifteen-year-old rationality.

"You will be, if you don't do as you're told," Ann promised. "Have you got your keys, John?"

He handed them over.

"There's not a chance Marguerite would be picked up by the killer," Brian said. "She doesn't fit the profile at all."

"Who knows how a psycho like that picks his victims? He probably takes what he can get."

"I don't think so," Brian mused. "There's a pattern."

"What kind of pattern? They all seemed different."

Except that they'd all been murdered. Henderson hoped that Marguerite had overlooked the sordid details.

Brian said, "They were all beautiful and they were all from different backgrounds. That's a pattern. There was a stockbroker, a lawyer, a waitress, a heavy equipment operator, a dancer and a college student. It could be that he's pointing out that no woman is safe. That any woman can be a sacrifice to our bloodlust. I wonder if he'll score a policewoman? Or maybe a nun. Hard to find one of those, though." He laughed.

"The police will get him before then," Henderson said. A psycho was bound to do something stupid eventually. That was why his own father always said not to do business with crazies. The old bastard should have taken his own advice.

"Brian, honey, I was so worried about you! Are you all right?"

"Of course I'm all right. Why wouldn't I be? I told you I was working late."

"I heard about that big drug bust in the South End and I thought you might be there. The news said there was shooting and I sort of panicked."

"The NSA has nothing to do with law enforcement," he snapped.

"I know that now," she said contritely. "The lady at the emergency number explained that to me."

"Emergency number?" Brian repeated blankly.

"911. I called and said I was worried about you because you might be there—"

"Did you mention my name?"

"No, of course not. I knew you wouldn't want me to. I just said my boyfriend was with the National Security Agency and who could I call to find out if he was there?

Because the NSA doesn't have a number listed in the phonebook."

"You shouldn't have called at all." The stupid cow. The 911 operator would have had this telephone number right before her eyes. They got lots of calls, though, including plenty from nut cases. Probably the operator wouldn't think twice about it.

"You aren't angry with me?" Tracy asked, hopefully. She really was pretty, with her childlike ways and submissive disposition. But his next girl was going to have more than two brain cells.

"Brian, I've got some news for you." From the tentative way she said it, he knew it was going to make him very, very angry.

"You're not pregnant?" he asked sharply. "Because if you are . . ."

"No, of course not, honey! You know I'm on the Pill."

"Accidents will happen," he said grimly. "What is it?"

"My mother decided to move out here. The farm equipment plant she worked at shut down last month, and she never did like South Dakota, so she thought it would be a good time to get out."

"I thought you didn't get along with your mother."

"I didn't, but I was younger then. She'd be company when you're out. I get a little lonely sometimes, Brian."

"Have you told her you're living with a man?"

"No, I thought it would be easier when she got here. Once she meets you, she'll understand. I told her I was seeing someone."

"Did you mention my name, Tracy?"

She twisted her fingers together and looked down at her red-enameled toenails. "Not your last name, Brian. I know you have to be careful. But I had to call you something." Her chin began to tremble.

"Don't cry, baby, it's all right." It wasn't, of course, but he didn't want to alarm her. "So you made up with your mom," he said casually. "When's she coming?"

"Not until she sells the house. A couple of months, I guess."

"I'll look forward to meeting her." He tilted Tracy's heart-shaped face up for a kiss.

The funeral was so small, they might as well not have bothered. Only one of Tracy's co-workers had come, more out of duty than sorrow. But Ann's arrangements, perfect as always, were worthy of a much larger audience. Old money always knew how to do the thing right.

Marguerite was looking suitably grave, having—at Ann's instructions—temporarily subdued her liveliness and curiosity.

Brian was exerting himself to charm the woman from Tracy's office and Tracy's mother, who had flown in the previous afternoon. Both women seemed a little overwhelmed by the house—Ann's old family home—the sterling silver tea and coffee service, the antiques and the Persian carpet.

"I don't know why you and your family should pay for the funeral," Mrs. Jorgenson said again, fretfully. "It's really my responsibility. Not that I could have afforded anything so nice. She would have loved the casket—all that pink satin and the panels with roses. Just like a jewel box . . ." She fished a limp handkerchief out of her purse.

"Tracy was a jewel. I wanted to take care of it," Brian said. "The money is nothing to me without Tracy. And we were as good as engaged, so don't I have a right?"

Henderson was slightly startled, then decided Brian was merely trying to make the woman feel better.

"Who would do a thing like that?" the other woman

demanded. "Running someone down that way and leaving her in the street like . . ."

"Like a dead dog," Marguerite supplied with more accuracy than tact.

"Marguerite," Ann said, "would you get Mrs. Jorgenson and Miss Perez some more tea?" They had returned to the house for what Marguerite insisted on calling 'the baked meats.' Having portrayed Hamlet's mother in a school play, she was full of apt quotations, and wanted to be a playwright. "Because I don't have the bone structure to be an actress," she explained.

"It must have been some drunk or doped-up kid," Brian told them. "The car was stolen. The police found it abandoned a mile away."

"What was she doing in that part of town at night?" the Perez woman asked. "There's nothing but warehouses and railroad tracks."

"There are some popular restaurants and galleries and a jazz bar within a few blocks," Brian corrected.

"I'd be afraid to go down there by myself or even with a friend. And I certainly wouldn't park there and get out of the car."

"If I'd known she was going there, I wouldn't have permitted it," Brian said. "But I was home with food poisoning that night. She said she was going out with friends . . . If I hadn't been sick . . ." Brian's voice shook.

"Don't blame yourself," Mrs. Jorgenson patted his arm. "Things happen, even back in South Dakota."

Henderson insinuated himself into the little group then, supplanting Brian, who seemed to be pouring it on a bit thick.

"We were very fond of Tracy," Henderson told her mother. "She was such a nice girl."

At last Miss Perez left and Mrs. Jorgenson was sent to

her hotel by limousine. Henderson breathed a sigh of relief.

"Ann, I'm going out for a while."

"I don't blame you. I wish I could, but I think I'll have a glass of sherry and then take a nap. Brian, will you be all right?"

"Yes, I'm going for a swim. I can't wait to get out of this suit."

Marguerite gave her brother a cynical glance. "You should be out prowling the streets, looking for Tracy's murderer."

"Tracy wasn't murdered," Brian snapped.

"She was done to death," Marguerite intoned. "What would you call it?"

"It was a hit-and-run, for God's sake."

Henderson stalked out. His nerves were raw.

When he returned, Henderson walked around the side of the house. If he knew his son, Brian would still be sunning himself by the pool. Marguerite, fair-skinned and inclined to freckle, would almost certainly not be present, and Ann preferred to swim early in the morning or in the evening. Maybe Brian and he could have a talk.

He never reached the patio. Approaching the windows of his library, open to catch the breeze, he heard Brian's voice.

"No, I'm doing all right. Yes, I guess you could call her my girlfriend, but it was no great romance. You know how it is, Amy. And she was out with friends—or *a* friend while I was home sick. It was a shock, though. So how about coming to Jazz Age with me next Saturday? To console me. Great, I'll pick you up at eight."

Very quietly, Henderson turned back to the front of the house and went to the library. He shut the door and closed the windows.

"That's going to make it hot in here, Dad."

"Probably." He dropped a cassette into the tapedeck and hit 'Play.' Henderson took off his dark suit jacket, hung it over the back of a chair and loosened his tie. "You're taking your bereavement very well, Brian."

Brian sighed and started to make a deprecating gesture with one hand.

"A little too well," Henderson added. "You did all right today. Maybe you hammed it up a little, but apparently that plays well in Peoria. But you have to maintain the act for a decent length of time afterwards—even when you're offstage—or it doesn't look good. The cops always suspect the husband or boyfriend, as it is."

"Sorry. But to be very frank, it's a relief she's dead. She told me she was pregnant. She wouldn't consider abortion and she didn't want money. She was insisting I marry her, Dad. I don't know what I'd have done, if she hadn't run into a bad driver. Or vice versa."

"Brian," Henderson asked, "you didn't mention her being pregnant to the police, did you?"

Brian grinned slyly. "Hell, no. They might have thought that gave me a motive."

"Well, don't mention it to anyone else." Henderson decided not to mention the autopsy results. If Brian had not thought of asking for them, let him go on thinking his bimbo was knocked up. Who'd have thought Tracy was the kind of girl to lie about it?

Apparently noting Henderson's expression, he said, "Don't worry, dad. Nobody could suspect me. After all, I haven't done anything."

"What are you reading, Brian?" Marguerite asked. He had been spending more time than usual at the house: perhaps he found the apartment lonely.

"It's a study of the psychopath. It's pop psychology,

but it's got some good grisly stuff in it. Though I'd rather see less of the psychologist's opinions and more of the psychopath's. I thought it might give me an insight into who's doing all those girls."

"Who needs insight?" Marguerite shrugged. "He's a wacko, that's all."

"He is not. He's making a point—if the police could see it."

"If he stands still long enough, the squirrels will carry him away," Marguerite asserted.

"You don't know anything about it—"

"Children," Ann said in her committee-taming voice. She had had considerable experience at stopping Brian and Marguerite's bickering. The two had never gotten along. Henderson guessed ten-year-old Brian had resented the arrival of a baby sister, which was understandable. But Marguerite, who liked almost everyone, had been noticeably cool toward her brother since she was a toddler.

Henderson looked up from the *Wall Street Journal*. "What's your theory, Brian?"

Brian tapped the book. "This distinguished Ph.D. and talk-show personality seems to think that serial killers choose women who remind them of their mother. That's a bunch of Freudian garbage."

"You said once that he was picking women from different backgrounds," Marguerite recalled. "That he was proving anyone could be a victim."

"Something like that," Brian said. He did not sound particularly pleased.

"But what's the point of doing such a thing?" Ann asked, sensibly. "I mean, there can't really *be* a point, can there? It's just madness."

"There's a point," Brian said. "I could figure it out if I tried."

"Brian," Henderson said, "leave the investigation to the police. That's what we pay taxes for."

"Sure," Brian said. "It's just an intellectual exercise, that's all. A little excitement."

Henderson regarded him thoughtfully. Brian's craving for excitement worried him.

"Lou, I want a tail on someone."

"No problem. I got somebody good. Roy used to be a private investigator until he got in trouble. Who do you want followed?"

"I'll tell him myself."

Lou nodded.

The ex-private detective looked like an insurance salesman. In a dark suit, he might have looked like a corporate lawyer. But no matter what he wore, he would not be taken for what he was. So much the better.

"My son has some idea about that serial killer. I want someone to keep an eye on Brian in case he actually finds the Wire Killer."

"The chances are, he'll never come within ten miles of the perp. If the police haven't got anyone, with this special task force and a computer, no amateur will," Roy stated flatly.

It was good to hear someone else say it. "Then just make sure he doesn't bother someone with a short fuse. I want regular reports." And if Brian picked up some other undesirable girlfriend, she'd need discouraging.

Marguerite and her friends made a video—in a Hitchcockian vein—called *Kent's First Case.* Marguerite's portrayal of the villainess, complete with platform shoes and black hat veil, provided unintentional humor, while the hero, who wore glasses but had been deprived of them for cinematic reasons, achieved an expression Ann called "bedroom eyes." To Henderson, it looked like myopia, pure and simple.

Brian did not attend the screening: he said he had a date. Henderson was inclined to be annoyed on Marguerite's behalf, although Brian and Marguerite were not close. On second thought, he supposed Marguerite was glad Brian was absent. She had once told Henderson that Brian was always putting her down. Maybe it was better that Brian, likely to be critical, was not present.

Ann won a trophy in a golf tournament the next day and seduced Henderson on the floor of his library that evening. Fortunately, Marguerite was out with friends, as the proceedings proved to be noisy.

He was feeling relaxed but slightly stiff next morning when he found the former detective waiting at the office to give his weekly report. The man looked nervous, but he gave the first part of his report unemotionally. There was nothing in it: Brian came home from work, went to his health club, went out for a drink with friends, took the banker's daughter to dinner. Stayed in one evening. Took a drive. Went to the grocery store and picked up his laundry.

"Now I've got to apologize, Mr. Henderson," Roy said. "The night before last, I lost him."

"How?" Henderson regretted the sharp edge in his voice.

"He left his apartment at eight-oh-six Wednesday evening and drove down Iris Avenue in his camper. At Fortieth, he parked near the Rose. That's a topless dance joint. A lot of hookers work that area. When he came out he had a very clingy female companion. Short shorts—you know, whore pants, boots up to here, shirt cut down to there. She had her head on his shoulder like she was swacked. He got her into the camper and drove off down Iris to 320th South. There's not much traffic down there: not after dark. So I couldn't follow close. It was about 323rd South that I lost him. I don't know if you know that area: it's like a little bit of the country: trees, curves, narrow road, drainage ditch on either side. Used to be farming country. There's no place to park on that stretch, just a few roads leading off to houses. He must have turned in at one of them and got the truck out of sight. I turned around and checked the ones I could, and there was no sign of the camper. But a couple had gates and 'No Trespassing' signs, and one was patrolled by a Doberman. And there was an old factory with a fence and a padlocked gate. I'm sorry, Mr. Henderson. But I figure where he went, it was someplace he knew, and the chances are he'll go there again. Next time he won't lose me."

"That's all right." He must have turned in at Pearcy Metal Fabricators. It had been closed for years, but one of Henderson's companies stored toxic wastes there before trucking them to a tract of land in the eastern part of the state. It would be years before the drums corroded in the dry earth. Brian had a key to the padlock, and to the buildings.

"So I went back to his apartment complex and waited. He returned at one-fifty-two yesterday morning. He went to work at the usual time, and after work he spent the evening at home."

"You've done a good job so far, Roy," Henderson said. "I've got no complaints. By the way, do you keep written records of your cases?"

Roy flushed. "Not like I did when I had a license. I've got a good memory. My clients . . ."

Preferred not to leave a paper trail, Henderson understood. "That's all right. I'll see you next week, Roy."

* * *

Now why in hell would Brian take some floozy all the way down there? Unless there was more to the affair than ten bucks and fifteen minutes. Oh God, Henderson prayed, don't let it be a whore with a heart of gold. Because if the bitch thought she'd landed a rich kid, she'd made the worst mistake of her life. And the last. Prostitutes o.d. all the time. Or get cut up by other tarts or beaten to death by customers or simply disappear.

At noon, Henderson decided to take a walk over to the waterfront park. Fresh air and a little exercise would do him good. He could get something to eat at one of the little carts that were so popular with the tourists and with his own office staff.

Sun and a fresh breeze from the Sound restored his sense of proportion. Brian was too smart to get involved with a hooker. But if he had, it could be fixed. Henderson knew some boys who would be glad to take her partying. She'd wake up forty-eight states away, so strung out on drugs she wouldn't remember her own name.

He picked up an order of fish and chips at the take-out window of a tourist trap restaurant on the pier and sat on a bench to eat them. Ann would not have approved. Someone had abandoned a copy of the afternoon paper. He glanced at the headline idly, then froze at an article halfway down the page.

VICE COP VANISHES

> An undercover officer posing as a prostitute disappeared Wednesday evening from her post on Iris Avenue. She was last seen wearing dark red shorts, high white boots and a V-neck blouse.

For a moment, Henderson felt so shaky and nauseated that he wondered whether he was having a heart attack, but he had to keep on reading.

> "She could take care of herself or she wouldn't have been where she was," according to her superior.

Not well enough, Henderson thought grimly. *"I wonder if he'll score a policewoman."* Oh God. The cops would never stop working on it. And eventually there would be headlines: *Grandson of Mob Boss Is Suspected Wire Killer.* Even if Brian were acquitted—not impossible, with money to buy the best defense lawyer in the country—he would never live it down. And all the old stories would be raked up. Ann would be humiliated. People in her circle were mentioned in the newspaper only when they married or died. Marguerite would pretend not to care, but nothing she did or became would save her from the notoriety. The papers and magazines would keep it alive.

"Lou. Get me a man from out of town. For a . . . special project."

"You mean like a t-t-troubleshooter?" Surprise made Lou stumble over the last word.

"Yes. Nobody else hears about this. Nobody. Got that?"

"I got it. Uh . . . Who for?"

"I'll tell him myself. Set up a meeting. He doesn't have to know he's talking to me."

"You shouldn't get involved, Mr. Henderson. I could—"

"Do it," Henderson snarled. "Or are you looking for a new job?"

* * *

The sight of the uniformed police made Henderson's skin prickle, although they were necessary. Reflexively, his arm tightened around Ann's shoulders. He felt her indrawn breath and understood without looking at her that she was trying to pull herself together, to present the right image—for him. He was grateful, but he could not face her pain. Not right now. Marguerite's expression was half stern, half angry, the way it had been the time she'd fallen off the porch roof and broken her ankle.

He wished he were alone, and not on display. There were undercover cops in addition to the uniforms, watching the crowd, his family, him, looking for the killer. Which made it a little embarrassing that in addition to Henderson's business associates, Ann's fellow golfers and club members, and Brian's acquaintances, a few of Henderson's old friends had shown up. Of course, anyone who knew anything about Henderson's past—like the police, the Justice Department, maybe a reporter or two—knew that Augie Green had been a buddy of his since they were kids in the South End. Cheerful, fat, sentimental Augie would never miss a wedding or a funeral, not when it concerned an old pal. It was kind of reassuring; one thing about Augie, he was sincere.

"A terrible thing," Augie murmured. "Some punk out to rip off what he could, I guess, thinking no one was home, and panicked when he found Brian?"

"That's what the police think," Henderson agreed.

Name That Tune

Charles L. Grant

Once, I don't know how long ago it was, I wondered what it would be like to kill someone. Sometimes it's just something you think about. Everybody does. It's the nature of things. The only thing is, sometimes you're ashamed of it, and sometimes you're not.

Some guy, maybe, he cuts you off on the interstate, and if it's been one of those really godawful days, your boss has been a pain or your wife's stepping out or your kid's mouthing off at you, you want to ride up right on this guy who thinks he owns the road, nudge him a little, send him over the barrier or into a ditch or into oncoming traffic.

You don't, of course.

You just don't.

Or maybe you're walking down the street on a perfectly nice day, and you see a woman smack a little kid across the face, grab his arm and drag him into a car or a store or just a few yards along the sidewalk, yelling, cursing, maybe screaming, the hand up to belt him again if he doesn't obey. Maybe she does smack him again. A good one, and now the kid's bawling and the other pedestrians are walking by, pretending nothing's wrong or giving her dirty looks but not saying a thing. You begin to wonder how bad the kid gets beaten when he's not out in public. If it's a real little kid, you may even think that it wouldn't be such a terrible deal for the world if this lady wasn't in it anymore. A quick hip to knock her in front of a bus, the subway train, a truck, and so maybe the kid doesn't have a mother anymore, but he also doesn't have a black eye and scars that aren't ever going to leave him. Ever.

You don't, of course.

You just don't.

It's like I said to Grace, that winter afternoon we were walking by the park pond in some city or other, "It's the kind of thing that makes us feel guilty and kind of weirdly happy all at the same time, you know what I mean?"

She had a long coat on, one of those Russian things, with a Russian hat, and big furry gloves. "Stan, that's a horrible thing to say."

I grinned. "Why, Miss Lanover, do you mean to tell me, you never got mad enough at anyone to want to belt them? I don't mean just slap them or anything. I mean, a good one, right in the chops, knock them down, make them bleed a little bit. Are you saying you never wanted to do that?"

Very liberal, Grace is. Anti-this, that, a lot of things. Peace on Earth. Save the whales. Plant trees. Don't execute anyone on death row, just lock them up forever, it's more humane that way.

But I caught the expression on her face before she said, "No, of course not." The kind of expression most people don't want you to see.

So I poked her with an elbow and laughed. "Liar." But nicely.

She stopped abruptly, the snow crunching quietly beneath her fringed boots. "I could never hit anyone like that, Stan. Never."

"I never said you would." I took her arm. Gently. We walked on. "But you've felt like it now and then, once in a while, here and there, right?"

I was still smiling.

That it was clear I wasn't really serious made her smile back, and kind of nod, sideways. "Well, yes, I suppose so. Not a lot, but yes . . . I guess so." Then she looked out at the ice, at the people skating there, calling to each other, holding each other up. "But God, Stan, I'd feel so *bad*." She looked at me quickly. "If I did it, that is. Which I wouldn't."

"I know you wouldn't," I whispered in her ear just before I kissed it. "I know."

Just like, I thought much later, somehow not being able to get the conversation out of my mind—like a melody you know you know but for the life of you, you just can't think of the title—just like I would never be able to hit her that way, or take her life, or anything like that. Don't misunderstand. I didn't love her, it wasn't that way between us, we were just good buddies the way men and women are sometimes, but I just couldn't imagine me doing that to her.

And I didn't know why.

Stupid, right?

Sure, I liked her. We talked about everything. I mean, just about every damn thing. Spent time together. Even went to dinner a couple of times a month.

So why didn't I know why I couldn't hurt her?

Because I liked her?

That was too simple.

So I asked Elana Trock, a neighbor in the building who's not really a friend, not like Grace, but I'd known her as long as I'd lived in the city, which had been, at that time, a couple of years. She has three kids, a beer-gut husband, and makes about the best damn meatballs in the universe.

She was fat. Not round and cuddly fat, but round and lumberjack-strong fat, if you can imagine it. Her kids never mouthed off at her, that's for sure. Never. One swat of that tree trunk she calls an arm and they'd be through the wall and into the next state before they could take a breath.

When she frowned, you looked for something to hide under. Fast.

She frowned at me across the dinner table that night. The kids were gone—*Uncle Peter will play with you later, get the hell out, watch TV or something*—her husband was on overtime. "What the hell'd that poor girl ever do to you?"

It took some fast explaining, talking a hundred words a minute, to explain that it was only a . . . a thing, I don't know the word, that we were talking about. We weren't mad at each other, we didn't have a fight, I didn't want to slit her throat.

"But the thing is, I don't know why I don't."

"What a stupid-ass thing to worry about," she said. Elana doesn't mince words; she spits them out in whole chunks. "You'd better worry about paying the rent. You find a job yet?"

I hadn't. I admitted it. She scolded me. I took the scolding. I didn't have any choice; it was, in those days, the price of the meal, and I'd known that going in. My old job, not such a hot one in the first place, went invisible when the company folded. According to Elana, living on unemployment was a worse sin than screwing around with your brother's wife.

Midway through it, with all of her arm-waving and looking to heaven for support and maybe a lightning bolt or two in the right place to make her point, I realized that I couldn't do anything to her, either.

"Well, thank you very much, Mr. Haglan," she said, dragging the dishes off the table and dropping them into the sink. She turned on the hot water. Steam smoked toward the ceiling. The pipes clanked and clanged. "I'll sleep better tonight, knowing you don't want to murder me in my bed."

"Very funny."

Some high-pitched yelling from the living room reminded us that I had promised to play with the kids while Elana did some late shopping down at the market. So I did. But not very well. It was that tune again, that not knowing why, and it was driving me up the wall.

When I finally got back to my own place on the third floor, four rooms and not all that bad for what I was paying, I didn't turn on the lights. Or the TV. Or the radio. I got undressed, put on a robe, and sat in the armchair by the window, looking down at the street. Shoppers down there, and people heading home, people heading for the movies, for their friends, for just a walk on a night when the air was like thin ice—not too cold, but brittle enough to remind you that it still wasn't spring and wasn't about to be anytime soon. Sometimes they reminded me of horses, their breath puffing clouds toward the sky; sometimes they reminded me of black beetles, all bundled up the way they were, hiding the fact that they even had arms; and sometimes they didn't remind me of anything at all. Just people. Walking. Going someplace, or going nowhere.

I fell asleep.

I woke up the next morning with a stiff neck and a headache large enough to blow out my walls.

And I still couldn't remember the name of that damn song.

You, I said to myself, are going to go nuts if you don't knock it off.

I agreed.

So after a quick breakfast, I showered, polished my shoes, put on my good suit. Sooner or later, I figured, it would come to me. Sooner or later. Despite the subject, it wasn't as if it was a matter of life and death. And if it wasn't important, I'd forget it.

That afternoon I had an interview with an accounting firm on the other side of the city, but when it was over, I knew I hadn't gotten the position. It wasn't that I wasn't good with numbers; I just wasn't what they were looking for.

That's when I started thinking about maybe traveling around a little, take a long trip. I never really went anywhere. I never had the time before. Every vacation that came around, there were things to fix around the apartment once I'd gotten good enough to fix them, and things to fix for Elana and Grace and a few others in the building. I couldn't refuse them. Besides, I liked it. And more than once, I'd thought about opening my own little shop, just like they used to have in the old days. A fix-it shop. You bring it, I'll fix it. Something like that.

So, since I seldom went anywhere, and didn't have a lot of things I was dying to buy, I had a fair amount of what they call liquid assets in the bank.

I could do it.

I could travel.

Pick up a few bucks here and there fixing things.

When I got tired of it, and before the money ran too low, I'd come home.

No family, only a couple of friends, and it wouldn't be like I'd be gone forever—it wouldn't be any big deal.

But, to keep unemployment happy since I still had a few weeks left to run and besides, who wanted to travel in the winter anyway, I went on another interview. Not giving a damn this time. Not getting the job. Not getting depressed.

Elana was mad.

Grace was sad.

They didn't know about my plans for the spring.

I wanted to surprise them.

I spent four days working it all out on paper, figuring the cost—best case to worst case—and thinking about where I wanted to go. Naturally, since I hadn't been anyplace, there were lots of places to choose from. Then I decided that there shouldn't be any specific destination. I'd just go, end up where I ended up, and come back.

What the hell.

I got excited.

I walked around the apartment a dozen times before realizing that I was going to bust if I didn't get outside.

So I did.

From just about midafternoon to just before midnight I walked all over the city. Streets I didn't even know existed. Stores with fancy windows that made me stare at them for what seemed like years. Movie theaters with movies I'd never heard of in my life. Where the hell had all this been all this time? I had a late lunch in a restaurant where I couldn't read the menu; I had dinner in a place that was more neon and loud music than decent food; I actually saw the tag end of a parade; I watched the way people looked at me oddly because I was walking with a snap and a stride and smile and a wink.

I felt good.

Until, not three blocks from home, someone grabbed

my coat collar and yanked me into a narrow alley. I didn't have time to breathe, to call for help, to even think about fighting back.

He had a gun.

He wanted my wallet, my watch, my sweater, my belt, my tie. I gave him everything. Numb. So angry I was numb, and too numb to be really scared. And when it was over, he swiped me across the forehead with the barrel of the gun, and the next thing I remember I was staring up at the starless sky from the sidewalk, blinking blood from my eyes. Dozens of people walked past before a lady stopped, kind of knelt down and saw the blood. She didn't wince or anything; she just helped me up, helped me into a cab, and helped me into the hospital. I don't think I said two words the whole time; I was too busy holding her handkerchief to my face and praying that I wouldn't bleed to death before the doctors got hold of me.

She left me in the Emergency Room, told me she hoped I'd be all right, and I never saw her again.

The nurse there took me to a bed hidden by some lightly stained curtains, made me take off my coat and shirt, and pretty soon had the bleeding down to a trickle, telling me it wasn't as bad as it looked, head wounds always bleed more, that's all.

"You know, I don't get it," I said, jaw tight from the pain, feeling a bit dizzy.

She looked at me as if I were some country hick—not like I was dumb, just innocent. "It happens all the time. Hold still, this is going to sting."

Her name tag told me she was Barbara Cruz. And she was wrong; it didn't sting, it hurt like hell. "No," I said when the pain eased enough to let me breathe. "I mean, that woman. She didn't even tell me her name."

"That happens too."

A small pulse throbbed around the gash on my head. "And those people . . . those damn people didn't even stop."

A doctor came in, stitched me up without saying a thing, all he did was hum some damn song or other, and told me to wait until Nurse Cruz returned with the paperwork.

I did.

And while I did, I thought and looked around and saw people lying and standing and bleeding and moaning and not a bit of it made me feel one way or the other.

I thought some more.

When Nurse Cruz came back, I asked her if she saw a lot of people like me, people who get mugged and nobody stops to help.

Dark eyes became darker. "All the time."

I signed some forms I didn't even read. "It's a bitch."

She patted my arm, helped me down and into my coat. "You'd better get straight home, Mr. Haglan, and change your clothes, okay? Sure it's a bitch. But they don't know you, they don't care. You don't mean anything to them, you know?"

I knew.

Boy, did I know.

The city was bigger on the way home, and colder. Halfway there, I figured it would have been the same in a small town, and that would have gotten bigger too. By the time I was back in the apartment, standing in the shower and being careful of the bandages on my head, I also remembered the name of that tune.

I'd almost forgotten the goddamn thing.

Except for trips to the corner market, I stayed in the apartment for almost a week, until I could take the bandages off and not look like Frankenstein's monster. Then I rode the subways for a while, for a couple of days, and walked the streets during the rush hour for a few days after that. I looked at the pedestrians, at their reflections in windows and passing cars; I watched bus riders and subway riders and messengers riding bikes; I tried to count how many of them I didn't know.

I wondered what it would be like to kill one of them.

It was easy.

A hip, a nudge, a poke, a gunshot on an empty street, and something that walks becomes something that lies down, and doesn't move.

It was easy.

They didn't know me.

I didn't know them.

And the best part is, I'm just like everyone else. Except that I'm not a coward, and I don't pretend to be something I'm not. When the time is right, and the circumstances are right, when I get the urge and the mood is just right . . . what the hell.

The day before I left on my trip, at the going-away party Elana gave me, Grace looked up from the newspaper and called the person who had murdered a teacher an inhuman beast who should be shot.

I grinned at her.

She blushed.

And I kissed her goodbye without telling her what I know—that people like me aren't inhuman at all.

God, no.

I was—best case, worst case—very human indeed.

And the last thing I told her was:

"Take care of yourself, dear. And watch out for strangers."

Taking Care of Georgie

Lisa W. Cantrell

"It's your wildest fantasy come true, little brother." Roger placed a hand on George's shoulder and gave it a conspiratorial pat. "A night of fun and games you'll never forget, I guarantee. And I've taken care of everything. All you have to do is go on up there and enjoy. You'll love it, I promise—with the tip I gave that broad, she'd better make it good. C'mon now. Trust me."

"I dunno, Rog." George shook his head slowly. The words were slurred, the product of too many Long Island iced teas at the party tonight—George's bachelor party. Tomorrow he would marry Susan.

Roger let his arm slide on around George's shoulders, a gesture of brotherly love. He began slowly steering them away from the car, past the old Le Grande Hotel the prostitutes used at night, toward the brownstone walk-up at the corner.

"C'mon now, Georgie, you're not going to turn down my bachelor present, are you? You wanna hurt my feelings?" He walked them to the bottom of the steps leading up to the brownstone.

"I just dunno, Rog," George said again, still shaking his head. "Doesn't seem quite, you know . . . right." But his gaze kept shifting up the cement staircase and the look on his face said he was weakening.

"C'mon, Georgie, it's not like you'd be cheating on Susan, not really. This girl's a pro, f'chrissake. All bought and paid for. And you're not married yet, so it doesn't really count." Roger edged them a little closer to the stairs. "Don't wimp out on me now, little brother. It's your last chance. Besides, it's too late to get my money back, so you might as well go on up and enjoy it—or I will." He chuckled wickedly.

"Well . . ." George peered up the stairs again, offering his brother a sheepish grin. With the back of his hand, he swiped at his mouth. "What th' hell. Okay, Rog, I accept . . ."

His expression suddenly clouded. "But you didn't tell the other guys about this, did you?"

Roger threw back his head and laughed, crooking his arm around George's neck and giving it a mock squeeze. "No, George. I didn't tell the other guys. I didn't tell anyone. This is just between you and me—nobody else will ever know, I promise."

He bent his mouth to George's ear and whispered: "Admit it now, Georgie. The idea of acting out a little uninhibited sexplay before you have to settle down to the tender husband role is a bit of a lure, isn't it? After those stag films . . ."

George laughed too. "Yeah, Rog, you got a point, there. So . . ." He glanced up at the building, swaying slightly inside Roger's supportive arm. "What am I s'posed t'do?"

Roger pulled a key out of his pocket. "Didn't I tell you I'd taken care of everything? She's on the second floor—Apartment 2-B. Up the stairs, first door on the left. Just let yourself in and she'll be waiting—in the bedroom." He winked. "But once in there, you're on your own."

George swiped at his mouth again and grinned.

Roger handed him the key. "That's the spirit. Off you go now, have fun. And don't let me see your smiling face until in the morning—*late* in the morning. I paid that broad for a whole night, what's left of it." He started back to the car, then threw: "And it better be a *big* smile, too, little brother," over his shoulder as George disappeared into the stairwell.

The call came at 3:57 A.M. Roger answered it on the fourth ring, remembering to fumble the receiver. It was the police. His brother George had been shot during an attempted rape. His intended victim had emptied her gun into him. George was dead.

Roger got up, dressed, drove to the hospital and police station where he identified the body, answered questions, filled out necessary forms. Afterwards, he drove around a while, just thinking on things.

The first slender brush of dawn was just climbing onto an edge of the night sky when he pulled into the driveway of the modest house where Susan lived. The lights were on; he'd called ahead to let her know he was coming, not telling her why. But she'd known something bad had happened. She'd known.

She opened the door as he neared it, her slender form hurriedly dressed in old denims and a baggy sweater.

He came in quietly, letting his face confirm her worst fear. Sitting down on the couch he dropped his head into his hands.

"Roger . . . ?"

He felt her sink onto the sofa beside him, put her hand on his arm, felt her tremble.

Tears sprang to his eyes as he shook his head slowly from side to side. "There's no easy way to tell you this . . ." He stumbled over the words. "I still can't believe what's happened."

"Tell me." The hand on his arm tightened.

He lifted his head to face her, feeling tears running down his cheeks—he didn't bother wiping them away—saw them echoed in the brightness of her own eyes. "George is dead, Susan. He was—" And now he hesitated, grief at what he had to tell her overcoming him.

"Roger, please. You have to tell me." Her voice was barely audible, but the hand clenched his arm spasmodically.

"George was killed, Susan—shot, trying to—rape the woman I've been seeing lately."

Her gasp was a knife, sharp and quick and deadly. It plunged into him and now the words gushed out:

"They said he had a key—*my* key. She'd given it to me recently." Roger shook his head in disbelief. "George had only seen her a couple of times, they hadn't even met. I still can't believe . . ." He bowed his head again, mumbled, "Oh, he'd made a couple of remarks, you know, just joking kinds of things. But I didn't think he meant—"

Roger took a moment to collect himself. "He knew about the key. But what he didn't know is that she kept a loaded gun in her bedside table. She'd told me never to come over late unless I called her first, or at least made sure she knew it was me coming in the door. It was the neighborhood she lived in, you see. She was constantly afraid that some rapist might—"

His voice broke and once again he buried his head in his hands. "It's all my fault," he muttered. "After the bachelor party tonight. George was so drunk. Acting strange, said he wanted to walk, get some air. But I never imagined anything like this—never."

He shook his head slowly from side to side, then buried it again in his hands. "I shouldn't have let him go off by himself," he murmured into his palms. "It's all my fault."

During this recital, Susan had said nothing. Now she touched his hand with her small, cool one, forcing him to turn his head and look up at her.

He held his breath.

"No, Roger." Her voice was bleak, her eyes were filled with so much pain. "You mustn't blame yourself. You didn't know—how could you? There was nothing you could have done. Nothing. I thought he loved me—" She quietly began to sob.

He breathed deeply, putting an arm around her shoulder, a gesture of brotherly love. Slowly, ever so slowly, he gathered her small warm body to his chest. She didn't pull away.

"I'm sorry, Susan." Gently he began stroking her silken hair. "So very sorry. George *did* love you, I know he did. He was just drunk—crazy!—I don't know. But he loved you, you have to believe that. And we'll get through this thing. Together. You'll see. We'll help each other through."

He laid his cheek against her soft, soft hair.

"Take care of your brother, Roger," their widowed mother had told him on her deathbed, the last words she'd ever spoken to him. *"Take care of my precious Georgie . . ."*

Well, tonight he'd taken care of George. And from now on he'd start taking care of Susan, the woman he'd loved ever since the first time he'd seen her with his brother. *The woman* I *wanted, little brother,* Roger thought with an inward smile, and held Susan just a little bit closer.

Fish Are Jumpin', and the Cotton Is High

S. P. Somtow

Every summer until the day he died, my dad used to take me on a fishing trip. He'd take a whole month off from work—when he had work, that is—and he'd throw the big trunk full of tackle into the back of his station wagon and he'd scoop me up and dump me in the front seat next to him and we'd just go, up or down I-95, until we reached a turnoff we'd never used before, then inland, down country roads, past towns with names a body couldn't pronounce, deep into cotton country, where they grew the best fish in America.

We always took Grandma with us on them trips. Not that she had much to contribute, but it felt good to have the whole family together. My favorite part of our times together was in the early evening, with the stars just fixing to come out, with the *dzzt-dzzt* of the chigger-buster and its weird blue glow, putting the tent up next to some winding creek, frying up a big old batch of bacon and flapjacks, hauling Grandma out of the suitcase and setting her up so the sunset'd shine right through her and stain them bleached old bones of hern the color of fresh-gushing blood.

Oh, Grandma was high after so many years on the road, but after we dusted her off and hung a brand new air freshener around her neck she was good as new, and it was better for her to be amongst her own flesh and blood than rotting away in some old hole in the churchyard back home.

I sure did love her. She was my favorite out of all my kinfolk, the only one that didn't mind my sassing.

When the fishing actually started, we'd pack her back up into the suitcase and stow her in the back of the station wagon. She was a sensitive soul.

I still remember that last summer we were all together like it was yesterday. The open road swimming in the heat, and us sitting in the cool air conditioning listening to Dad's favorite music, which was George Gershwin in any shape or form, specially the show tunes from *Porgy and Bess;* Dad telling me stories about what it was like in the Depression; Dad telling about all the fish he used to catch down Hannibal way, especially the wrigglingest ones, the ones that got away. . . .

"This time of year is best, Jody," he told them. "This time of year's when the fish are jumping."

The name of the town was I think Sweetwater. I don't recollect the county. We cruised in about sunset, and the fish were already gathering. Along the main street was the best place to start looking. Maybe outside a beauty salon or a bar. Likely as not a town like this would only have one.

I spotted one first: she had them droopy earrings and her skirt hitched up almost all the way to her panties, and her lips were painted blood-red and her eyes were lined in heavy black. "Slow down, Dad," I said. "Look, there, against that lamppost."

"Bullcrap, sonny-boy," he said. "Ain't no more'n a minnow."

"With all that makeup plastered on her face?"

"Too much makeup. You gotta look beneath the makeup. She can't be no more than twelve years old. Beneath the makeup, sonny. See that one now—there's quality."

I knew what he meant. Her bust was about busting out of her blouse, and her face was painted, every inch of it, in eye-popping red, black, and blue. She had a beehive hairdo. Her ass was all crammed into her jeans and she was smoking a cigarette as she leaned against a mailbox outside the town drugstore.

"Now that," said my Dad, "is a fish."

"How we gonna catch her, Dad?"

"The usual, I think. The worm on the end of the hook on the end of the line."

"You want me to play the worm, Dad?"

"Sure thing, son."

He laughed. I sure was glad he was in a good mood, 'cause that meant he'd let me help with the whole job from start to finish. If he was in a bad mood, he'd lock me out of the good parts, and if he was in a really foul mood, he was liable to make me spend the night with Grandma.

We shadowed her for a couple of blocks, which was all there was to that town anyways. She never did notice. They never do. She was looking at her watch and cussing to herself. That was good. They're more ready to take the bait when they think they've just been stood up. After a bit she started taking bigger steps, like she was fed up and decided to walk home even though it was probably a fair piece from the town itself. She had good legs for walking, though, firm and muscular.

The town won't hard to figure out. It didn't have but

one stop sign and then it run up against open fields. Dad stopped shadowing her, took off, and let me off at the side of the road about a mile on down, just the other side of a slope, so she wouldn't know I was there till she practically tripped over me. He cuffed me a couple times in the mouth, to make it look convincing. I always hated that part.

I laid myself down and, soon as I saw her coming, I started moaning, and it won't all play-acting neither. My Dad was a mean slapper and I had a tooth loose.

"Lordy," she said, "what happened to *you?*"

"Oh, ma'am, please help me," I said, "my Daddy done wore me out with his belt and tossed me out of his car and I don't know where the hell he is."

"Why, that son-of-a-bitch!" she said, and knelt down beside me. "Report him to the CPS, you ought to. You know what that is? Child Protective Services. They can fix you up, honey. My sister's a social worker."

"Damn straight I know about them CPS folks, ma'am, they's what got me into this . . . they took me from my parents . . . that man which beat me, he's my *foster* father." Bleeding hearts were the easiest to confuse.

"Lordy," she whispered, and I could see she was mighty perturbed.

"Don't tell the social workers, ma'am, they'll only find out about the time I shoplifted a box of candy from Woolworth's, but ma'am, I couldn't help myself, I hadn't et in four days. . . ."

"Honey, are you *hungry?*" She rooted around in her purse and produced half a Twix bar. I usually prefer the peanut butter flavor but I had to pretend I was desperate for food, so I gobbled down the whole thing and then threw in some good retching sounds for good measure.

"What's your name?" she said.

"Um . . . Jody," I said. I always used my real name—what the hell, they weren't about to kiss and tell.

She kind of leaned down and I gripped her wrist in both hands, hard as I could. I was pretty strong even though I was only in the seventh grade. She didn't think nothing of it, just figured I was clinging on to her because I wanted attention. But it was because I heard Dad's station wagon lumbering on up the hill.

Before she knew what was happening, Dad lassoed her out of the open window, slammed on his brakes, and started reeling her in. I hung on as she got herself whip-dunked down against the car door.

"Shit, Jody, you run and call 911 right now, you hear?" the fish screamed, but that was before I got the duct tape out of my jeans pocket and shoved a snotty old handkerchief in her mouth and wound the tape around and around her face. She kicked some, but the lasso pinned her arms to her sides, and pretty soon we had her trussed up real good, like a pig.

"We oughta use her for a hood ornament," I said, laughing.

"Nah, sonny-boy, they only do that with deer."

We hauled her inside and stacked her up next to Grandma's suitcase. She made whinnying noises, and she thrashed around a mite, but she won't near as much trouble as some.

There was an empty barn on some abandoned farm which me and Dad'd staked out, about sixty miles down the road, which looked like about the perfect spot for our headquarters that summer. I couldn't wait to get there so we could start gutting the first fish of the season. We'd spent the whole night preparing for it, cleaning out the special room we were gone use, sharpening our tools.

It was about sunset when we pulled right into the barn. The air was hot and dank, but it didn't smell of cowshit or nothing; there'd been no folks on this farm for a long, long time. Dad said it was because of the recession; it'd made his job a whole lot easier. There won't no electricity there but we had hung up some lamps in the loft, and we had most of the equipment laid out.

"Go put your Grandma somewhere decent," my Dad said. "You know she's a sensitive soul and she don't even like to buy meat at the supermarket."

I drug Grandma's suitcase over to a far corner so we could gut and clean without upsetting her. Then me and Dad carried our prize up the steps into the loft. She was trussed too tight to squirm much, but her eyes wiggled back and forth like lime Jell-O. We tossed a rope through a metal ring hanging from the rafter and hoisted her so she was about an inch or two off of the floor, and then I started cutting the clothes off of her.

Meanwhile, Dad was getting the instruments ready, polishing them until they shone.

"Measure her," he said, "and then we'll take off the gag so we can tell what she's thinking."

I got out the tape measure. She was 37-25-39; not a bad specimen. It was a pity we couldn't stuff her and mount her. The people back home just wouldn't understand. I wrote the numbers down in the ledger so we'd always have a record. Then I put the book away in the tackle trunk, and I got out the big old Bible we always carried with us on our fishing trips.

"Ready?" I said.

"Ready."

I ripped off the duct tape from her mouth.

"Fuck you!" the fish screamed. "What are you, some kind of sex killer?"

Dad slapped her across the face. "Don't you ever say that!" he shouted. "I ain't one of them sick perverts which interferes with women and then kills them. I never do no interfering. Ain't that right, son?"

"Yeah, Dad."

"I am an angel of the Lord, and you ain't nothing but a painted whore of Babylon. Thou shalt not suffer a witch to live. We're doing the Lord's work here, and don't you forget it. We're gone pray with you, and watch with you, and show you the error of your ways, and when we's through with you you will beg us and plead with us to send your soul flying right into the arms of the Lord's compassion. And now, Jody, let's have the harmonica."

I fished it out of the trunk and handed it to him. He played and I sang:

I will make you fishers of men,
Fishers of men,
Fishers of men,
I will make you fishers of men,
If you fol—low me!

It was hard to sing on key because of the way she was hollering. Finally my Dad had to whup her across the face a couple of times. "You're supposed to sing, not scream," he said. "Sing, bitch." I knew how he hated getting the paint of Babylonish whoredom on his hands. She never did seem to appreciate what we were doing for her immortal soul. Well, he just went on slapping her until she started to croak out the words of the hymn.

After a while my Dad told me to open up the good book and read aloud some of the parts that had to do with lusting and whoring. The important texts were highlighted in neon yellow. I read about adultery and the sins of the flesh. Didn't rightly know what some of them things were, but I knew they had to be mighty bad to deserve the kind of punishment the Lord had called us to inflict. While I read, my Dad unleashed his staff of chastisement from his pants—I did the same—and the power of the Lord went into it and made it hard and strong. It was a high honor to be allowed to help with this part of the ceremony. I could feel the rapture seizing hold of my whole body.

"Why don't you just rape me now and get it over with?" she said, spitting in my face.

"You still don't get it, do you?" Dad said. "Keep reading, sonny-boy."

He shucked her nipples with a paring knife and dropped them in the mason jar with the others. He made a series of crisscross cuts on her belly. She screamed. He swung his staff of chastisement against her flesh and I did the same with mine, even though it only reached up to her thigh. I felt bigger than myself, like the wind of the Lord was blowing through my soul.

I held the Bible with one hand and went on reading.

"Oh Jesus it hurts it hurts," she shrieked, "I'll do anything I'll let you fuck me if you want just make it stop make it stop—"

Dad sighed. "She thinks this is all about . . . lust. I've told her I ain't gone interfere with her in any way, but she still don't understand. She's too far gone to understand."

"For them that's too far gone," I said, "ain't but one answer." I ripped off one of her fingernails. Her squalling never stopped.

"Shut the fuck up!" he shouted. "There's a lady present here! You want to wake my mother?" He hit her over the head with piece of pipe, and that seemed to calm her down a tad. It was enough for us to finish the business of anointing her with the milk of the Lord's mercy, which come spurting out of our staffs of chastisement just at that moment.

We revived her by sloshing a Diet Coke over her face, and our ministry to her went on into the night. We sliced, we diced, we chainsawed and we roto-rootered. But just like Dad promised, we didn't send her into the world hereafter until the moment she pled for it, because we won't no killers.

When we were done, we were filled with joy, and though we were tired we knew it was an honest day's work and that we were storing up wages in heaven.

"Praise be to God," Dad whispered as the fish breathed her last, "for we have saved you from the everlasting fire."

The Lord rewarded us with provender. The butt meat was always the best. We had us a small fire, fetched Grandma out of her suitcase so she could enjoy a nice family meal; and, in the wee hours before the sunrise, my Dad and I laid down on our pallets and talked about life, and birth, and death, and about the Lord; about all the things that mattered in our lives.

It being high summer, it turned rainy all of a sudden. The moisture seeped into the barn and we like to drowned from breathing it in. I loved the sound of that rain.

Dad told me the story of how the Good Lord had called him to this ministry. He had told the story so often I almost had it by heart, but I didn't mind hearing it again because it was a bond between us and every time he told the story it made me admire him more. "Were you real little?" I asked him.

"Littler'n you," he said dreamily.

Mosquitoes danced in the light of the lantern. "We lived in a two-room shack up in the hills in them days. Every day I studied the Bible with Brother Michael down at the Church of Light. Sometimes he'd use his rod on me, and anoint me with the milk of mercy, but I paid the pain no mind because it was bringing me closer and closer to God. And every evening I swept the house clean and said my prayers and fell asleep in your Grandma's bed. She worked late and I'd never see her until morning, when I woke up to the smell of frying bacon."

"Sounds like a piece of heaven," I said softly, because all I'd ever known was the wrong side of town, where the bigger boys lay in wait for you after school and beat you till the crap ran down your pants.

"Oh, sonny-boy, that it was. Until the night I slept fitfully, and the Lord woke me from a dream. The dream was of hills and a river. The river was beating against the wall of a dam and the hills were pulsing with electricity. The river was full of power. It was full of fish. That dream disturbed me and I woke up. It was a thundering night. And I saw the most hellish sight that I ever did see. My mother was awake, and she was nekkid, and her face was painted. Her lips and her cheeks was rouged and her eyelashes blackened. There was a man on top of her, and he was bare-ass nekkid hisself, and he was interfering with her. He was sticking his rod where it shouldn't be stuck. And I was full of the wrath of the Lord, because Brother Michael done read the Bible with me that day, and we talked about sins of the flesh.

" 'Stop interferin' with my mother, you hear?' I shouted.

"But your Grandma, she was too far gone. Instead of realizing the error of her ways, she done pushed me off the bed and said, "Interferin'! Where d'you think *you* come from, you little bastard, if it won't for interferin'?' I landed on the hard wooden floor and banged my ass up bad. Then I crept away to the kitchen to look for a knife."

I could feel the horror of it as clear as if I'd been there myself. Each time Dad relived it, it became more real to me.

"What did you do next, Daddy?"

"I saved her, sonny-boy. I saved your Grandma, praise be to God, I saved her from the everlasting fire. And now—"

"Now we're a family again." I could feel the warmth of our love deep in my heart and in my bones. We were a special family. Fishers of men. Dad kissed me and I wrapped my down bag tight around myself and listened to the pelting rain until I fell asleep.

That was how our summer began and it was like every summer as far back as I could remember. After we buried the fish in a ditch about twenty miles from the barn, we went on from Sweetwater to Wild Horse and from Wild Horse to Ocrapocah and Dumb Holler. We found a fish in every town and brung her back to the old barn to minister unto her. We never had to pay for our supper but once, when we stopped at a McDonald's to remind us of the lean times. My Dad never once spoke a harsh word to me, and he only hit me when he had to.

The trouble started I reckon the day we reached a town called Spring Oaks. It won't that small of a town—it actually had more'n one traffic light. Dad decided to get a copy of the local paper. It had a photograph of fish number one of the season right there on the front page. At first Dad was pleased. He pulled off the road next to a cotton field to read it.

CRISSCROSS KILLER STRIKES AGAIN, the headline read. They'd found our first fish in that ditch. Kids'd been playing there. Somehow they'd figured out it was the same person who'd done a bunch of slayings down in Florida three years back; that was what they'd named him that time, because of the pattern of the knife cuts on her torso.

"So, what does the press have to say about me this

time?" Dad said, pouring hisself a cup of coffee out of the thermos. I skootched up closer to him and read it over his shoulder. He was a slow reader and I would sometimes help him with some of the words, whenever I seen his lips stop moving.

I read: "Severe lacerations . . . limbs missing . . . genital area mutilated . . . some semen stains found on buttocks suggest sporadic attempts at penetration. . . ." It was the usual bullcrap. Then there was this part that said, "Turn to page four for a specialist's profile of the suspect," and Dad turned to that page in a hurry.

In the article, some fancy psychiatrist from Massachusetts had studied all the victims of the Crisscross Killer and compared them all. This is what he said: "The evidence would indicate a white male in his mid-to-late thirties. There is nothing about his general appearance to provoke suspicion. He has probably had an extremely traumatic childhood experience which resulted in the transformation of normal sexual impulses into an arcane and private ritual involving death and mutilation. Doubtless he has been imprinted with the wrong set of symbols. The danger is to oversimplify, to invest the killer's personality with a *Psycho*-like Pavlovian response to the trigger stimulus. . . ."

"What in God's holy name does this mean?"

"Don't understand a word of it, Dad," I said, "honest I don't."

"Well, I do. This high-and-mighty Yankee witch doctor's saying I'm a pervert, that's what. He's saying I'm a sick, demented, sex-crazed, psycho killer instead of a ministering angel of the Lord."

"Is that what he means, Dad?"

"Are you mocking me, sonny-boy? I ought to tan your hide right here and now and—"

"Dad, I didn't mean no—"

"Shut your damn mouth, Jody."

Right then and there I knew that good times was over for the summer. The bad mood had come over him at last. Sometimes it came after only one or two fishes; this time we'd managed to stretch our precious time together through five of them—what a summer! the best I'd ever known—but the better it'd been, the worse the mood he went through when it was near over. Best to try to ride it out somehow. He just couldn't help hisself.

What I said next I reckon I shouldn't have: "Dad, but that psychiatrist fellow was right guessing your age, won't he?"

"Be *quiet!*"

"And it's true, ain't it, that your sex feelings ain't the same as ordinary folks'?" I thought this must be true because I always listened to the way the boys in school talked about fucking, and I never could get it to jibe with Dad's way of reckoning the facts of life. I knew Dad was right, of course, but it was a curious thing, how so many kids my age could be so ignorant, and not know the danger they stood in of eternal damnation, which meant their parents must not know nothing neither, and so on, back through the generations, all the way through to the original sin of Adam.

"I don't know what you're talking about," he said.

"Oh, Dad, you know . . . you never stick your dick into them. I never seen you stick your dick into *nobody.* Shit, Dad, I never even seen you beat off."

I saw him go beet-red. He ripped the paper up and he threw it out of the car window and he slammed me against the dashboard and put his arms around my neck and like to strangled me. "Don't hurt me, Daddy," I whimpered, but he only said, "Into the back. In there with your Grandma. I don't want to see hide nor hair of you until we get home."

"But Dad—"

"Get in there before I whup your ass with a bundle of thorns."

I crawled into the back and opened my Grandma's suitcase and got in alongside her. Sometimes Dad would relent but this time I heard him stick the key in the padlock and I heard Dad shriek out at the top of his lungs, "My God, my God, why hast thou forsaken me?"

It was dark. It smelled bad. Grandma's bones rattled around and the air freshener had stopped working. I held my breath a long time. The key in the padlock never turned. I could get out if I wanted to, but I knew I'd get a sound whupping if I tried. All's I could hear was the muffled sound of my Dad cussing, cussing, and cussing.

After a while I could feel the car moving again. The whole suitcase shuddered and the bones kept slipping and sliding. Maybe there was another fish to fry. When the bad mood took my Dad, the most we could squeeze out of a trip was maybe one more. I put my ear up to the lid and tried to listen. The station wagon was slowing down. Dad was using the charm approach. I could hear him speaking softly. He was probably driving alongside somebody, wooing her as he steered her toward a deserted street. It seemed to be going smoothly even without using me as bait. Pretty soon I heard the car door open. This was going great. She won't even putting up a struggle, just coming along voluntary. That only proved she was one of them whores of Babylon—only a whore'd get into a stranger's car without no coercion.

I heard her laughing. Well, it was more of a nervous giggle. "You have a coffin in the back of the car!" she was saying.

"Ain't no coffin," said my Dad. "It's a suitcase."

She had just gone and pushed one of my Dad's buttons. Dad's mood always darkens anytime a body calls

Grandma's suitcase a coffin. I was curious about what was gone happen so I cautiously lifted the lid about a half inch. I saw the back of the new fish's head and it was enough to realize she was the best and biggest of the summer. Her hair was red as the autumn hills and I could smell that perfume—I was right grateful that she'd used so much because I'd about had a noseful of the stench inside the suitcase—and it didn't take much imagination to realize she probably had tits like balloons. My Dad can really pick them every time.

Dad turned onto the road toward our barn.

The fish said, "You won't hurt me, will you?"

There was a pause. "I don't hold with interferin' with women," he said.

She'd just done pushed another button. I could feel Dad's rage uncoiling. I could imagine his hands just shaking and shaking on that steering wheel and his mind racing on ahead, thinking about the ministry, about the terrible cup the Lord had given him to drink from.

"So you're a fag?" said the fish. Teasing. Taunting.

That was the third button.

"Bitch! Don't say them things! Brother Michael was a good man . . . a good man, do you hear? and he showed me the way of the Lord." He let go of the steering wheel and grabbed the fish by the neck, both hands, and started to choke her. The car was zigzagging all over but won't nobody else on the road.

I was thinking: Dad, if she dies now before we've had a chance to save her, she's gone straight to hell and we'll be guilty of murder. But I daresn't say nothing because I'm afraid of my Dad's temper.

Then, all of a sudden, everything changes.

She ain't just a-kicking and a-scratching like other fish. There's a purpose to what she's doing. She's getting the better of him, and all of a sudden she whips out a pair of handcuffs and next thing you know, he's cuffed to the steering wheel as the station wagon veers off the road and into a tree.

Then she pulls out a gun.

"I'm Lt. Flora Harberd," she said. "FBI. You have the right to remain silent. . . ."

"What the hell are you doing, ma'am?" said Dad, and he suddenly sounded ineffective and vulnerable. Almost as though Grandma were telling him what to do. Almost like a little boy. "I was happy to pick you up. Won't no call to start calling me names, and then picking a fight with me. You ain't no detective. You were dolled up like a who'."

"David Lee," she said. "Or should I say, Billy Joe Blackburn? Johnny Raitt? How many aliases have you used, Mr. Crisscross Killer? Or are you the Swamp Thing? The Macon County Terror? Oh, yes, we've been watching you for a long, long time. I was chosen to bait you, Mr. Killer, because I was the closest match to your preferred victim type. 98%! They made us take a test. Computer-matched our photographs with pictures of your mother when she was a young woman working the streets. Well, mister, you're hooked now, and we're going to reel you in."

It stung me that she was talking about fishing. It was like she didn't have no understanding of the world at all. It won't her place to talk about the Lord's work. She was a fish, not a man.

My Dad, he was just shivering and sweating all over, and I think his faith was wavering. Especially when she shoved that pistol of hers right between his lips.

"Want to suck on this, mister?" she said. "We have Brother Michael in custody, you know. He talked. Boy, mister, he squealed like a pig, he sang."

My Dad wailed. Like a little baby. What was wrong

with him? Why won't no thunder and lightning coming down from the sky?

"I could shoot you dead right here and now, mister," said the fish turned fisherman. "I know you're just gonna cop an insanity plea and spend the rest of your life in some asylum. It ain't right. You're scum. You should be dead."

"Damn Yankees," my Dad said.

"Shut the fuck up and let me finish reading your Miranda rights."

I could only see a slit of what was happening. But I could tell that my Dad won't doing nothing to defend hisself, it was like all the fight'd gone right out of him. There was only me left to do something about it.

She didn't know there was anybody else in the car. I didn't have no weapon. I just grabbed a hold of the first thing I could. I took a deep breath. She was talking about how they could use anything he said against him in a court of law. I bust out of that suitcase and smashed it down hard on the fish woman's head. She looked at me with wide surprised eyes and just slumped over in the seat.

"That was close, Dad," I said. "Another minute and she could've blowed your brains to kingdom come."

"You . . . you . . . look what you done to your Grandma, Jody . . . oh, how can you look your Daddy in the eye . . . ?"

And I saw what I was holding in my hand. Grandma's skull. I was right horrified at what I done. Carefully, I put it back in the suitcase and shut the lid back down. "Sorry, Grandma," I whispered.

"Didn't tell you you could come out of there," Dad said angrily. He aimed to slap me across the face, but he was still wearing his cuffs.

"Come on, Dad . . . you have to be strong." I leaned

over and started looking for her keys. "I know she almost had you but we can deal with her now." I fished out the keys, drug out a coil of rope from the back of the wagon, and started to truss her up the way Dad'd taught me, good and tight. Then I unlocked the cuffs. Dad just sat there, looking at his hands. Seemed like he didn't believe it could've happened, what with the Lord protecting him and all. "For God's sake, Dad, help me."

"You tore your Grandma apart!"

"Grandma's dead."

"You *killed* her!"

"No, Dad. You did. A long time ago. You done told me so yourself. You saved her from the everlasting fire. Praise be to God."

He looked all confused. "You reckon?" he said.

"Come on, Dad. Let's get her on down to the barn."

"Oh. Yeah."

We carried her up to the loft just like we done all the others. We moved Grandma's suitcase back inside. We slung the fish from the rafter through the iron hook. She was unconscious, so we didn't even bother to gag her. Everything was as it always was, but I could see that my Dad's heart won't in his work no more. I wished he would just slap me a time or two; even his bad moods were better than this. His eyes had gone lifeless; won't no fire in them; they stared ahead like the eyes of a fish.

We cuffed her ankles with her own cuffs and we laid her piece alongside the sacramental tools of deliverance.

All the time Dad was sharpening them tools and opening the Bible to the right page for the start of the ritual, he was mumbling to herself, "I ain't pure enough, I ain't . . . I ain't the perfect servant of the Lord . . . I have strayed . . . oh, God, I have strayed, and now you're showing me the error of my ways. . . ."

"Dad, what do you mean, you've strayed?" I couldn't believe what I was hearing. I loved my Daddy with all my heart. He wasn't the straying kind. He was a pillar of strength to me. He didn't waver. The man I was seeing now, he won't like my Dad. He was more like me.

"Once, sonny-boy, once and once only . . . I interfered with a woman."

The fish-detective hung from the rafter and swayed back and forth. She was still out cold. I couldn't believe my ears. I thought I had heard every story my Dad had to tell about his past. This was a new one. I had the feeling everything was about to change forever. He was unlocking the secretest chamber of his heart to me.

"I was new to fishing," he said. "My understanding was still poor. I didn't even know then that fishing was what it was. I loved the Lord, and I wanted to bring these sinners to his bosom, but there was things I was too simple to grasp. In them days I was still fishing far from home, up north. I caught me a fine one, tied her to a bedpost, and began my ministry unto her.

"I didn't rightly know what I was doing. And she taunted me. She teased me with honeyed words. She mocked me. 'That rod of chastisement of yours don't hurt me one bit,' she said. 'It don't hurt unless to poke it right inside of me, unless you stoke the fires of hell inside my belly.' I believed her. So trusting I was, and so ignorant of the desires of the flesh! Before I knew it I'd pierced her in that place. And no sooner'd I spent my milk of mercy than she screeched, 'You've given me a baby, by the grace of God; now you can't torment me, because you can't take away the life from the innocent child.' "

As he told me this, his hands were trembling. He paced back and forth. He stumbled. The other stories he told me, they were like pebbles, rubbed smooth in the river of his mind. This won't that kind of story. This was raw and jagged and full of pain.

"What did you do next, Dad?" I said. I was afraid we'd never get to the main business of the evening.

"It was true! The Lord revealed to me in a vision that a baby was growing inside her—to remind me of my sin—flesh of my flesh! What could I do? I kept her chained up, of course, cleaned the filth off of her twice a day, fed her on scraps from your Grandma's table."

"Did you let her go, Daddy? Did she give birth to me? Is she my mother?"

"Don't talk about such sins, sonny-boy. It's enough that the Lord pitied my transgression and gave you to me as a token of his mercy." He went on polishing his knives, but half-heartedly.

"But Dad—"

I couldn't get no more information from him, because the policewoman started to stir. She didn't kick and she didn't scream, she only glared at me and my Dad with spiteful eyes. Oh, she was painted all right, painted in lurid colors, and her clothing was the fishiest I'd ever seen. Even if she was a policewoman like she said, there was a bit of whore deep inside her, and we could still ferret it out and save her soul.

"Let's get to work, son," he sighed.

I took out the measuring tape. She was the finest yet. I slit the clothes off of her with an X-acto knife. I found her police badge in a pocket. She hadn't been lying about that. I took out my Bible and began the reading.

"Shame on you," said the fish, "Mr. Lee, or Blackburn, or Raitt. It wasn't enough that you should go around killing defenseless women; you had to corrupt the mind of an innocent child too. After you're in custody, CPS will take care of him, but it's going to take years of therapy before he can live a normal life . . . fucking up your own kid like that, mister."

My Dad didn't even have the sense to slap her into silence.

"Pay her no mind, Dad!" I said, and started to read the story of Jezebel out of the big old Bible.

"You're not going to get away with this," said the fish. "I have a homing device planted on me. The police in four counties have been tracking me. Even if you kill me, they're all going to be converging on this place in just about two minutes."

Dad's face paled. "Don't listen to her, Dad!" I shrieked. "She ain't got no device. Look at her, bare-ass nekkid and hanging from the rafters. There ain't no device. She's just resisting the word of the Lord is all."

"Where's the device?" said my Dad. The old spirit was starting to come back into his face. "Where is it?"

She spit in his face.

"Where's the fucking device?"

He was yelling at the top of his lungs now. I felt pride. He was gone make it through. His faith was gone come back to him. He grabbed one of her tits and pinched it until it started to turn purple. But she didn't seem to break.

"Ma'am," I said, "you'd best tell him what he wants. You ain't endured the kind of pain my Dad can give. He gives it with love, for the sake of your soul. Go on, tell him."

I've never seen so much hate in a woman's eyes. She didn't have no fear, though. It was like she didn't mind nothing—not even dying—as long as she could carry my Dad with her. She had the sureness of an avenging angel. The Lord giveth, the Lord taketh away. Maybe she had been sent to us. In any case, the look she gave him was enough to make him stop pinching her.

"Where's the fucking device?" he said, but it came out more like a croak.

"Guess," said Lt. Flora Harberd. "You're going to have to fuck me to dislodge it, you shit-eating white trash scumbag."

I heard the sirens wailing in the distance. A dozen sirens coming from all directions. I was afraid.

"Never," said my father.

He picked up her piece and shot her through the heart.

Then he just stared at the smoking gun, peered so hard it looked like he was crosseyed. I thought he was gone point it at hisself.

I said, "Dad, Dad . . . we never watched with her and prayed with her . . . she never did plead for us to send her into the hereafter . . . Dad, you done *murdered* her!"

The sirens were nearer now. And it started to rain.

"Why did you *murder* her, Daddy?"

"It was the onliest thing left for me to do, sonny-boy. She wanted me to interfere with her to save my own life. What is my life compared to the work we've been doing? Listen, sonny-boy, listen! I've been strong! I done resisted the last temptation!"

It thundered above the wailing of the sirens. But all I could think of was the way she jerked, and the way the blood come squirting out in all directions, like a soda fountain gone wild. This was scary. Her death was permanent. She won't never gone enter into the glory and the rapture. Oh, I was heartsick for her, and I knew that my Dad had stepped over the fine line that divides saintliness from madness.

Then there come a great big echoing voice: "Come out of the barn with your hands in the air or we're gone start shooting!"

My Daddy laughed. "My trust is in the Lord. Death ain't but the beginning."

"Dad, ain't no use," I said softly. "Go on out there."

"Not in front of your Grandma! I don't want her to see me be a yellow coward! Not after all we been through together!"

"Daddy, she's dead." I could feel tears running down my cheeks.

"Now don't you cry, sonny-boy," he said with a tenderness I'd rarely seen in him. "We all gone meet again on t'other side. Go on now. Go and be with Grandma. Get in that suitcase and stay there till they come for you."

He kissed me on the cheek and walked me downstairs and made sure I had the lid down, though he didn't use the padlock. He trusted me after all we'd been through.

The thunder came again and again and again, and the sirens shrilled, and presently come the big electric voice again, telling my Dad to come out of the barn. And I heard my Daddy laughing, and laughing, and laughing, and finally I heard shots ring out . . . repeating shots . . . ten, twenty, a hundred of them.

I couldn't take it anymore. I shoved aside the coffin lid and I saw my Dad, wounded, crawling toward me.

"Daddy!" I screamed.

He hadn't been wounded in but one or two places, for all their gunfire. But I knew he won't gone last but a minute or two. I ran to him and I cradled his head in my arms.

The voice called to us again. It was closer now.

"I got one last thing . . . to tell you," Dad said to me. "One last thing."

"Save it, Dad . . . hold your talking . . . you gone be fine."

"No. No. It's important . . . it's about you . . . about

the secret of your birth . . . about how special you are, sonny-boy. You done asked me if that whore of Babylon was your mother, and I didn't answer you. Well, she won't your mother. Even though she bore you inside of her whorish belly for nine long months while I tried to bend her to the worship of the Lord. She won't your mother! The Book of Job says, 'Man that is born of a woman is of few days, and full of trouble . . .' "

" '. . . he cometh forth like a flower, and is cut down; he fleeth also as a shadow, and continueth not. . . .' " I said, because like him, I knew the Good Book well, almost by heart.

"You won't born of a woman, Jody. I ripped you from that belly soon as you were big enough to breathe without that woman's help. I am your mother and your father, sonny-boy. That's how much I love you."

"And in ripping me from her . . ."

"I found my calling. Because only when she knew she was gone die did she call on the Lord . . . only when she was in her final torment did she plead for the mercy of the Lord . . . and the milk of His mercy gushed forth onto her belly as I carved it open. It smells like a fish, sonny-boy . . . the opening of a woman that tempts man to sin . . . it smells like a fish. That's how I knew I was gone become a fisher of men. You were that angel, sonny-boy, who come to me from the belly of the woman. You were the life that come leaping out of the dust of death. You're special, son. I only come to prepare the way. You won't born of no woman, and your life gone be free of trouble. You're blessed, sonny-boy."

"Oh, Daddy, Daddy," I said, "oh, save your breath, don't leave me, oh, Daddy, I love you more than anything in the whole wide world."

"Then fetch me my harmonica."

I found it and brought it to him. I held it to his lips.

He played but a few notes, and, as the rain streamed down and the thunder burst and the police came breaking down the barn door, I sang the words of his favorite spiritual:

My Lord, he calls me,
He calls me by the thunder. . . .
The trumpet sounds within-a-my soul,
I ain't got long to stay here.

And then I closed his eyes for him, because he won't breathing no more.

The CPS, they done took good care of me. After my Grandma's funeral, they sent me to social workers and psychiatrists, and finally they sent me to a big old ranch in Northern California with horses and cows. I liked the ranch and I liked my social workers and I liked the other kids that'd been sent there, most of them from troubled homes, abused children who hadn't known the kind of love me and my Daddy shared.

It's good to know that I ain't sick in the head or nothing, just that I been through some hard times, and I can be healed of the nightmares. My supervisors say I'm coming along just fine, and that maybe I'll be able to go to a foster home soon. The best thing is, a couple of the doctors here, they got excited when they heard me sing, and they think maybe when I'm older I could try out for the Grand Ole Opry. They've promised to send me to a voice coach over in Sacramento, and I sing in the church choir every Sunday.

Last week a girl named Nikki took me to the hayloft behind the stables and wanted to look at my thing. She showed me hers, too.

"You can play with it if you like," she told me "Go on. Touch it."

It felt good. I felt the stirrings of the old rapture. My loins were about bursting with it. I kissed her, too. I'd never tasted living human flesh before. But when I lifted my finger to my nose I could smell the taint of stale fish, and it brought back all the memories.

I killed her.

It Takes One to Know One

Robert Bloch

Kevin Ames took the elevator to the thirty-fifth floor, thinking about earthquakes all the way. When he arrived his involuntary sigh of relief echoed along the carpeted corridor as Ames made his way to the double doors at the far end. Here he halted to read the gold-lettered legend identifying the offices of *Tischler, Tischler, Phelps, Obendorrf & Associates.*

This time his sigh was voluntary. It was easy for him to understand why attorneys band together; obviously there's safety in numbers. But why did they list so many names? Wouldn't it be simpler to assume a group identity, like *Ali Baba and the Forty Thieves*?

Kevin Ames shrugged, then squared his shoulders, forced a smile and opened the right-hand half of the door guarding a reception area beyond.

Its decorous decor did little to put him at ease as he entered, and the matching receptionist behind a glass partition added no comfort to the occasion. Her prim lips parted in a smile of greeting usually reserved to welcome child-molesters at Disneyland.

"Good afternoon," he said. Apparently it wasn't, not for her anyway, because her smile went blank.

There was no change of expression in her unlifted face as he gave his name and received the *whom-did-you-wish-to-see?* routine in return. But when he answered that question her reaction was unmistakably evident.

"Mr. Tischler *senior*?" Her voice italicized her incredulity.

Ames nodded. "I have an appointment. For four-thirty."

"One moment, please." There was a flicker of disbelief in her eyes—the kind of look you'd give someone who brings a doggie-bag to the Last Supper.

Concealing his impatience, he stood waiting as she turned to address the intercom. "Grace? Did he come in this afternoon? No, they didn't say anything to me. Do you have something down about a four-thirty appointment? There's a Mr.—"

"Ames. Kevin Ames." His answer filled her pause, but he wasn't really listening. He'd started taking inventory of her desk.

Not much to see, really. No papers, no pads; it all goes on tape or into computers nowadays. But there was still the bud vase with the single rose, always a single rose in a pricey office like this, and a single receptionist who wouldn't be caught dead at a singles bar. At a certain age she still might or might not manage a face-tuck just to keep up appearances, but in any case or any age you could bet that her bra would always be a white one.

His speculation ceased abruptly as she switched off the intercom and addressed him. "Mr. Tischler will see you now, Mr. Ames."

Did he imagine it or was there a new note of respect in her voice, a warmer current flowing under the ice? If so, the thaw was generated by Tischler's name, not his.

Somewhere inside his skull, soundless queries emerged from cerebral silence. *Kevin? Kevin who? Never heard of him. What does he do?*

Practices anonymity, he responded, his answer as unvoiced as the question. That's the nice thing about talking to yourself, you never have to worry about being heard. And you always get the last word. Come to think about it, writing was also a way of getting the last word. Perhaps that was one of the reasons he'd been attracted to such a career. Or, more accurately, a profession. People who remain anonymous after a lifetime of effort can hardly claim their futile efforts towards recognition actually constitute a career.

"Good God! Has it really been that long?"

This voice he actually heard, and it wasn't coming from inside his head but from here, inside the private office. The paneled, polished claustrophobic quarters of Danton Tischler, Sr., attorney-at-law to the great, the near-great and the ingrates of Greater Los Angeles.

The voice didn't sound in the least as he remembered it. A once-hearty baritone was now a cracked, almost falsetto whisper—*probably through falsetto teeth,* Ames reflected—which one might expect from an elderly man. But then, this was an elderly man speaking; the young Danny Tischler he'd once known wasn't an occupant of Century City, because Century City didn't even exist in those days. The young Danny lived in memory as the sole resident of a bungalow-courtyard law office somewhere out along the wilds of Ventura Boulevard, where Edgar Rice Burroughs still ruled Tarzana.

Just how long ago *had* that been? Ames didn't need to ask, for the old man was already providing the answer.

"Forty years," he murmured.

Impossible. But there it was, in black and white, on

the upper left-hand corner tab of the file folder which Tischler tapped as he spoke. His fingers, Ames noted, were like breadsticks.

"That's right," Ames said. "Time flies when you're having fun."

Tischler glanced down at his breadstick fingers. "You call old age fun?"

Ames shrugged. "Perhaps it's all a matter of viewpoint. If you look at it another way, life is an ongoing obituary."

The elderly attorney managed a dry chuckle. "You should have been a philosopher instead of a writer."

"No percentage in it," Ames told him. "And I'm not just talking about money. Have you ever heard a pretty little girl say, 'When I grow up, I want to marry a philosopher'?"

"So you went in for writing instead?"

"One of the reasons, I suppose. When you're young you think that way."

"Then how come you never married?"

"Because I grew up and stopped thinking that way."

"Any regrets?"

"I'm grateful just for having survived," Ames said. "Regrets are for the others who didn't make it."

"You stayed friends over the years?"

Ames frowned. "I wish I could say that. Remember, we used to meet for lunch at that Chinese place in Sherman Oaks every week and talk shop? But then we started moving around, job to job. Before you know it you've lost touch. When I think of how close we were when all of us started out doing horror for the magazines—"

"Right." Tischler's glance strayed again to the folder before him. "That name you fellows picked—*The Skull Club.* Maybe you thought it was a gag back then, but it's sure appropriate today." He looked up abruptly. "Know something? I never expected you'd be the one."

"I'm a little surprised myself," Ames told him. "Maybe 'shocked' is a better word. At least that's how I felt last week when I read about Jesse."

"Hadn't seen him lately?"

"No reason to. And you?"

"The same." Tischler nodded. "I did send him an invite when we had the party to open the new offices here, but he didn't show up. For that matter, neither did you."

"Sorry, I was out of town."

The breadstick fingers flicked in a gesture of dismissal. "No sweat. There was such a mob scene here that night I probably wouldn't have spotted you. Everybody who wasn't out of town came running for the free Dom Perignon." Tischler paused. "Which reminds me. Better get down to business." He opened the folder and squinted at its contents. "Guess there's no point reading this again. Nobody's touched it in all those years." He reached down to pull out an oblong manila envelope, raised its flap, and extracted a small sheaf of papers. "Besides, I have these."

"What are they?"

"Copies of the death certificates. Care for a look?"

Ames shook his head quickly. "Not necessary. I know they're dead."

"Never hurts to be sure." Tischler slid the sheaf back into the envelope.

"Once a lawyer, always a lawyer," Ames said. "Do you want me to take a medical examination to prove I'm still alive?"

"A notary's statement will do." This time the attorney actually smiled. Rising, he crossed the room and pulled out the bottom drawer of an oaken filing cabinet. Ames watched him as he stooped, scrabbled, and straightened up again, gripping the straw-covered bottle.

"Here's your wine," Tischler said.

He returned to his seat behind the desk, depositing the rounded broad-based bottle in Ames' outstretched hands as he moved past.

Ames blinked. "I thought you kept this in your safe."

"I did, at first, but you're talking forty years ago." Tischler's chuckle was still dehydrated. "Every time the firm expanded we moved, but we kept running out of room. By the time we came here last fall, even a walk-in vault wouldn't hold all the sensitive material. When I ran across the wine I just stuck it in here where there was room, and I knew it'd be safe. Not that anybody would want to steal a bottle of cheap Chianti."

Ames glanced at what he was holding. "Cost us ninety-eight cents plus tax. All we could afford back then." His glance rose. "Brings up a point. What do I owe you?"

"No charge." Tischler nodded. "My pleasure."

"But you're entitled to something for storage and keeping your eye on it," Ames said. "If you hadn't volunteered, the five of us would have been stuck with safety-deposit box rental for forty years—"

"—and I would have missed the chance to tell my learned colleagues about the tontine." Again Tischler was smiling as he broke in. "Gave me something different to talk about. There aren't many lawyers around today who even know Lorenzo Tontine's name." He added a few wrinkles to his forehead. "Come to think about it, I don't believe I did until you told me. Getting a bottle of wine for the last survivor of the bunch was your idea, wasn't it?"

"I guess so. Though it was Everly who brought up a tontine to begin with. At first he was thinking along the regular line—everybody putting some money into a special account, letting the interest accumulate." Ames shrugged. "In the end, we had to settle for a fifth of Dago Red. That's what they used to call it in the old days."

"It's the sentiment that counts." Tischler nodded. "Do you plan to drink it?"

"Of course. As you say, it's the sentiment that counts."

Kevin Ames thought about sentiment as he drove home through the darkened downpour on drenched streets. It didn't rain very often in what TV weather forecasters refer to as the Southland, but who cared? Rain or shine, he had the wine. And should it prove sour, the taste would still be sweet.

Revenge is sweet.

Now there's a sentiment for you. Sentiment enough to compensate for sediment, if forty years had produced any in this bottle, this priceless bottle, more precious than the finest champagne.

Out of the corner of his left eye he caught the flicker of neon from a restaurant window, and his stomach responded with a warning growl. Perhaps he ought to stop for dinner.

He slowed down just long enough to note that in spite of rain the small parking area to one side was full, and there were no openings at the curbside nearby. All right, the lot was full and he was empty, but there'd be plenty of time to eat later. Waiting a few hours for a meal was nothing, not to a man who'd waited forty years for a drink. First things first.

Or was it last things last?

Ames was the last, Last of the Mohicans, last of his tribe—all those ignoble redskins who'd once whooped around the campfire fed by pages they'd produced for the pulps at a penny a word. When it went out they went on, following fresh trails to fresh fires sparked by the scattered sheets of paperback novels or the multicolored revisions of television scripts. The flames were fitful, but enough to keep the young braves warm.

In time more seasoned warriors could fuel their fires with hot properties, but even the blaze of glory hadn't warded off the chill forever. They were cold now, all of them, and only he knew warmth.

Warm car to heated garage, heated garage to comfortable kitchen, comfortable kitchen to dark den. Or was it a rec room?

Names kept changing. At the time Ames managed to put a down-payment on the place it was just a cheap tract-house in the boonies. Now it was a desirable residential property on a choice view lot.

Too bad he couldn't boast of equal improvement in forty years! Entering the room Ames switched on the light and its reflection bounced off the picture-window, transforming the surface into a mirror. For a moment he caught a glimpse of his reflection, and winced at the gargoyle in the glass. He drew the drapes hastily, trying to avoid looking at the backs of his hand as he did so. He hated the sight of blue veins, corded and crisscrossing like the routes on a freeway map. Next would come the liver spots.

Or would they? Nothing wrong with his liver; he'd never been much of a drinker. Until now, that is.

Now was a matter of putting the bottle down on the counter, shucking his jacket, opening the cupboard to search out a wine-glass from the bottom shelf.

Wonder of wonders, he actually found one, and after circling its inner surface his forefinger came away dust-free. He located the corkscrew next, a fancy-looking gadget at the back of the top shelf, still nestled in a gift-box and still unused. Corkscrews were metal mysteries to him.

Actually, employing it wasn't as much of a challenge as he'd anticipated. Once he fitted the twisted tip into the top of the cork and clamped the hood over the bottle's neck, he tightened the levers at both sides, pulling the cork out as they retracted. Simple as brain-surgery.

The wine poured easily, no specks of sediment surfacing as it rose to fill the glass. There was nothing you could call a bouquet—what the hell do you expect for ninety-eight cents?—but he thought he did detect a slight musky smell. Or was it merely the usual musty smell emanating from those moldering paperbacks and ancient pulp magazines lining the bookshelves row upon row?

If he'd had any sense he'd have dumped the lot years ago. They had no value to dealers or collectors, and no value to readers, either. But these tattered, battered specimens with their garish covers wrinkled like the faces of old whores held value to him. They represented the sum total of his lifework. No matter how they smelled, this was all he had to show for forty-odd years of effort.

On the lower shelves were the hardbacks—not his, but those of contemporaries and colleagues. If he was starting out again he wouldn't waste his time and talent on penny-a-word short stories and cheap paperback originals. Hardcovers were solid and substantial, made to last; the pages and their contents didn't smell. No doubt about it, this was the route he'd go.

But you can't turn back the odometer. And maybe it wouldn't matter even if he could. Let's face it, he *had* aimed for respectable publishing markets when starting out, just like his friends were doing. The difference was that they made it and he didn't.

There'd been no way of knowing where any of them would end up, no sure road-map to success. Forty years ago, high school kids didn't study genetics; they read the Declaration of Independence and graduated believing that all men are created equal. So if a half-dozen of those kids from roughly-similar backgrounds decided on a writing career, why shouldn't their chances of success be just about equal too?

Luck was a factor, of course, but at first luck seemed to be everybody's good buddy. Luck brought them together—Everly, Jesse and himself in class, the other two through mutual acquaintances. Hanging out together but working separately, they made their first sales to the same few remaining pulp magazines, their first breakthroughs into the expanding paperback markets.

Come to think of it, there'd been a sixth candidate for the Nobel Prize in Literature back then whose name he had trouble recalling today. Frank Osric, that was it. For a beginner, Frank was a pretty good candidate for a full-time career. But he'd also been a sexual athlete, world-class, who married a bimbo whose father owned a factory. So with a baby on the way, he ended up punching a time-clock instead of a typewriter.

The Skull Club members were the five who stuck together. Funny how they'd all written pretty much the same sort of stuff back then; a little science fiction, and a lot of fantasy before it split up into dark, light, or shocking pink with polka-dot stripes.

It was only later that they branched out individually into the mystery markets, spy-thrillers, police procedure product. It was after television moved from New York to Hollywood that they really broke up, as their lives split up into deals, deadlines, and rewrites over the weekends.

Kevin cupped his glass, wondering as he did so why

nobody ever spoke of glassing their cups. English is a strange language, and writers are strange people.

Or maybe he was the strange one, the way he'd tried to keep in touch with his friends during the early years of their rise to fame and fortune. And he had tried, dammit. Phoned for lunch-dates and got excuses. Then, as their success soared, he got secretaries. And finally, thanks to the miracle of modern technology, he got answering machines.

After the others scattered, leaving the Valley for more trendy territory, contact with them dwindled to Christmas cards. Eventually even the cards stopped Hallmarking the passage of years, and that's when he got the message.

It was about time because the message had been awaiting his attention for ages, delivered by a diversity of sources. It had come from New York agents who couldn't sell his books to the right publishers, it came from agents out here who couldn't peddle his spec-written scripts to television or films. And while his work continued to appear in the lesser genre zines or paperbacks, the message came from critics loud and clear, in the form of silence.

Kevin ignored it for a long time, telling himself to hang in there, do the job, have patience. So he hung, and he jobbed, and eventually the patience ran out.

Reading was what scared it away; reading articles, essays and books about the work of his colleagues. He was shocked to see the first references, perhaps a dozen years ago; shocked not so much by their content as by the realization that so much time had passed since the days they'd all started out together. His mirror had already begun to tell him the same story, and he was tempted to try shutting his eyes while shaving. But he couldn't close his eyes to the facts. Pimply punks, who didn't even exist when the Skull Club was alive and flourishing, had been born, grown up, and become critics. Critics who knew genre fiction and its writers, who even mentioned the Skull Club in passing when discussing the work of the others.

The others. That's who the critics wrote about, the others. Jesse and Everly, Rondbeck and Fargo. Everybody except Kevin Ames.

Turning away from the bookshelves, he grimaced in rueful recollection. To be fair about it, his name actually had been mentioned, several times in several places, but only in passing, one of a long list of lesser or at least less-known talents. And one creep had managed to misspell it. *Kevan Aims.* So much for critical perception.

But none of the others suffered such careless treatment. No critic had a problem identifying Roy Fargo.

Kevin paused to confront the wall beyond the shelves. That's where the pictures were, the photographs from newspapers and magazines he'd clipped and pinned to a corkboard during the past decade, just for old times' sake.

Or so he'd told himself at the start. Now, of course, he knew the truth. It had never been for old times' sake, not even at the beginning.

Roy was the beginning, the first to go up, and that in itself had been hard to take. Not that Roy Fargo was much more of a success than Kevin himself. True, he lived in Beverly Hills, but his apartment was on the very tip of the south-of-Wilshire area, and this was before the real-estate boom. Roy never made it into the megabuck neighborhood: all he wanted was a chance to move from paperback to hardcover markets. By then the major publishers were concentrating on clones of Stephen King, but small specialty houses sprang up to feed the nostalgia craze for Golden Oldies from the Golden Age. They sold mainly through mail-order, putting out signed and limited editions, including genuine leather bindings for the true collector and/or greedy speculator.

At first, established writers shied away from small advances and small printings, so specialty publishers took what they could get. One of the first they got was Roy Fargo, who soon became a familiar name amongst the literary leather-freaks. His timing was right, because pop art was becoming popular with those who took credit for turning obscurity into celebrity.

That's when critics started paying him serious attention, cannibalizing each other's articles and reviews, pumping up a new audience for an old name.

And that's when some genre-oriented zine published the photo of Fargo which, haloed by a fringe of other newsclippings, occupied the left-hand side of Kevin's corkboard display. Below it was the story headline—*ROY FARGO, MASTER OF MYSTERY, WINS WIZARD AWARD.*

Kevin squinted at the picture in the dim light. A good photo, yes, but not a good likeness. Maybe because the Fargo he'd been familiar with was a younger man.

The passage of those subsequent decades had fattened the face, thinned the hairline, wrought wrinkles and wattles. Only the set of the fish-mouth remained unchanged; Roy Fargo was the kind of man who only smiled at funerals.

Even so, that headline should have made him laugh out loud, because he'd never written a real mystery in his life. To Kevin the only mystery was why editors accepted such dated whodunit fare, such hardboiled potboilers with their dumb-dick antihero and his gat, rod, heater, equalizer or piece aimed to put a notch in somebody's crotch.

Kevin thought of what he himself had written over

the same period of time, genuine mysteries with authentic backgrounds, not just updated slang and the same old phallic fallacisms.

What right did Fargo have to steal Kevin's blood-and-thunder? If there was any justice, that should have been his prize. Both Fargo and himself had been nominated for the Best Paperback Novel award that year; it had been Kevin's first and only time. When he heard about it he'd felt a surge of encouraging excitement. The Wizard Award was prestigious; it meant something to editors who paid winners more attention, and higher advances. Ten years ago it would have given Kevin Ames a chance to snuggle under hardcovers with a major publisher.

If there were any justice.

But there was no justice, and Fargo was the one who accepted his trophy at the annual banquet, Fargo who signed a three-book hardcover contract, Fargo who was photographed.

Kevin stared at the photo and the photo stared back. That's the way they'd stared at each other ten years ago, just two months after Roy accepted his prize.

The phone rang and Kevin started at the sound, then realized there was no ring, merely an echo. An echo sounding down the corridors of time; an echo of the phone's sudden and surprising ring on that evening a decade ago. Actually the surprise had not been in the ringing but in the voice which responded when Kevin answered the call.

"Kevin, old buddy—how are you? This is Roy."

"Fargo?"

"As in North Dakota."

"Well I'll be damned!"

"Your prediction, not mine." A sort of chuckle sounded over the wire, a muffled sound which might issue from a fish-mouth. Or the mouth of someone who'd been drinking like a fish, as they used to say long years ago.

Only they didn't say it about Fargo, since he drank very little in the old days. Couldn't afford to, for one thing. But times and fortunes change, because he'd obviously had a few and he was calling from the bar at some steak-house off Melrose that Kevin never heard of before.

"What're you doing down there?" he asked.

"Tell you about it when I see you," Fargo said.

"See me?"

"That's right. They've got great steaks here. I'm inviting you to dinner."

"Now—you mean tonight?" Kevin hesitated. "But—look, I have plans for the evening—"

"Change them."

He did, and they met.

When Kevin arrived at the crowded side-street restaurant his host was already seated in a booth just off the noisy upfront bar. Recognizing Fargo came as a shock, for his photo had scarcely hinted at the ravaged reality, the flab of flesh, the face with its mottled veins broken like pledges to Alcoholics Anonymous. But the greatest change was in the fish-mouth, now set in a permanent smirk of smug satisfaction.

Coming here on impulse had been a mistake, but Kevin realized it too late for retreat; he could only sit down and lighten up.

Tonight, a decade later, he couldn't pretend to recall any of their preliminary greetings or small-talk. Drinks before and during dinner helped ease his tension, and Roy had already achieved an alcohol level which would intoxicate any vampire who drank his blood.

But the steaks were every bit as good as promised, and it was over dessert that their conversation really began. Instead of coffee, Fargo opted for a double Turkey-and-rocks. Kevin, conscious of his own limited ability to handle liquor, settled for a small cognac. Now he felt a trifle more relaxed, but it was still hard to equate this bloated and aging stranger with the Roy he'd once known, or thought he'd known, so well. *I wish I hadn't come,* he told himself.

"I'm glad you came," Fargo told him. "Been wanting to get hold of you for a long time."

"I should have called you," Kevin said. "When I heard the news—"

"About the prize?" Fargo shrugged. "No problem. Charlie Rondbeck was at the awards banquet so we talked there, but I haven't heard word one from old Jesse or Everly either. And I didn't expect to hear from you, considering."

"Considering what?"

"Considering you're the guy who should have gotten the award in the first place." Fargo raised his glass with a flourish that ruffled the Turkey's feathers. "Cheers!"

Kevin downed his drink, feeling its warmth mingle with the glow kindled by Roy's words. It was difficult to resent a man who admitted the truth. Fargo wasn't just flattering him; he must be feeling guilty about what happened, or else why would he bother inviting him to to dinner?

"Thinking about you when I was at the bar earlier," Fargo said. "How we lost touch all this time, and then the award business coming up. So I called."

Kevin found himself smiling. "You still haven't told me what you're doing down here."

"Oh, that." Fargo set his glass down, rattling the rocks. "Got myself a Volvo last week. Runs like a dream."

"Good for you," Kevin said.

"Not so good." Fargo captured his glass again in a

pudgy grip. "Yesterday some bastard put a dent in the left rear fender while I parked at the market. This afternoon I took it over to the dealer's body-shop around the corner from here. Figured straightening out the fender would be a ten-minute job, which just goes to show you how long it's been since I owned a new car. Turns out that now they replace the whole damn thing on these models. Costs you an arm and a leg because it's not covered by the warranty, but what can you do? So I told them go ahead, and wandered over here."

Kevin's inner glow had faded during Fargo's wordy account, replaced now by a rising resentment.

"So that's why you got hold of me," he said. "You need a lift home, right? Been cheaper for you just to call a cab."

Fargo shook his head. "You got it all wrong, old buddy. Shop stays open 'til nine, so the car'll be ready by now. I was just killing time."

"And wanted me to kill it with you," Kevin broke in.

"Knock it off." Fargo groped for his glass, eyed its emptiness, and signaled to the passing waiter. "Want a refill?"

"No. I'd better be going." Not only had Kevin's glow faded; what he felt now was an icy numbness, and he made no effort to keep the chill from his voice. "Seeing as you don't need me—"

"But I do need you! That's why I called." Fargo leaned forward as the waiter returned to switch the empty glass with a full one. "Told you I got to thinking. That's how I came up with the idea."

"Get to the point."

"Remember I said you should have won that award?" Fargo reduced his double to a single as he spoke. "Just knowing it was enough to put me on a guilt-trip, but I'm getting off at the next station."

"Talk sense."

"I'm talking dollars and sense, for both of us. I'm talking collaboration."

Kevin opened his mouth but Fargo gestured with his glass, intercepting interruption. "Heard about my new deal, right? Three-book contract, no options. Upfront advance is—they don't want me to say, but take my word it's a good chunk of cash. And this idea of mine will fix things so you'll get your share."

"You want to write those books with you?" Kevin said.

Fargo lowered his gaze and his voice. "I want you to write those books *for* me."

"You're drunk."

"Damn' right I am. I've been working at it ever since I signed that contract."

Unprepared for such an admission, Kevin scarcely knew how to respond. "Does your agent know about this?" he faltered.

"Yeah." Fargo nodded. "He says he's seen it before. Guy's used to being kicked around all his life, then something like this happens and he goes into shock, can't cope. Every time I think about doing these books for that kind of money, I freeze. You don't jump from the Little League into the majors, not at my age."

"Writer's block," Kevin said. "Get some help to dry out, find yourself a good shrink—"

Roy gestured with his glass again. "A shrink can't write those books for me. You can."

"But there are plenty of full-time ghost writers around. Ask your agent."

"No way! I don't want this to get out. Got to have somebody I can trust to keep their mouth shut. Somebody who'll work in my style, only better. That's you."

Sharp flattery or blunt truth? Kevin realized it didn't matter. Another question did, and he asked it.

"Okay, perhaps I could do the job. But why should I?"

"For old times' sake. Because we're friends. Because you need the money."

"I'm doing all right."

Fargo shook his head. "Cost of living's rising, but your sales aren't going up with it."

The little ball of anger that had formed in the pit of Kevin's stomach was starting to roll. He tried to halt it as he spoke. "Who told you that?"

"Never mind, I checked it out. You're hurting, old buddy." Fargo set his empty glass down. "But not to worry, help is on the way." The fish-mouth fissured in a grin. "Money talks, and all you got to do is listen. My proposition is we make a work-for-hire deal, no royalties, just a flat fee, half up front, half on delivery. And seeing as it's you, I'm willing to go ten thousand per book."

Kevin couldn't control the roll of rage so he concentrated on controlling his voice. "You've got to be getting a lot more for those books, just in advances alone. Plus the royalties to come, paperback and foreign rights, maybe even film or TV sales somewhere down the line."

Roy Fargo was having his own vocal problems. "Who knows?" He wagged a fat finger. "All you gotta know is there's thir'y grand in it for you, guar'nteed. Way you grind stuff out, shouldn't take more'n two months apiece. How long's it been since anybody paid you thirty thou for six months' work?"

"Never got that much," Kevin said. "But if I ever do, it won't be for something that has your name on it."

"Think you're too good to ghost for me?" Fargo's forefinger jabbed air. "Well, let me tell you somethin', old buddy. I don't think you're good enough! On'y reason I called is I felt sorry for you, wanna give you a break. So what thanks do I get—"

"That's enough," Kevin said. He was amazed that he could speak so calmly while feeling the ball rolling deep inside him. "Get out of my face."

"I'm gone." Roy Fargo slid out of the booth and rose askew but upright as he spoke. "I got no time to waste on you, old buddy. You're jus' a hack, always will be. Jus' a hack—"

Kevin watched him weave down the aisle; not until after his host departed did he realize Fargo had left without paying the tab.

Adding insult to injury came to a total of seventy-eight bucks for drinks, dinner, tax and tip. A sizable bite, ten years ago.

But at the time Kevin scarcely felt it. What he felt was the ball in his gut, grinding as it grew, *way you grind stuff out, just a hack, always will be.*

Somehow he paid and made his way to the exit, the ball rolling, the rage swelling, the rain falling.

Kevin blinked. There hadn't been any sign of rain when he arrived. But then there hadn't been any sign of Fargo's pretended pity or that insulting suggestion to sell out, betray his talent for thirty pieces of silver. All right, so it was thirty thousand pieces. Probably came to about ten percent of what Fargo was getting as an advance alone. He'd still end up with most of the money, and all of the glory.

Hell with it. Hell with him. Hell with this goddam rain, coming down in buckets, turning the damn' potholes into swimming pools. Dark as pitch, too; no light except the one way down at the corner. Where was his car parked? Oh yeah, down here. Next question—

where're the keys? Got 'em. Final question—how'd you get so loaded?

And loaded he was. Load in his gut. Stop rolling. Put key in ignition and start rolling. Now.

Windshield wipers working. Back and forth, to and fro. Don't look at them, dummy—look past them. Keep your eye on the road. Potholes. Water. Splashing.

There, that's better. Car revving up, stomach settling down. Forget Fargo. Forget the bastard playing him for a sucker, laughing up his sleeve all the way to the bank.

It didn't matter, didn't matter a damn. Into each life some rain must fall and that's what mattered now, rain on the windshield, headlight beams blurring across puddles in the street, flashing over the figure that staggered out from the crosswalk and slipped on the wet pavement.

Fargo fell, in what seemed like slow-motion.

Everything happened in slow-motion, except the sudden resurgence of rage. It was still there after all, but it wasn't still, it was rolling, the car was rolling, hands whirling the wheel, foot flooring the gas-pedal.

A crunch, a bump, a shriek of brakes. And then he was around the corner, gunning the motor, *don't look now, they may be gaining on you.*

But they didn't gain.

Kevin could grin because they'd never gained on him, not in ten years. If they had, of course, he'd have explained it was an accident.

At the time, in his drunken and panic-induced flight, he'd really believed this, or wanted to. Not until long afterward did he admit it was murder.

In a way it was actually premeditated murder, because he'd killed Fargo many times before, in his dreams. Of course nobody knew about the dreams, let alone the reality.

Nobody knew he and Fargo were meeting. And when they did, neither had been recognized in the crowded restaurant. They weren't seen arriving or leaving together. And there were no witnesses on the rainy street when a drunken pedestrian was struck down in the dark by some hit-and-run driver.

Kevin had committed what mystery-writers strive to achieve—the perfect crime.

How about a Wizard Award for *that*? Or at the very least, perhaps a Sorcerer's Apprentice?

He lifted his glass to the fat face framed on the wall before him, then drank deeply. Cheap wine, and bitter; not at all comparable to the cognac he'd enjoyed during that last meeting with Fargo a decade ago. And yet bitter was better, infinitely better, because it quenched his thirst. Years and years of thirst for just this moment, the moment of triumph.

Kevin gripped the lumpy neck of the straw-wrapped bottle and refilled his glass before moving on past Fargo's wall-eyed stare. Carrying the Chianti with him for convenience's sake, for old times' sake, he scanned the corkboard for a faded Polaroid print of Arthur Rondbeck in out-of-focus closeup.

This face was thin and drawn, just as he remembered it, the face of a diabetic asthmatic cancer-riddled and heart-damaged hypochondriac.

Even as a young man Rondbeck had never enjoyed good health when he could revel in illness. Here was someone who purchased pills for extra energy but lacked the strength to swallow them: a man who was too tired to lie down. And yet, Kevin noted, he was probably the most prolific member of the Skull Club group. The only problem being it seemed hard to tell if his work was the product of a word-processor or an enema.

Where had he found time to turn out a book of critical

essays on his fellow writers, and why would a publisher accept him as an authority? But a publisher *did* accept him, and his manuscript too.

Kevin squinted up at the Polaroid, trying to bring Rondbeck's bleached-out features into focus. What had that sallow face looked like seven years ago?

For the life of him he couldn't recall; apparently he lacked a photographic memory. But he did remember the letter Rondbeck sent him with a copy of the chapter on Kevin's work, a labor of love entitled *Blood Brothers.* And seven years later he still remembered that enclosure, every vicious word of it. Words like *derivative, stock characterization, predictability, over-obvious plots.* The labor of love was actually a labor of hate.

But Rondbeck hadn't sent the chapter to ask for an opinion; what he wanted was verification of biographical data dealing with Kevin's career which preceded the pages that demolished it.

His letter had arrived on a bad day. Kevin's immediate impulse was to pick up the phone and, for the first time in many years, communicate with his old friend—communicate his anger at this unprovoked and unwarranted attack. But as luck would have it, the phone was disconnected and would remain so until he paid his long-overdue bill. And that wasn't about to happen until Kevin finished the novelization, also overdue, of the sleazo film-script he'd been stuck with.

His second impulse, to write Rondbeck a letter of rebuttal concerning his errors of judgment as well as fact, was equally impractical, because that very morning his typewriter had conked out. Another three days and God knows how many dollars shot to hell, no wonder he had one of those pounding headaches, now on top of everything else this letter arriving to make his day—

There was only one thing to do; drive out to West LA

and confront Rondbeck face to face. Tell him that under no circumstances would he allow such an attack to be published. With this kind of garbage spread around, pretty soon Kevin wouldn't even get assignments to novelize bad movies, let alone contracts for books of his own.

Driving west, Kevin's anger mounted as the sun sank, its slanted rays blinding him as he crawled through the homeward-bound traffic.

Blinding. But he could see Rondbeck plainly enough, standing in the abandoned hallway after he opened the front door of the old two-story house just north of Pico.

See but not hear, because of the pounding in his head. *Pounding headache.* Didn't have to hear, because just the sight of that stupid face and sickly grin told him all he needed to know, more than he needed to know about Rondbeck's motives, about his deliberate attempt to smear his name, his reputation, his whole damned life-work. Kevin told himself not to listen, and he didn't listen, but all the while Rondbeck kept on talking, talking as he led the way up the stairs and into his workroom. Here was the printer fed by the word-processor, here was the word-processor fed by the stupid, grinning character-assassin who couldn't stop talking because he was afraid.

Yes, that was it, Kevin could see it now; the fear behind the grin, the apprehension in the eyes, the alarm. There must have been something in his own face, his own silence, which triggered the alarm to go off and sent Rondbeck into a flurry of excuses, explanations, apologies.

And without needing or heeding the actual words, Kevin knew what Arthur Rondbeck was saying and why. He'd turned off deliberately because he didn't want to get the message, there was only one way to deal with the headache, get rid of it, stop the pounding, and now that his mind was made up there was no point getting confused by apologies.

There'd been enough confusion anyway, and Kevin had to make a deliberate effort to keep calm. Cool, calm and collected. Don't do whatever you did with your face to scare Rondbeck that way, keep your voice down, just tell the man it was all a mistake, your turn to apologize, let bygones be bygones, we'll both forget it ever happened, sorry but I've a pounding headache, got to go now.

Go to the hall. Go to the landing. Let Rondbeck lead the way. And over the pounding, when push comes to shove—

The crash.

The crash as the railing gave way, the sudden gasp, the rush of air, the thud.

Sprawled at the foot of the stairs far below, neck twisted to an impossible angle, lay the figure. The body. The corpse.

That's all it was now, just a cold, contorted thing, its head stamped with a bloody caricature of Arthur Rondbeck's face. The grin was gone. And so was the grinner.

Kevin was gone too, as soon as he'd run his handkerchief over the inner and outer doorknobs and made sure the front door itself was locked behind him.

He looked around for his car and couldn't see it. For a moment he froze, then relaxed, realizing he'd parked around the corner.

It wasn't until he was almost home that he realized something else. There'd been no reason for him to park where he did. No conscious reason, because he'd been hiding it behind the headache. Behind the headache was the rage and behind the rage was the reality. He'd gone to Rondbeck intending to kill him from the very first.

Another premeditated murder? But how could that be? He hadn't planned anything in detail, any more than he'd planned the death of Roy Fargo. Murder involved a risk that should only be taken when fully warranted, when utterly necessary to eliminate a threat or an enemy.

Or a rival?

Kevin saluted Rondbeck's photo-face with a full glass, then remedied its emptiness before moving on.

Seven years ago he'd confronted the *rationale* of his behavior. Or misbehavior; it didn't matter which. What mattered was that Fargo and Rondbeck were dead. Just as he wanted them to be, just as he wanted all of them to be, because they were the ones who drank the wine of life and left him the dregs, but he'd have the last laugh, the last laugh after they'd drawn their last breaths.

And they would, all of them. Once he'd made that resolve he was willing to wait. And wait he did, without fear of suspicion; two of his four rivals were in their graves and neither had risen to point a bony finger at him.

Rondbeck's death, recorded as accidental, was scarcely incidental, and merited only brief mention in fine print. But both Lloyd Everly and Jesse Cross had been the subjects of occasional interviews. In recalling their early careers, each made a passing reference to the Skull Club. Just a few words of nostalgia, yet one never knew; if a third and a fourth member met accidental death in the near future, somebody checking old news articles for an obit could note the tie-in, perhaps even get curious about the survivors.

So best to wait, Kevin had decided. There was no personal reason to resent those two as he had the others; it was only their success he hated.

Only their success, and his failure. Neither had been deserved, but then everything's a matter of luck, and if you want justice you have to go after it yourself. Even if it means waiting five more years.

That's how long Kevin waited before he paid his visit to Lloyd Everly. Five long years of reading and hearing about Everly's latest novels and movie sales, with no consolation for Kevin except the knowledge that time was on his side. Everly's appearances on television talk-shows revealed a steadily-receding hairline and a steadily-advancing network of wrinkles. If Kevin's tentative plans worked out, death from natural causes would be a logical verdict. And he'd no longer have to put up with the sight of that aging have-a-good-day face on the TV screen. It was bad enough seeing the autographed photo on the corkboard with a *printed* signature if you please, or even if you don't please.

Kevin hadn't requested anything at all; the glossy 8 × 10 showed up unannounced and uninvited in the day's mail. That's what did it—the photo and the accompanying message.

Compadre:

Long time no, sí*?*

Thought you might like this. Why don't we get together one of these days and compare swimming-pools?

—Lloyd.

Yes, that's what did it, all right. Only a jerk like Everly would come up with a smart-ass way to point out he had a pool and Kevin didn't, never would. But unwittingly he'd pointed out something else: the method for murder.

Discarding his earlier plan, Kevin made his move. This time he prepared in advance. Three days beforehand he cased the dead-end street in the pricey neighborhood abutting Bel Air. A block away from the house was an ideal place to park without being seen by traffic, because there wasn't any. His next move required immobility, sitting in the car for two full days to learn the comings and goings of local residents, their gardeners or other hired help. He noted no nannies or other live-ins; Everly himself was a widower who'd lived alone here since his wife died, so that didn't complicate matters. Some of his neighbors employed maids or cleaning-ladies, but they all cut out sometime between four and five, when the wives came home from Rodeo Drive. It wasn't until six or later that the husbands drove in from Century City and the Cedars-Sinai Medical Complex.

Obviously the safest interval would be from five to six. He mustn't call about stopping by until just before driving up; that way left less chance of Everly mentioning his impending visit to anyone else. The rest was obvious. Wear washable jeans and jacket, and don't forget the rubber gloves.

Kevin chuckled as he thought back on it now. Old Haji never wore rubber gloves, but that's what he was doing—playing Haji. Just the way Otis Skinner and Ronald Colman played him in those ancient movies, just the way Alfred Drake did in the old musical they'd made out of *Kismet.*

Funny that he'd remembered their big scene, and now he got the chance to do it himself. Grabbing the villain and silently submerging his head in the pool until he drowned, then pushing the body in. So simple, once Everly let him in and they had a quiet poolside drink together. Whisky straight, that's what Lloyd Everly wanted, but he ended up with water for a chaser. Lots and lots of water.

Remembering it, Kevin almost choked on his drink.

The way Everly had choked, but it wasn't all that funny to him. *Kismet* means fate in Arabic, doesn't it? Well he met his fate all right. And it was all right, no problems except to carry away the second glass so as to leave no evidence of a visitor when the pool-man came by two days later and found his employer drowned.

So Everly had been liquidated. Clever phrase, clever method, clever man; Kevin felt a surge of self-apprecia-tion, or was it just the wine?

But no, he wouldn't be here drinking the wine if he hadn't been the cleverest of the lot. Fargo, Rondbeck, Everly—all so-called mystery writers, but none of them could come up with complex plots and simple solutions. All they'd done in their careers was to go with the flow—the flow of blood, the rising red tide of—

Why the lecture? This was supposed to be a celebra-tion. "God bless," Kevin said, gesturing toward Everly's photo with his empty glass and refilling it from the half-empty bottle. Half-empty? No wonder he had this warm feeling, felt good all over.

That's how he'd felt after Everly was deep-sixed two years ago, because it was almost all over. Only one other survivor to deal with, down and dirty, just slip him the Ace of Spades.

Kevin had waited so long with the others, so pa-tiently, but these past two years had been real torture. Or imaginary torture, because he was always thinking about what he'd do when he finally got his shot at Jesse George.

It wouldn't be an actual shot, of course; nothing that obvious. Or that quick. Timing was everything. Perhaps he could use a variation of the method he'd worked out for Everly before the pool idea came to him. But what-ever he decided on, he'd have to cool it before he cooled Jesse. And there were problems.

One of the problems was a young wife Jesse had recently acquired, some little bimbo with naturally-stringy hair and the usual wifely problem of her own—there wasn't any room in her clothes-closet and she didn't have a thing to wear. Kevin picked up these fascinating tidbits from gossip columns in literary journals sold at supermarket checkout counters.

True or false, the setup made for complications, but Kevin knew simplicity was still his best bet. Only it couldn't be a bet, couldn't be a gamble; he needed a sure thing. Which was why waiting became torment as he tried figuring how to mark the cards, load the dice, rig the game.

Up to now Jesse looked like the winner. He'd always been the biggest winner of the whole gang, and during the past two years his success seemed incredible as he made the complete career-leap, from the Skull Club to the Book-of-the-Month Club. The novel following stayed on the chart for nineteen weeks, then sold to films on a deal that included a percentage of the gross.

Halting before the fourth picture, Kevin peered at it with narrowed eyes. Hard to make out because it wasn't even a photograph, just a caricature from some article in a magazine he'd stolen from his dentist's reception-room. Over the years Kevin hadn't found any photos; old Jesse was either camera-shy or just plain cautious. It might be both, because he didn't do TV or book-signings or any personal appearance shots. His success had come without any Wizard Awards, critical acclaim or paid publicity. In spite of the news items about his career, he shunned the spotlight.

Maybe it was smart to play it that way, living somewhere in the mountains up near Santa Barbara and avoiding the Hollywood scene. Safer too, because Kevin had all this trouble finding a way to kill him.

And when he finally did—or thought he did—old Jesse outfoxed him again. Just like that, no warning, he dropped dead. Keeled over from a heart attack right there in his own home, only a week ago.

"Party-pooper!"

Kevin lifted his glass with a frown of annoyance. He'd really been looking forward to taking care of Jesse himself, closing the books on his Book-of-the-Month, outgrossing that gross-out film.

He hadn't read the book or seen the movie, but it didn't matter. What mattered was that others did, thousands of readers, millions of filmgoers. Jesse George got fame and acclaim, and though he never sought celebrity, hundreds of mourners were at his graveside.

If Kevin ever had a funeral, it would be attended by a crowd estimated at nearly twelve people. Which wasn't fair, seeing as how the others, except for Jesse, wouldn't even have had funerals if it weren't for his efforts. Efforts which were, as usual, unappreciated and anonymous. Story of his life.

Kevin squinted at the caricature on the corkboard and the caricature squinted back. Ugly artwork. Now that all four of the other Skull Club members were gone he could take their pictures down, tear them up. Too bad he never got a chance to tear up the real Jesse. It would have been great, seeing him die, feeling the surge of adrenaline, the taste of triumph on the tongue.

That was the secret, wasn't it? All these years, this lifetime, writing about psychopaths and never knowing why they did what they did or what they actually got out of their efforts. But he knew now.

He knew the greatest moment was when the anger or envy that drove you to the deed disappeared in the doing. All those inhibiting emotions vanished; there was no fear, no shame, no guilt, no empathy for anyone or any thing. To inflict rather than endure—that was the real victory. Which was more than Roy Fargo, Arthur Rondbeck, Lloyd Everly and Jesse George would ever learn. They'd lost, he'd won. Let them keep their fame, he had the game.

Damn betcha, he'd won. That's why he was here now. And here he'd stay. Maybe get rid of Tischler next, just in case that legal mind of his started working overtime. No law said he had to stop with the lawyer, either. He could go on to anyone he liked. Or disliked. Truth is, each time had been easier, kept getting better and better, and—admit it—now he *wanted* to go on.

In vino veritas. Damn betcha.

Nodding, Kevin raised his hand again and the wine sloshed in the glass. "Easy does it," he said, suppressing a belch. Little too much of that *vino veritas.* But who had a better right? Not this imitation Rogues' Gallery on the wall, these phonies pretending they understood what they wrote about. All they ever did was write. He was the only one who *lived* it.

"So this time, here's to me," he told himself. And gulped.

The drink really hit him. Sledgehammer wrapped in cottonwool. Better lay off, too much booze.

Kevin tightened his grip on the bottle in its straw wrapper, its straw cradle. Like Jesus. Little Lord Jesus in the cradle on Holy Night, when the Wise Men came.

But he was the wisest, not those fools on the wall. Hot in here. And hard to hang on to the wine. Why did they always wrap Chianti in straw? And why was the straw creased on one side?

Wait a minute. There was something stuck underneath there, wedged down, only the edge of the corner showing. See if you can grab hold and pull it out. Careful, don't tear it.

Kevin tugged and freed a sheet of blue paper; it was folded over, just thick enough to make a slight bulge under the straw. Did somebody put it there on purpose, to be found?

A letter, that's what it was. Goddam handwritten letter. Hard to see in this light, hard to make out the words. But the salutation, whatever they call it, was his name.

Dear Kevin:

Just a line to congratulate you. Because it is you, right?

When Fargo died I wondered a little, but accidents happen. And when Rondbeck fell victim to another accident I began to wonder more. Nothing to go on, just a hunch, but if there was anything at all to my crazy idea, the logical suspect was Lloyd Everly.

Then Everly became the third accidental death, and I knew. Knew what you were doing, knew what you were after.

Kevin blinked, trying to clear his vision, clear his thoughts. Jesse was the letter-writer. But what was he trying to do, prove how smart he was? Much good it did—he was dead like the others, and dead is dumb.

Kevin peered down again, peered at squiggly lines on crumpled paper.

I knew I'd be next, so I'm getting out of town, going where you won't be likely to find me. But if something goes wrong, chances are you'll be reading this and gloating over winning. I can understand, because the two of us are basically very much alike. And as they say, it takes one to know one.

Again, heartiest congratulations,

Jesse

Yes, it really said that. *Heartiest congratulations!* Kevin had to laugh, laughed so hard he couldn't stop, laughed until his sides hurt. Sides and stomach and chest. The room started to spin and he slid down the side of the wall, clenching his fists. Through blurring eyes he saw that he'd dropped the letter as he fell, turning the page over to expose what was written on the other side. Through shimmering waves of pain he read the final words.

P.S.:
Sorry you missed old Tischler's party. I went, but he didn't notice me in that mob-scene. It was easy to sneak into his private office without being seen. After all, it only took a few minutes—just long enough to find the bottle, pull the cork, and poison the wine.

The Lesson

Billie Sue Mosiman

Jodie was a boy who knew the stakes and how to win the game. He thought himself invincible, that nothing could ever stop him.

He knew the house and the old couple well before he ever approached the rusty screen door. He knew their routines, their meal and bed times. He knew the old man favored Red Man tobacco and the old woman Brewton snuff. He knew the endearments they used in place of each other's names. He knew they missed their grandchildren who had moved to California.

He knew enough to manipulate them the way he wished.

He tapped on the frame of the door and waited with the appropriate waifish, lost look on his small grubby face.

It was the old woman who came to answer the knock. He stepped back to allow her room to push open the screen. "Now who do we have here?" she asked pleasantly.

He did not like the bitter, snuffy smell of her, but that did not show on his face. He grinned winningly and glanced down at his feet as if in embarrassment. "I'm Jodie Weavers," he said.

"Well, hello, Jodie Weavers. Are you lost?"

He knew she would ask that. He shook his head so that his long sandy bangs flipped around his high forehead. "Just traveling through, ma'am. I was wondering if I could do some chores for you, maybe spend the night . . ."

"Traveling through!" The old woman turned in the shadowy doorway and called to her husband. " 'Miah! There's a boy here."

Jodie waited. Shuffled his feet in a way that indicated he was somewhat afraid of coming harsh judgment. The old woman pulled him to her side, and he found his right cheek smothered against her big, floppy old woman's breast. He fought the urge to jerk away. He held his breath and counted to ten.

Jeremiah Davis came through the cool interior shadows of the hallway. "What's this?" he asked.

"This boy says he's traveling through. Wants to stay the night. Doesn't that beat all? It's children on the roads this year."

This year was 1930. Surely they had seen children come by the old farmhouse before, Jodie thought. The old woman was pretending to be shocked for his benefit.

"Then bring him inside," Jeremiah said. "Here, boy, let me take your bag." He reached for Jodie's dirty torn-sheet baggage, but Jodie pulled it back before the old man's gnarled hand could touch it.

"No, that's okay, it's not heavy. Just a couple changes of clothes I got."

The old woman ushered him indoors and guided him down the hall behind Jeremiah to a back room that Jodie knew would be the big open aromatic kitchen. His mouth salivated so much he had to swallow twice. He hadn't eaten for hours and hours.

"It's a shame about children put out on their own. You can't be . . . more'n ten!" The old woman scrutinized his thin arms and legs. She brushed the unkempt bangs from his forehead.

Motherly. He let her touch him though he wondered briefly if he was going to be able to stand all this pawing. Well, he'd just have to. To get what he wanted, he always had to play the silly games. Pretend he was a little innocent boy beset by hunger (he was), a poor child in need of care (he was not).

"I'm nearly eleven," he said quietly. And shuffled his feet again, licked his lips while glancing at the plate of biscuits on the wide bleached oak table.

"Here, sit down, let me feed you. Bet you haven't had a square meal in days."

"No ma'am, I ain't eaten regular in some time."

Jeremiah took a chair and offered one to the boy. "Where you hail from? I don't recognize you from 'round here."

"I'm from Kentucky." Jodie pulled the tin plate the old woman set before him closer to his chest. He watched her pour a stream of golden maple sugar syrup into it. Syrup! He hadn't had sweets in ever so long. It might be all right here for more than a day or two. If only *she* didn't smell like old spit and *he* didn't ask too many questions.

"Why look at him eat, 'Miah. Makes my heart squeeze shut to see children hungry in this country. It just ain't right, going to bed without a bite to eat."

"Kentucky?" Jeremiah asked. "That's a far piece for a boy your age to come from. Where's your folks? They still up there?"

"Dead. Died."

The old woman clutched the material of her flour-sack dress at the neckline. "Oh, that's just awful," she said. " 'Miah, ain't that just awful? An orphan he is, poor little thing."

"Terrible," Jeremiah agreed. "How'd it happen?"

Questions. Couldn't even let him eat, so many questions. Damn ole rednecks. "Milk fever," he mumbled, mouth full. He swallowed noisily. "I don't drink milk. I didn't get sick."

The old couple exchanged sad looks. "You poor thing," the old woman said. "All alone in the cold world."

Jodie endured the rest of the afternoon during which the old woman prattled her pity and the old man went to work filling a galvanized tub with water heated on the wood cook stove for his bath.

That night bathed, fed, dressed in a pair of Jeremiah's overly large cotton longjohns, Jodie sat at the window of the bedroom he had been given and looked out at the rising moon. He hated Louisiana. It was the end of the earth in his opinion. Too flat down here and too swampy and too Suffering Jesus sultry hot even at night.

He'd have to finish off the old couple in a few days. He needed to leave this state and head west to Texas. He had heard East Texas was a lot like Kentucky. Hilly, forested, cool. And there he'd find more old people, that's for sure. In this day of families breaking apart, moving on to find work, the elderly were left behind to hold down the homesteads. Easy pickings. Unsuspecting, eager to help out a young boy on his own. In the cold world . . . the cold, cold, world.

They thought they were adopting him. He let them think it and played to their lonely passions. He even wangled a new set of overalls from the country store ten miles distant and the old woman took a scissors to his hair.

While Jodie made himself useful—hauling water, fetching wood, rising early to start the stove fire—he found time to scout the old couple's bedroom when they were otherwise occupied. He found a real gold pocket watch Jeremiah had received on retirement from the railroad. He found an opal and pearl brooch the old lady told him she wore on her wedding day oh so long ago. He also found the hoard. They always hoarded, these backwoods types. It was never a fortune, but plenty enough to get him to where he wanted to go. Six silver dollars and assorted change. Plenty.

Full as a hound tick, rested from his travels, Jodie prepared to move on. He had the stolen treasures securely tied in his sheet satchel. The old woman had cooked a yard turkey and made a pile of cornbread dressing. This ensured he would have food for the trip.

He had used a butcher knife on his parents. But he liked variety. He thought he needed practice with different weapons in order to be ready for anything. Some of the old folks he'd run up against were tough as rawhide. The last old geezer, a widower and a mean, hateful, suspicious viper at that, took the shotgun right out of his hands, and him with a hole big enough to wade through gaping and dripping from his belly. You just couldn't depend on things going right. If Jodie had learned anything, that was it. Things could mess up in a hurry and you had to think quick to save your skin. He'd had to club the widower across the head with a stick of pine kindling. Messy business.

"My, but you're looking better," the old woman crooned the morning of her death. She tousled his hair. He winced and drew back.

"What's wrong?" she asked. "Didn't you sleep good?"

Dumb old biddy. What did sleeping well have to do with disliking her touch? Oh, the old could be so stupid. Jumped to conclusions. But if they didn't, he'd never have been able to cross the country and be sure of safe havens and traveling money along the way. Yet he was losing patience with all these unexpected caresses. It put the chill on his back and made him shiver down near the bone. Just because he was small, did that give them permission to constantly maul him? What would they do if he grabbed them and hugged them in a bear hug, wouldn't let them go? Bet they wouldn't like it. Nosirree.

"It's nothing," he said. "Can I have eggs for breakfast?" She usually served up gummy oatmeal. Their chickens had not been producing much since they had to cut back on buying laying mash.

"Sure you can," she said. "You want them fried or scrambled?"

"Scrambled," he said. When her back was turned he pulled the scythe he'd hidden behind the kitchen wood pile and struck her a killing blow.

Jodie knew how to put power behind his skinny arms. One day he figured he'd have muscles, he thought, standing over the prone woman. Huge, ripplings forearms strong enough to wield a bale of hay on his own. Or a wood axe. One or the other.

She sighed where she lay upon the cracked linoleum floor. Her eyelids fluttered at him. Her wrinkled lips tried to form words, but all that came from them was a brown Brewton snuff spittle to mix with the pooling blood. What a disgusting sight she was. How he wanted to stomp in her face right there, wipe that look off forever.

Jodie watched the life fade from her watery blue eyes before he went to the stove and removed the black iron skillet from the burner. Didn't want to start a fire. Not just yet.

He ate a biscuit stuffed with sausage on the way to the barn where Jeremiah sat upon a turned over bucket milking the cow.

"Hey there," Jeremiah called. "Come to learn how to milk? I can teach you if you want. Only take a few minutes."

A chaw of Red Man bulged his cheek and made his speech slurred.

"I just come to watch," Jodie said.

"Had your breakfast?"

"Have now." Jodie raised what was left of the sausage biscuit to show the old man.

He checked the milk bucket and saw the milking was almost done, the foamy white liquid more than halfway filling the container. The cow snorted, flicked her snake-like tail at flies.

Through the open barn doors buttery yellow morning light spilled onto the hay-strewn earth. Soon it would be so hot outdoors the ground would crack like peanut brittle and the cow, let out to graze, would instead slump down in the shade of a chinaberry tree and chew her cud. Hades couldn't hope for worse temperatures come summer noon in Louisiana.

"How do you like it here?" Jeremiah asked, squinting back over his shoulder at the quietly-standing boy. "You happy with us?"

He senses something wrong, Jodie concluded. He's asking his questions again. Nosy bastard. Be glad to be rid of *him*.

"Aw, I like it all right." He moved toward the stacked hay in the corner in an aimless, just-messing-around way. The pitchfork was speared into a bale, its blond handle worn smooth and dark from a thousand sweaty palmings.

He jerked the pitchfork free and hefted it in his hand

like someone ready to throw it a few yards to see if it would stick in the dry ground. Just aimless play. That's what the old geezer would think he was doing. Boys fooled around. You couldn't stop boys from being boys, all the old people knew that.

"Say your folks died of the milk fever?"

"Uh huh. Got real sick. Doctor couldn't help."

"And you didn't have any brothers or sisters, huh?" Jeremiah paused and flexed his fingers before tackling the heifer's teats again. He had paid no attention to the boy's play with the pitchfork.

"Nope. Was just me."

"And you never liked to drink milk, did you?"

The pinging of streams of milk hitting the side of the bucket was the only sound in the barn.

"Never did like milk." Jodie moved across the barn floor silent as a wraith. He now stood near enough Jeremiah to stab him in the back, but he hesitated bringing the pitchfork up into the air above his shoulder. He wanted to hear these particular questions. Something about the direction they were taking intrigued him ungodly. Just what was it the old man was getting at?

"Must have changed your mind. About milk, that is," Jeremiah said, rising from his sitting position, wiping his hands on his denims. He turned to stare sternly at Jodie, his gaze taking in the pitchfork before going back to the boy's sturdy, emotionless face.

"Why's that?"

" 'Cause I been noticing the milk jug's always half empty every morning. Now that must mean you been snitching a couple glasses every night unless we got rats and they've taken a liking to milk I ain't never heard of before."

Jeremiah stepped closer to the boy. He was scowling.

He spit tobacco juice to the side, but his stony gaze never left Jodie.

"I don't reckon you hate milk all that much. I don't reckon you *ever* hated milk, by my lights. I don't even reckon your folks up and died of the milk fever like you said."

"Did too." Damn him to hell! He knew he should have stayed out of the kitchen at nights, but days on the road made him take risks when it came to food. He never seemed to get enough. And he couldn't drink milk in front of them, not after the lies he'd told.

Jeremiah shook his great gray shaggy head. "I don't think so, boy. I think maybe there's another story you got to tell, now ain't that right? One that might not be good to hear. Ain't that right?" He spit again and moved even closer.

Jodie could not throw the pitchfork now. He hadn't the room to maneuver. It was all going bad, going sour and deadly as pork on a blistering day.

Suddenly Jeremiah clamped his big hand around the handle of the pitchfork and took it from Jodie. "Let's go inside and let's talk about where you come from, Jodie Weavers. And where you're going."

As Jodie walked ahead of the sharp tines of the pitchfork poking him in his bony young back, he wondered how in the world it had all come tumbling down this way. He wondered why he'd thought this old farmer stupid. He wondered if he'd ever make it to East Texas.

Somehow he thought not, at least in the foreseeable future. Unlike the widower, Jeremiah, upon seeing his dead wife, would not be disposed to let her killer make even the slightest move.

Sweet suffering Jesus. Going to prison down south in Louisiana had to be just about the worst fate Jodie might ever have envisioned.

It was so hot here. Swampy. Flat.

Some of the people were too smart to die when the time came. He never should have hesitated in the barn. He'd let his curiosity get the best of his good sense.

He ever got free, he'd remember that. Next time—and there'd be one since he was just a little kid. They couldn't keep him locked up forever. And next time . . . next time he'd take them out first opportunity presented itself. He had learned his lesson.

No hesitation. No mercy.

By the time the sheriff arrived Jodie was calm and wearing his most contrite face. He was almost looking forward to the coming punishment.

At the door when the law had him by the neck collar to lead him to the car, Jodie turned and grabbed Jeremiah's old shaking hand. "Thank you, sir. Thank you so much for your hospitality."

The last thing he saw was the old man rubbing the palm of his hand along his overalls as if he'd just stuck his hand into a pile of horse manure.

The sheriff said, "Don't you be laughing, boy. You in a peck of trouble."

Jodie held in the laughter until it felt like a balloon was blowing up his chest. When he let it out as weeping and the sheriff turned in his seat to look over at him, he thought he saw a ghost of sympathy cross the swarthy country face.

The balloon deflated, the tears stopped, and all the way to town Jodi ingratiated himself to his captor.

Every day he was learning more of the fine points of winning the game.

Nothing was ever going to stop him.

Fee Fie Foe Fum

Ray Bradbury

The postman came melting along the sidewalk in the hot summer sun, his nose dripping, his fingers wet on his full leather pouch. "Let's see. Next house is Barton's. Three letters. One for Thomas Q., one for his wife, Liddy, and one for old Grandma. Is *she* still alive? How they *do* hang on."

He slid the letters in the box and froze.

A lion roared.

He stepped back, eyes wide.

The screen door sang open on its taut spring. "Morning, Ralph."

"Morning, Mrs. Barton. Just heard your pet lion."

"What?"

"Lion. In your kitchen."

She listened. "Oh, *that?* Our Garburator. You know: garbage disposal unit."

"Your husband buy it?"

"Right. You men and your machines. That thing'll eat anything, bones and all."

"Careful. It might eat you."

"No. I'm a lion-tamer." She laughed, and listened. "Hey, it *does* sound like a lion."

"A hungry one. Well, so long."

He drifted off into the hot morning.

Liddy ran upstairs with the letters.

"Grandma?" She tapped on a door. "Letter for you."

The door was silent.

"Grandma? You in there?"

After a long pause, a dry-wicker voice replied, "Yep."

"What're you doing?"

"Ask me no questions, I'll tell you no lies," chanted the old one, hidden away.

"You've been in there all morning."

"I might be here all year," snapped Grandma.

Liddy tried the knob. "You've locked the door."

"Well, so I *have!*"

"You coming down to lunch, Grandma?"

"Nope. Nor supper. I won't come down till you throw that damned machine out of the kitchen." Her flinty eye jittered in the keyhole, staring out at her granddaughter.

"You mean the Garburator?" Liddy smiled.

"I heard the postman. He's right. I won't have a lion in *my* house! *Listen!* There's your husband now, *using* it."

Downstairs, the Garburator roared, swallowing garbage, bones and all.

"Liddy!" Her husband called. "Liddy, come on down. See it work!"

Liddy spoke to Grandma's keyhole. "Don't you want to watch, Grandma?"

"Nope!"

Footsteps arose behind Liddy. Turning, she found Tom on the top stairs. "Go down and try, Liddy. I got some extra bones from the butcher. It really *chews* them."

She descended toward the kitchen. "It's grisly, but heck, why not?"

Thomas Barton stood neat and alone at Grandma's door and waited a full minute, motionless, a prim smile on his lips. He knocked softly, delicately. "Grandma?" he whispered. No reply. He patted the knob tenderly. "I know you're there, you old ruin. Grandma, you *hear?* Down below. You *hear?* How come your door's locked? Something wrong? What could bother you on such a nice summer day?"

Silence. He moved into the bathroom.

The hall stood empty. From the bath came sounds of water running. Then, Thomas Barton's voice, full and resonant in the tiled room, sang:

> Fee fie foe fum,
> I smell the blood of an Englishmum;
> Be she alive or be she dead,
> I'll *gurrrrr-innnnnd* her bones, to make my bread!

In the kitchen, the lion roared.

Grandma smelled like attic furniture, smelled like dust, smelled like a lemon, and resembled a withered flower. Her firm jaw sagged and her pale gold eyes were flinty bright as she sat in her chair like a hatchet, cleaving the hot noon air, rocking.

She heard Thomas Barton's song.

Her heart grew an ice crystal.

She had heard her grandson-in-law rip open the crate, this morning, like a child with an evil Christmas toy. The fierce cracklings and tearings, the cry of triumph, the eager fumbling of his hands over the toothy machine. He had caught Grandma's yellow eagle eye in the hall entry and given her a mighty wink. Bang! She had run to slam her door!

Grandma shivered in her room all day.

Liddy knocked again, concerning lunch, but was scolded away.

Through the simmering afternoon, the Garburator lived gloriously in the kitchen sink. It fed, it ate, it made grinding, smacking noises with its hungry mouth and vicious hidden teeth. It whirled, it groaned. It ate pigs'-knuckles, coffee-grounds, eggshells, drumsticks. It was an ancient hunger which, unfed, waited, crouched, metal entrail upon metal entrail, little flailing propellors of razor-screw all bright with lust.

Liddy carried supper up on a tray.

"Slide it under the door," shouted Grandma.

"Heavens!" said Liddy. "Open the door long enough for me to poke it in at you."

"Look over your shoulder; anyone *lurking* in the hall?"

"No."

"So!" The door flew wide. Half the corn was spilled being yanked in. She gave Liddy a shove and slammed the door. "That was close!" she cried, holding the rabbit-run in her bosom.

"Grandma, what's got *into* you?"

Grandma watched the knob twist. "No use telling, you wouldn't believe, child. Out of the goodness of my heart I moved you in here a year ago. Tom and I always spit at each other. Now he wants me gone, but he won't get *me,* no sir! I know his trick. One day you'll come from the store and I'll be nowhere. You'll ask Tom: what happened to old Grandma? Sweet-smiling, he'll say: Grandma? Just now decided to hike to Illinois! Just packed and *left!* And you won't see Grandma again, Liddy, you know why, you got an inkling?"

"Grandma, that's gibberish. Tom *loves* you!"

"Loves my house, my antiques, my mattress-money,

that's what he loves dearly! Get away, I'll work this out myself! I'm locked in here till hell burns out."

"What about your canary, Grandma?"

"*You* feed Singing Sam! Buy hamburger for Spottie, he's a happy dog, I can't let him starve. Bring Kitten up on occasion, I can't live without cats. Now, shoo! I'm climbing in bed."

Grandma put herself to bed like a corpse preparing its own coffin. She folded her yellow wax fingers on her ruffly bosom, as her moth-like eyelids winced shut. What to do? What weapon to use against that clock-work mechanic? Liddy? But Liddy was fresh as new-baked bread; her rosy face was excited only by cinnamon buns and raised muffins, she smelled of yeast and warm milk. The only murder Liddy might consider was one where the victim ended on the dinner platter, orange sucked in mouth, cloves in pink hide, silent under the knife. No, you couldn't tell wild truths to Liddy, she'd only laugh and bake another cake.

Grandma sighed a lost sigh.

The small vein in her chicken neck stopped throbbing. Only the fragile bellows of her tiny lungs moved in the room, like the ghost of an apprehension, whispering.

Below, in its bright chromed cage, the lion slept.

A week passed.

Only "heading for the bathroom" ran Grandma out of hiding. When Thomas Barton throttled his car she panicked from her bedroom. Her bathroom visits were frantic and explosive. She fell back in bed a few minutes later. Some mornings, Thomas delayed going to his office, purposely, and stood, erect as a numeral one, mathematically clean, working on her door with his eyes, smiling at this delay.

Once in the middle of a summer night, she sneaked

down and fed the "lion" a bag of nuts and bolts. She trusted Liddy to turn on the beast at dawn and choke it to death. She lay in bed early, hearing the first stirs and yawns of the two arising people, waiting for the sound of the lion shrieking, choked by bolt, washer and screw, dying of indigestible parts.

She heard Thomas walk downstairs.

Half an hour later his voice said, "Here's a present for you, Grandma. My lion says: no thanks."

Peeking out, later, she found the nuts and bolts laid in a neat row on her sill.

On the morning of the twelfth day of imprisonment, Grandma dialed her bedroom phone:

"Hello, Tom, that *you?* You at *work,* Tom?"

"This is my office number, *why?"*

"True." She hung up and tiptoed down the hall stairs into the parlor.

Liddy looked up, shocked. "Grandma!"

"Who else?" snapped the old one. "Tom here?"

"You *know* he's working."

"Yes, yes!" Grandma stared unblinkingly about, gumming her porcelain teeth. "Just phoned him. Takes ten minutes for him to drive home, don't it?"

"Sometimes half an hour."

"Good." Grandma mourned. "Can't stand my room. Just had to come down, see you, set awhile, breathe." She pulled a tiny gold watch from her bosom. "In ten minutes, back up I go. I'll phone Tom, then, to see if he's still at work. I might come down again, if he is." She opened the front door and called out into the fresh summer day. "Spottie, here, Spot! Kitten, here, Kitt!"

A large white dog, unmarked, appeared, yelping, to be let in, followed by a plump black cat which leaped in her lap when she sat.

"Good pals," Grandma cooed, stroking them. She lay back, eyes shut, and listened for the song of her wonderful canary in his golden cage in the dining room bay window.

Silence.

Grandma rose and peeked through the dining room door.

It was an instant before she realized what had happened to the cage.

It was empty.

"Singing Sam's gone!" screamed Grandma. She ran to dump the cage upside down. "Gone!"

The cage fell to the floor, just as Liddy appeared. "I thought it was quiet, but didn't know why. I must've left the cage open by mistake—"

"You *sure?* Oh my god, *wait!*"

Grandma closed her eyes and groped her way out to the kitchen. Finding the kitchen sink cool under her fingers, she opened her eyes and looked down.

The Garburator lay gleaming, silent, its mouth wide. At its rim lay a small yellow feather.

Grandma turned on the water.

The Garburator made a chewing, swallowing noise.

Slowly, Grandma clamped both skinny hands over her mouth.

Her room was quiet as a pool; she remained in it like a quiet forest thing, knowing that once out of its shade, she might be set on by a jungle terror. With Singing Sam's disappearance, the horror had made a mushroom growth into hysteria. Liddy had had to fight her away from the sink, where Grandma was trying to bat the gluttonous machine with a hammer. Liddy had forced her upstairs and put ice compresses on her raging brow.

"Singing Sam, he's killed poor Sam!" Grandma had sobbed and wailed. But then the thrashing ceased, firm resolve seeped back. She locked Liddy out again and now there was a cold rage in her, in company with the fear and trembling; to think Tom would *dare* do this to her!

Now she would not open the door far enough to allow even supper in on a tray. She had dinner rattled to a chair outside, and she ate through the door-crack, holding it open on the safety chain just far enough so you saw her skeleton hand dart out like a bird shadowing the meat and corn, flying off with morsels, flying back for more. "Thanks!" and the swift bird vanished behind the shut door.

"Singing Sam must've flown off, Grandma." Liddy phoned from the drug store to Grandma's room, because Grandma refused to talk any other way.

"Good *night!*" cried Grandma, and disconnected.

The next day Grandma phoned Thomas again.

"You *there,* Tom?"

"Where *else?!*" said Tom.

Grandma ran downstairs.

"Here, Spot, Spottie! Here, Kitten!"

The dog and cat did not answer.

She waited, gripping the door, and then she called for Liddy.

Liddy came.

"Liddy," said Grandma, in a stiff voice, barely audible, not looking at her. "Go look in the Garburator. Lift up the metal piece. Tell me what you see."

Grandma heard Liddy's footsteps far away. A silence.

"What do you see?" cried Grandma, impatient and afraid.

Liddy hesitated. "A piece of white fur—"

"Yes?"

"And—a piece of black fur."

"Stop. No more. Get me an aspirin."

Liddy obeyed. "You and Tom must stop, Grandma. This silly game, I mean. I'll chew him out tonight. It's not funny any more. I thought if I let you alone you'd stop raving about some lion. But now it's been a week—"

Grandma said, "Do you really think we'll ever see Spot or Kitten again?"

"They'll be home for supper, hungry as ever," Liddy replied. "It was crude of Tom to stuff that fur in the Garburator. I'll stop it."

"Will you, Liddy?" Grandma walked upstairs as in a trance. "Will you, really?"

Grandma lay planning through the night. This all must end. The dog and cat had not returned for supper, though Liddy laughed and said they would. Grandma nodded. She and Tom must tie a final knot now. Destroy the machine? But he'd install another, and, between them, put her into an asylum if she didn't stop babbling. No, a crisis must be forced, on her own grounds, in her own time and way. How? Liddy must be tricked from the house. Then Grandma must meet Thomas, at long last, alone. She was dead tired of his smiles, worn away by this quick eating and hiding, this lizard-darting in and out doors. No. She sniffed the cooling wind at midnight.

"Tomorrow," she decided, "will be a grand day for a picnic."

"Grandma!"

Liddy's voice through the keyhole. "We're leaving now. Sure you won't come along?"

"No, child! Enjoy yourselves. It's a fine morning!"

Bright Saturday. Grandma, early, had shoved a note under the door, into the hall, suggesting her two relatives take ham and pickle sandwiches out through the green forests. Tom had assented swiftly. Of course! A picnic! Tom had laughed and rubbed his hands.

"Goodbye, Grandma!"

The rustle of picnic wickers, the slamming door, the car purring off into the excellent weather.

"There." Grandma appeared in the living room. "Now, it's just a matter of time. He'll sneak back. I could tell by his voice: *too* happy! He'll creep in, all alone, to visit."

She swept the house with a brisk straw broom. She felt she was sweeping out all the numerical bits and pieces of Thomas Barton, cleaning him away. All the tobacco fragments and neat newspapers he had flourished with his morning Brazilian coffee, clean threads from his scrupulous tweed suit, clips from his office supplies, out the door! It was like setting a stage. She ran about raising green shades to allow the summer in, flooding the rooms with bright color. The house was terribly lonely without a dog making noise like a typewriter on the kitchen floor or a cat blowing through it like silk tumbleweed over rose-patterned carpets, or the golden bird throbbing in its golden jail. The only sound now was the soft whisper that Grandma heard as her feverish body burned into old age.

In the center of the kitchen floor she dropped a pan of grease. "Well, look what I did!" she laughed. "Careful. Someone might slip and fall on that!" She did not mop it up, but sat on the far side of the kitchen.

"I'm ready," she announced to the silence.

The sunlight lay on her lap where she cradled a pot of peas. In her hand a paring knife moved to open them. Her fingers tumbled the green pods. Time passed. The kitchen was so quiet you heard the refrigerator humming behind its pressed-tight rubber seals around the door.

Grandma smiled a pressed and similar smile and unhinged the pods.

The kitchen door opened and shut quietly.

"Oh!" Grandma dropped her pan.

"Hello, Grandma," said Tom.

On the floor, near the grease spot, the peas were strewn like a broken necklace.

"You're back," said Grandma.

"I'm back," Tom said. "Liddy's in Glendale. I left her to shop. Said I forgot something. Said I'd pick her up in an hour."

They looked at each other.

"I hear you're going East, Grandma," he said.

"That's funny, I heard *you* were," she said.

"All of a sudden you left without a word," he said.

"All of a sudden you packed up and went," she said.

"No, *you,*" he said.

"You," she said.

He took a step toward the grease spot.

Water which had gathered in the sink was jarred by his moves. It trickled down the Garburator's throat, which gave off a gentle chuckling wet sound.

Tom did not look down as his shoe slipped on the grease.

"Tom." Sunlight flickered on Grandma's paring knife. "What can I *do* for you?"

The postman dropped six letters in the Barton mailbox and listened.

"There's that lion at it again," he said. "Here comes someone," said the postman. "Singing."

Footsteps neared the door. A voice sang:

> Fee fie foe fum,
> I smell the blood of an Englishmun,

Be he alive or be he dead,
I'll *grr-innnd* his bones to make my bread!

The door flew wide.
"Morning!" cried Grandma, smiling.
The lion roared.

About the Authors

Robert Bloch is a world-renowned author of fantasy and suspense, including hundreds of short stories and over a score of novels. Perhaps best known for his novel *Psycho,* which was filmed by Alfred Hitchcock, Bloch's other suspense novels include *The Kidnapper, Lori,* and *The Jekyll Legacy* (with co-author Andre Norton). He lives in Los Angeles.

Lawrence Block has won virtually every award an American mystery writer can win, for his suspense and mystery novels, including his very popular Matt Scudder books. He lives in New York City.

Ray Bradbury is the bestselling author of such classic works of imagination as *The Martian Chronicles, Something Wicked This Way Comes, Fahrenheit 451,* and many others. His *oeuvre* includes science fiction, fantasy, contemporary fiction and suspense. He has also written for the movies and television and has had many of his works adapted for film. He lives in Los Angeles.

Kathleen Buckley has had outstanding short stories published in various magazines and anthologies. She lives in Seattle, Washington.

Ramsey Campbell is the author of numerous short stories and a number of fine horror novels, including *The Doll Who Ate His Mother* and *The Count of Eleven.* His works have earned him World Fantasy Awards and other honors. He lives in England.

Lisa W. Cantrell is the author of the suspense thrillers *Boneman* and *The Manse,* the latter of which was awarded the Horror Writers of America's Bram Stoker Award for Achievement for a First Horror Novel. She lives in Madison, North Carolina.

Jonathan Carroll is the author of such brilliant, disturbing novels as *The Land of Laughs, Outside the Dog Museum,* and *A Child Across the Sky,* as well as a number of memorable shorter fictions. He lives in Vienna, Austria.

John Coyne is the acclaimed author of *The Searing, Hobgoblin,* and other works of suspense. He lives in New York state.

Ed Gorman is the Shamus Award–winning author of many mystery and suspense novels, including *The Autumn Dead.* He has written horror novels under the name Daniel Ransom. A noted editor of anthologies, Gorman is co-publisher of *Mystery Scene* magazine. He lives in Cedar Rapids, Iowa.

Charles L. Grant is the World Fantasy Award–winning author of fine works of horror, fantasy and science fiction. His recent novels include *The Pet* and *Raven.*

Grant's numerous short stories have been published in a wide variety of magazines and anthologies. As an editor, he created the *Shadows* series of original horror anthologies and the *Greystone Bay* books, among others. He lives in northern New Jersey.

Richard Christian Matheson has had a number of horror stories published in magazines and anthologies. He has written original works for film and television, and has published one novel, *Created By.* He lives in Los Angeles.

Billie Sue Mosiman's chilling short stories appear in various magazines and anthologies. She lives in Texas.

S. P. Somtow is the author of several horror novels, including *Vampire Junction* and *Valentine,* as well as many unusual short stories. He writes fantasy and science fiction under his real name, Somtow Sucharitkul. A prolific composer of music, he lives in Los Angeles.

Steve Rasnic Tem is a gifted creator of horror stories, and has collaborated on works with his wife, Melanie Tem. He has published one novel, *Excavation.* He lives in Colorado.

Robert E. Vardeman has written horror, fantasy, and science fiction short stories. He has published a number of novels, in collaboration and on his own, including the *Demon Crown* series. He lives in Albuquerque, New Mexico.

Chet Williamson is the author of memorable horror novels, including *Reign,* and the suspense novel

McKain's Dilemma. He lives in Elizabethtown, Pennsylvania.

J. N. Williamson is the author of numerous short horror fictions and novels. He edited the *Masques* series of original horror anthologies. He lives in Indianapolis, Indiana.